Praise for *In the Company of Witches*

"In Auralee Wallace's *In the Company of Witches*, a charming New England town, a historic B&B, and a bevy of magical aunties—and one eccentric uncle—make the perfect backdrop for Brynn Warren to track down a troublesome guest's killer. *In the Company of Witches* is a fun and compelling mystery, but there's more: it explores how grief can sometimes rob us of magic, while love, and community, can help bring back our sparkle. A welcome addition to the magical cozy genre!"
      —*New York Times* bestselling author Juliet Blackwell

"*In the Company of Witches* is an entertaining read, with a compelling plot and a cast of engaging and humorous characters—including a crow named Dog! This is the perfect blend of mystery, magic, and mayhem."
      —*New York Times* bestselling author Sofie Kelly

"Fans of the paranormal will enjoy the series debut of the Warrens, who go way beyond quirky."
      —*Kirkus Reviews*

"Wallace's wonderful Connecticut setting and quirky characters make this a fun new cozy mystery series."
      —*Library Journal*

T0014944

Evenfall Witches B&B Mysteries

IN THE COMPANY OF WITCHES

WHEN THE CROW'S AWAY

When the Crow's Away

AN EVENFALL WITCHES B&B MYSTERY

AURALEE WALLACE

BERKLEY PRIME CRIME
New York

BERKLEY PRIME CRIME
Published by Berkley
An imprint of Penguin Random House LLC
penguinrandomhouse.com

ISBN: 9780593335857

First Edition: April 2022

Printed in the United States of America

Book design by George Towne

For my dad,
the self-proclaimed old highcooer.
Love you.

Chapter 1

PINK AND PEACH clouds, fiery in the sun's dying rays, rolled slowly across the baby blue sky. A riot of birdsong rang out from the trees as a gentle breeze twirled fluffy seedpods in the air. Spring had finally come to Evenfall, Connecticut.

"I just love this time of year," the woman beside me said. "That feeling of warm sunlight on your face. The sight of all the flowers popping up their sleepy heads. The smell of rich, fresh earth bursting with new life." She sighed happily. "Isn't it just magical?"

"I've never cared for it."

I darted a look over to the woman seated on my other side, doing my best to suppress a smile. Some things never changed. While my aunt Izzy tended to see the very best in everyone and everything, my aunt Nora, well, she made an art form out of being perpetually unimpressed.

Then there was me. I was right in the middle. Literally.

I was seated between the two of them on the back porch of our family's Queen Anne tower house, Ivywood Hollow

Bed and Breakfast. My aunts had suggested we come outside to enjoy the spectacular sunset. It was hard to say if we were succeeding in that particular goal just yet.

"But it's *spring*," Izzy persisted. "What is there not to like about spring?"

"Quite a bit actually," Nora said, flashing her long, crimson fingernails in the air. "Where should I begin? The sun is blinding in the early morning hours. You can't work in the garden without getting completely covered in mud. And then there is all this nonstop *twittering*." She cast a disapproving glance at the trees.

In fairness, she was more of an autumn person.

Izzy sat up in her seat. "Well, all that may be true, but—"

"Then there's the people," Nora went on, not quite through with her rant. She propped an elbow on the armrest of her chair and pointed at us. "Everyone behaves so nonsensically this time of year. They're practically overflowing with hope and excitement. And for what? A mild breeze and a bit of sunshine? Ridiculous." Suddenly a bluebird swooped in out of nowhere and landed on Nora's finger. She blinked at it. "You, my tiny feathered friend, are only proving my point."

The bird twittered prettily, then flew away.

"But, Nora," Izzy said with a nervous laugh, "wasn't it your idea for us to come out here to enjoy all that spring has to offer?"

"Oh no, Sister. Don't you dare try to pin this on me."

I frowned. *Pin what on who now?*

Izzy huffed a breath. "I knew I shouldn't have included you in this." Her eyes widened when she caught me looking at her. "In this viewing of the sunset," she added awkwardly before looking back at Nora. "You haven't liked spring since high school. Wasn't it your junior year when—"

"Absolutely nothing happened." Nora pulled down her oversized black sunglasses to give her sister a ferocious look. "And I do not *hate* spring." She pushed her sunglasses back up and laid her forearms delicately on the armrests of her chair. "I simply think it's overrated."

Izzy held up her hands in defeat.

"Wait, what are we talking about?" I asked, finally getting a word in. There was clearly a great deal being communicated under the surface here. I had a lot of questions, but I opted to start with, "What happened junior year?"

"Absolutely nothing," Nora repeated in a clipped tone.

I twirled my long black braid between my fingers as I looked back and forth between my aunts.

The two of them painted a contrasting picture. Nora was looking rather elegant this evening—if not a touch severe—in her black silk jumpsuit. She had her fiery red hair twisted up into a tight bun on the top of her head, accentuating her long neck and perfect posture. Izzy, in comparison, appeared fresh and sweet in her pink floral dress with ruffled hem. Her strawberry blond hair sat loose and curling about her shoulders, wavering charmingly in the breeze.

I had to admit I felt a bit shabby in my wrap sweater and jersey leggings. But, in fairness, no one had told me I needed to dress for the occasion. Not that this was an occasion. We were just taking in the sunset. At least I thought that's what we were doing. Suddenly I wasn't so sure.

"Why are we even talking about spring? Or unremarkable junior years?" Nora asked grumpily. "I thought we were supposed to be out here talking about Brynn?"

And there it was. I should have known.

I gripped the armrests of my wingback rattan chair to force myself up into a less relaxed posture. "And what is it exactly about me that needs discussion?"

"I have no idea what your aunt is talking about," Izzy said, forcing an overly bright smile. "Have you tried the tea, darling?" She reached for a cut glass mug. "It's a ginger and jasmine mix. I flavored it with honey, cloves, orange slices, blackberries, and just a touch of red pepper for heat."

I eyed the tall pitcher filled with amber liquid, sparkling

in the slanted rays of the setting sun. Beside it sat a plate covered in freshly baked tarts with ruby-colored filling.

"They're raspberry," Izzy prodded, following my gaze. "Your favorite."

They looked delicious. I could practically feel the flaky crust breaking apart in my mouth. But we both knew those weren't just any old tarts. I pinned my aunt in my gaze. Her eyes widened again, this time to unparalleled levels of innocence. It was pretty adorable. But I wasn't about to be distracted by her cuteness. "Izzy? What is going on?"

"Oh, just tell her why you've dragged us out here," Nora said with an exasperated sigh. "I'm about to spontaneously combust in all this golden sunlight."

"Are you sure you don't want to try the tea first, darling? Or the tarts?" Izzy asked hopefully.

I raised an eyebrow. "I think I'll wait."

My aunt sighed, then cleared her throat. "This wasn't quite how I wanted to bring the subject up," she said, cutting her sister a look. "But, well, Brynn, your aunt and I have noticed that you seem distracted lately. Like something might be bothering you."

Was that all this was about? I chuckled with relief.

"And Izzy here has a theory on what that *something* might be," Nora said with a sniff. "She also has some ideas about how to fix it."

My chuckle died a swift death. My aunts speculating on my well-being was always disconcerting, but the idea of their *fixing* any of my theoretical problems was downright terrifying. Time to nip this in the bud. "You don't have to come up with any theories. Or ways to fix anything." I stared off into the endless sky beyond the sorbet-colored clouds. "And you don't have to worry. I know I've been a bit distracted lately, but I promise you it's nothing."

"What's nothing?" Nora asked sharply.

I could feel her studying me, but I kept my gaze on the sky. "It's hard to explain, but I've had this funny feeling lately. I think it's the changing of the seasons. Spring fever maybe."

In fairness, I could see why my aunts might be concerned. A few days ago, I had been kneading dough with Izzy, and she had caught me staring off into space. I had been quite still for several minutes without realizing it. Then a day or two after that, I may have snipped the side of my finger with gardening sheers helping Nora trim the dead branches off of a rosebush. It was a little strange. I wasn't normally so careless. When the feeling came on, it was like I had to stop everything I was doing, still all my senses, in order to pick up on *whatever* it was. It was like listening for a soft noise somewhere in the distance. Or trying to catch a faint scent on the breeze. It almost felt like something might be coming. But the funny thing was, as soon as I did focus on the sensation, the feeling would disappear, like it had never existed at all. Again, I had chalked it up to the season. What is spring if not the feeling of anticipation? I was sure it was nothing to worry about.

I knew my aunts might have a bit of trouble with that though. They had raised me since the age of five after my parents died in a car accident. Worrying was a part of their job description, even if I was now over thirty.

I didn't have to look at Nora to feel her gaze narrow in on me. "Spring fever? Since when do you suffer from *spring fever*?" The tone in her voice made it sound like we were talking about malaria or maybe West Nile virus. "Are you sure this strange feeling of yours doesn't have something to do with your work?"

"Or maybe something else?" Izzy asked sweetly, clutching her hands to her chest. Stars above, what was going on with her? She was practically batting her eyelashes at me.

I gave her a look that spoke to the fact that I thought she might be a touch dangerous, then said, "I don't know. Maybe."

"You are not doing a very good job of explaining yourself," Nora said.

I let out an exasperated grunt. "Because there's nothing much to explain. I just keep getting this feeling like something is about to happen, but then nothing ever does. Really, you guys don't need to worry." As if on cue, a warm breeze gusted by, making the trees whisper. I eased back against my chair. Hopefully we could let this conversation go now and just enjoy the evening.

"But what is it exactly you think is about to happen?"

I groaned. Loudly. "I don't know. That's what I'm trying to tell you. Oh! Look! Bunny!" I pointed at a small cottontail hopping across the lawn. I darted glances at both my aunts to see if they had spotted it too. But no, they were both still focused on me with matching expressions of concern. "What? Now we don't like bunnies?"

"They eat my vegetables," Nora replied. "Don't change the subject. You do realize that we Warren women are not ones to ignore feelings. Have you spoken to your uncle about this?"

"No, I haven't told Gideon anything. There's no reason to. It's nothing. I'm sure of it." I really was sure. The whole thing was silly. But at least I was getting some tarts out of it. I reached for the biggest one on the plate, picked it up, and took my long-awaited bite. Chills rushed over my body. It was beyond good. Sweet. Tart. Buttery. It was also, funnily enough, quite relaxing, and encouraging, and dare I say, *prodding*. Like suddenly I had the urge to give up all my secrets.

I shot Izzy a look.

She smiled and scratched the back of her neck.

"Why didn't you guys just ask me what was going on?" I mumbled, bringing a hand up to cover my mouth. "You didn't have to plan this elaborate ruse." Truth be told, though, I already knew why. Not that long ago I had gone through the darkest period of my life, and I hadn't shared much of anything with my family, but I had come a long way since then. They knew that.

"We didn't know how you would react, darling. You can be quite private."

I swallowed hard and wiped the crumbs from my mouth and then my lap. "Okay, well, next time just talk to me." I held my hands up. "Really. I have nothing to hide." I turned my palms inward, looking at the crumbs all over my fingers, then quickly grabbed a napkin. "Now, tell me. What was your theory on what was bothering me?"

"It's nothing," Izzy said, shaking her head so quickly it almost looked like a shudder.

I was about to interrogate her further but was distracted by a young couple entering the garden from the side gate. They were newlyweds spending a couple of days at the B&B. Neither one had spotted us yet. They only had eyes for each other.

"They are so sweet together," Izzy mused, a dreamy look coming over her face.

My chest tightened.

They were so sweet together, and so much in love. It was impossible not to see it. It was in every gesture, the way the distance between them closed when they entered a room, the look in their eyes when they said each other's names, even in the way they held hands. It was precious. Truly precious. I had been in love like that once.

"Ridiculous," Nora muttered.

I smiled.

We watched the couple in silence for a little while before Izzy asked, "Don't *you* think they're sweet together, Brynn?"

I shot up in my seat. Wait a minute.

"What?" Izzy asked nervously. "What is it?"

"Did you know those two would be out here? Is that what you really wanted to talk about? *Love?*" I was using the same tone to speak about love that Nora had used when she was talking about spring.

Izzy's hand flew to her chest. "Brynn, do you really think I would be so conniving as to have that sweet young couple involved in some sort of scheme?"

"Hello!" the young man called out to her with a friendly wave. "Did we come at the right time?"

Nora laughed. Actually, it was more of a cackle.

Izzy smiled weakly. "Yes, just in time for the sunset. Lovely, isn't it?" She sank back into her chair. "Nora is so much better at conniving."

"I'll take that as a compliment," her sister replied, turning her face to the sun.

"Listen," I said in a much gentler tone, "I can see what it is you're trying to do here, and I know you mean well, but you are way off base."

I watched the newlywed husband lower a branch from our magnolia tree for his wife to see up close. Just as it neared her sightline, I heard Nora whisper something under her breath, and one of the pink buds swirled open, much to the couple's delight.

When Nora caught me looking at her, she shrugged and rolled her eyes.

"But, darling," Izzy said, stealing back my attention. "It has been some time now. Isn't there a part of you that misses it?"

"Of course I miss it. I miss *him*. The two can't be separated for me." That was the simple truth of it. I had lost my husband, Adam, to an undiagnosed congenital heart defect almost two years ago. It was a devastating loss. In truth, it had nearly killed me, but I had come a long way since then. I gave my aunt what I hoped was a reassuring smile. "But I can miss those things without feeling like my life is missing something. I am at peace with where I am now. I've had the greatest love anyone could ask for. And even though that part of my life is over, I'm grateful to have had it." I meant the words deeply. It wasn't something I had ever articulated out loud, but I was glad I finally had so that my aunts could understand.

"Now you're just being stubborn," Izzy said with a pout.

I blinked. Normally I would have expected that kind of comment from Nora. "I'm sorry?"

"Is it the family history that's holding you back?" my aunt asked. "Because you know all that curse nonsense is just that. Nonsense."

I didn't answer. The Warrens did have a history of being unlucky in love. Some might call it a curse, and, at times, it had certainly felt that way to me. But no, that was not what was holding me back. I wasn't being held back.

"You are a young woman, Brynn," Izzy went on, undeterred by my silence. She took a sip of tea, then smiled. I think she impressed herself with how good it was. She recovered quickly though. "You have a long life ahead of you. How can you be so certain that you will never experience love again? Life could very well surprise you."

"I just know." I could have explained further—told them that it was impossible for another man to ever fill my heart the way Adam had—but a slight prickle had come to my eyes, and I did not want to encourage that prickle to grow into something more. "Besides, how could I miss love when I have so much of it? I love you. I love Nora. I love Gideon." Just then an enormous cat jumped up onto my lap. "And I definitely love you," I said, rubbing the feline's soft ears. "In fact, right now, I think I love you most of all." Faustus, the B&B's resident Maine Coon cat, closed his eyes in pleasure as I ran my thumb over the bridge of his nose. He was a lovely large beast with all black fur, except for the dignified frosting of gray around his face.

"Oh, well, you and the cat should be very happy together," Nora said dryly.

"See?" Izzy said, throwing out a hand in her sister's direction. "Even the *hater of spring* agrees."

"No. No," Nora said. "Leave me out of this. I'm just here as a spectator."

I studied my aunt, but her expression remained hidden behind her sunglasses. She was being uncharacteristically quiet for this conversation.

Clearly Izzy thought so, too, because she said, "You're not getting off that easily. Tell the truth, is Brynn being stubborn?"

Nora regarded me a moment. "Yes, definitely stubborn. But I've always thought of stubbornness as being more of a virtue than a vice. It shows conviction. Well done, Brynn."

I frowned. "Thank you. I think." I was having trouble following all the twists and turns this evening was taking. I was never going to look at sunsets the same way. "But I have to disagree. I'm not being stubborn. It's just fact. I've had a great love. I'm grateful for that. And right now, I couldn't be happier. I'm completely fulfilled. This is the life I am meant to be living. Even if some areas are going a bit slowly right now."

All of that was true.

I loved running Ivywood Hollow with my aunts. I loved living in the loft above the carriage house. I loved that I was now reconnecting with old friends I had lost touch with over the past few years. And I loved the fact that I had a calling in life that allowed me to help people—the work Nora had referred to earlier. Although it had been a while since I'd truly been able to help anyone. That was the one area of my life that was moving slowly. I guess you could call me a grief counselor of sorts, and living in a small town like Evenfall, there were sometimes dry spells of, well, death.

"Ah. I see what's wrong with you now," Nora said knowingly. "It's not love that you're missing. You want someone to die."

I gasped. "What? I would never! How could you even suggest—"

I saw the corner of my aunt's mouth twitch.

My shoulders dropped from my ears. "You're horrible, you know that?"

"I know," she said happily, reclining further into her seat.

I frowned again.

"All teasing aside," Izzy said, "your well-being is of the utmost important to us, darling. We just want to know you're happy."

"I am happy. Very, very happy. Couldn't be happier in fact."

Faustus jumped down from my lap, hitting the porch floor with a loud thump. I guess he didn't like my particular brand of happy.

"You know, I think this conversation has run its course. Why are we wasting time bickering when we are surrounded by all this beauty? I bet everyone in Evenfall is enjoying this sunset."

Suddenly a disembodied voice called out, "Well, I'm not!"

I jumped in my seat. Chills raced up my arms as I spotted a gust of wind swooping over the tall iron gate of the backyard. I realize one can't usually see a breeze, but this was no normal wind. This short stream of air was colored with silvery sparkles that danced and gleamed as it cut a path through the air, bending and twisting like a ribbon caught in a storm. The current rushed up to us; then, in a flash, the twirling sparkles coalesced into the shape of a man, standing right in front of me, his legs going straight through the coffee table.

I could feel my aunts looking at me, wondering what was happening, but I couldn't take my eyes from our newly manifested visitor.

I recognized him instantly. He had quite the distinctive style of dress. The red and white striped collared shirt. The smart-looking suspenders. The fun garters on his sleeves. The bow tie. I had never seen him wear anything else.

Probably because I had only ever seen him at work. No, the only difference in his appearance now, from the last time I had seen him, was the shimmering glow and the fact that he was slightly transparent.

"Brynn?" Izzy asked, staring blankly into the space I had focused on.

"It's Mort Sweete. From the candy shop. He's here."

Or at least his spirit was.

"Oh dear," Izzy said softly.

"Oh dear!" the man shouted. "I think that's an understatement. I'm dead!"

"I am so sorry," I said quickly. "I realize this all must be a shock for you. But I'm here to help. If there's anything I can do, please don't hesitate to ask."

"Okay then," the man said, leaning back and pulling on his suspenders. "I've been murdered. Can you help me with that?"

Chapter 2

WHAT IS IT, Brynn? What's happened? You look like you've seen a ghost," Izzy dropped her voice to a whisper. "I mean, of course, you have, but, well, you know what I mean."

I did know. There was no need for her to explain.

"I'm not entirely sure what's going on just yet."

"What do you mean you're not sure what's going on? I just told you what's going on," Mr. Sweete spluttered, puffing his chest out as though he were still breathing. "I've been murdered!"

I couldn't deny the sincerity of belief evident on the confectioner's face. He looked ready to tear his hair out. It was a startling change to his normal demeanor. Mr. Sweete always had a big personality, never a wallflower, but I was used to seeing him in very different circumstances.

Mort Sweete was the public face of the Sweetes' Shoppe, Evenfall's one and only confectionary store, and the sixty-something-year-old candymaker epitomized what it meant to be young at heart. Mort was known for his booming laugh and endless stream of jokes, and he always seemed to be surrounded by wide-eyed youngsters. They knew, at any time, he might find a candy tucked away behind someone's lucky ear. As a child, I wondered quite seriously for a time if he might in fact be Santa Claus in disguise—candy making did seem like an appropriate off-season job—but he didn't have the beard.

I gave each of my aunts a look. "Could you two give us some privacy?"

"Of course, darling," Izzy said, gathering up her tray, which was not exactly what I had intended—one tart of Izzy's was rarely enough—but if I'd heard Mr. Sweete correctly, this wasn't exactly a dessert conversation.

"Call us if you need anything," Nora said. She snapped her fingers, and my chair glided back several inches, making room for her to walk past. "A Warren's work is never done."

It was hard to argue with her on that point.

There was, of course, an explanation for why I could communicate with Mort Sweete's spirit, why Izzy could influence people with her food, and for Nora's ability to induce flowers to bloom with just a few words whispered under her breath.

We were witches. All of us.

The Warrens had been practicing magic in Evenfall for nearly four hundred years. We used our powers to help the citizens of our small town; and while we couldn't solve every problem, we did our best to use our gifts to help when we could. I had been raised to believe that magic came with responsibility. It was a gift, but one that was meant to be shared with others.

Izzy, of course, was a kitchen witch. She was a maestro with food. Even without magic her recipes were enchanting. I had seen the most stressed and distracted guests lose themselves in the experience of sampling her dishes. Just a few weeks ago, a patron shed tears of joy when he asked

Izzy if we served dinners and she surprised him with her fresh-caught lobster thermidor. He was near inconsolable by the time the white chocolate cheesecake with blueberry compote arrived for dessert. But my aunt's gift extended far beyond the taste sensations she created. Izzy had the ability to make her food with *intention,* and those intentions were rarely lost on her samplers. You see, Izzy could get anyone to *feel* just about anything with her food. Not exactly against their will. She was very careful with her powers. She was a good witch, after all. But her creations were definitely encouragements. Usually they bred light feelings, such as comfort, romance, and confidence; but on rare occasions, and only when necessary, she did induce darker emotions, like anger, jealousy, and regret. But, again, Izzy was judicious when it came to her charmed culinary creations. She believed in a feather touch.

Nora, on the other hand, was primarily a garden witch. She had a connection with plants and the earth that few ever got to experience. She understood the miracle of life and growth—and in balance—death and decay. And while she was a master student of botany, she somehow also just knew what plants could be used for. Nora believed wholeheartedly in the power of nature, and nature it seemed believed in her too. I had seen trees shift their branches to offer her shade on sunny days and the occasional vine tendril literally seek out justice on her behalf. Actually, I had more than seen it. As a child, I once ran my finger along the icing of a cake Izzy had set out for Nora's birthday, and before I managed to bring the sweet dollop to my mouth, I felt a vine tighten its grip around my ankle. It was a very disturbing sensation, especially considering I had been inside at the time. Unlike her sister, Nora preferred bold magic, and she wasn't always a fan of following the rules.

Now, I didn't specialize the way my aunts did when it came to creating and nurturing magic. My talent just *was.*

You see, I was a friend of the other side.

Or to put it more bluntly, a witch of the dead.

For as long as I could remember, I'd had the ability to see and talk with ghosts just like I would anyone else.

I had lost this power for some time after my husband passed, and going through the experience of losing both him and my ability had taught me what a gift it truly was to be able to help those who had gone over to the other side. I made a promise to myself to never lose sight of that again. So, while Nora was right in that a Warren witch's work was never done, I wasn't complaining.

I waited for my aunts to leave, then gestured for my ghostly visitor to take one of the open porch chairs. He wouldn't need rest in his current form, but I found ghosts were often comforted by following living conventions.

"I don't want to sit!"

Or not. My instincts were a little off these days.

"Why are you so calm? Didn't you hear me? A heinous crime has been committed, and you're just sitting there with pastry crumbs on your lips."

I smiled apologetically at the ghostly confectioner and brought a napkin to my mouth. Izzy's tarts certainly were flaky. "I'm so sorry, Mr. Sweete. I didn't mean to come across as unconcerned. You have my complete attention. Why don't you tell me everything you remember?"

I really didn't mean to come across as unconcerned. Declarations of murder were quite concerning. But truth be told, I wasn't particularly alarmed.

Yet.

Ghosts, rarely, if ever, remembered the hours leading up to their deaths. Sometimes they'd lose entire days. That fact alone made me question Mr. Sweete's certainty that something untoward—well, something other than death—had happened to him. And speaking of death, the transition was difficult for even the most soft tempered of souls, especially when it came unexpectedly. That could some times lead a spirit into searching for something or *someone* to blame.

"The last thing I remember was being at the candy shop, feeling as fit as a fiddle. As strong as a lion. As vital as a—" He cut off himself off, looking perplexed. I suspected he was having difficulty making another comparison. "And then this!" Mr. Sweete waved his hand through his torso, the edges of his body swirling like water around his fingers as they passed through. "This isn't right!"

"I'm very sorry. That must have been a terrible shock."

"I'll say it's a terrible shock. Once I figured out how to make this form work, I headed right over here. I've heard the stories about you and how you can talk to people in my condition. I guess they're all true."

This was one of the difficulties that came with living in a small town. Word did get around. Nobody in Evenfall really believed that we were witches. Well, with the exception of one person, but that whole situation was a problem for another time. Still, our friends and neighbors did know we were helpful, and perhaps a bit *different*. We had found more lost pets than could be comfortably explained, and we always seemed to be preventing accidents. Izzy, in particular, was wonderful at catching toppled dishes before they smashed to the floor. But it was even more than that. Nora, for example, gave near miraculous gardening advice to those who were brave enough to ask for it, and she also had quite the knack for producing homemade cosmetics. She had helped many a supplicant go from feeling beaten down to bombshell with a single jar of face cream. And, in addition to preventing accidents, Izzy's donations were reliably top sellers at local bake sales; and she always seemed to have just the right dish on hand to help a neighbor in need, regardless of the circumstance. She had brought many a feuding family together over a roast turkey. As for me, well, I, of course, could be counted on to offer a cup of tea and consoling words to the bereaved. I knew there was talk about my being a medium, but it was not something I encouraged. It was best for everyone for us to lie low. We could do more good that way.

"Mr. Sweete, I'm not sure what you've heard," I began, but he cut me off before I could finish.

"I also heard you were the detective that solved Constance Graves's murder."

And then there was that.

Not exactly my best effort at lying low. Months back, a guest staying at the B&B had been killed in one of our rooms; and I suppose you could say I helped solve her murder, but I certainly did not consider myself a detective. "That would be an overstatement of my abilities, Mr. Sweete."

"Stop calling me Mr. Sweete," he snapped, dispelling all of my previous Santa Claus impressions. "If we're going to work together to bring my murderer to justice, you might as well call me Mort." He frowned down at the purring cat walking circles around where he stood in the coffee table. Faustus loved ghosts.

I took a breath. "All right. Mort. But solving murders is not what I do. That was a very special circumstance. My specialty, if you want to call it that, is to help spirits find peace. Usually by connecting them with their loves ones." As soon as the words left my mouth, the very air around us went cold, and I could have sworn Mort's pallor blanched even beyond its new ghostly state.

"Loved ones?"

"Mort, are you all right?"

"What am I doing here?" He shook his head, sending tiny sparkles spiraling into the air. "I should be with Angie."

I was confused until I realized that Angie was Angela Sweete, Mort's wife. I didn't know her well, but enough to say hello.

The ghost's eyes trailed off to the distance. "I have to go."

"I understand," I said, scooting forward to the edge of my seat. "But would you like me to come to your house? Talk to your wife?"

"No! You can't come to the house. Are you crazy?" He looked back at me, his fading eyes bulging. "You'll only upset Angie."

"Oh, I wouldn't want to do that. I—"

"Just be ready tomorrow morning. Bright and early. We're going into town." Mort was almost gone. I knew he had already begun to manifest elsewhere, opting against riding the wind this time around.

I rose to my feet, trying to steal back his attention before he disappeared entirely. "Why town? What's there?"

"What's there? My murderer! Haven't you been paying attention?"

"And you want me to . . . ?"

"Catch her, of course!" Mort yelled just before he disappeared.

I dropped back down into my chair, blinking. "Of course," I muttered, throwing my hands in the air. "I'll just *catch* her."

Izzy stuck her head outside one of the French doors. "Everything all right, darling?"

I looked over at her, probably appearing as bewildered as I felt. "I really have no clue."

Nora stuck her head out next.

"Well, you're the one who wanted more ghosts."

Chapter 3

IT DIDN'T TAKE long for me to realize that settling for the evening would be easier said than done after my ghostly visitor. Normally a cup of chamomile tea and a bit of reading in my armchair by the fire did the trick, but my mind was far too busy to relax tonight.

My loft in the carriage house certainly wasn't as grand as the rooms in Ivywood Hollow, but my little apartment had to be my favorite place in the world. It truly was my home. The structure was original to the B&B, and it had served many purposes over the years. My great-grandmother had converted this upper level into a magical workshop nearly a hundred years ago—her cauldron still hung in the fireplace—and while we had made a number of additions to keep the space livable, we'd tried to preserve the atmosphere she had created. I wasn't about to let anyone touch the exposed beams of the peaked ceiling or the wide-plank wood floors that creaked beneath my feet.

I closed my book and placed it on my lap. I tried to focus

on the soothing crackle of the fire burning low in the hearth, but my thoughts were jumping. I didn't know what to think of Mort's visit, and funnily enough, his claim of murder wasn't what was preoccupying me the most. No, it was the desperately sad look on his face when he spoke of his wife. I couldn't help but wish he had accepted my offer to go visit with Angie. I knew firsthand how precious the opportunity to speak to a deceased loved one could be.

I certainly wished I had been given that opportunity before my husband passed into the light.

That's right. Witches of the dead couldn't make contact with their departed loved ones. It was the one caveat to the power, a safeguard of sorts for those with the gift. How could you possibly move on if you could still see and talk to your loved one as though nothing had happened? Not to mention the fact that in that scenario there would be little to compel the departed to leave this mortal plane. It was a necessary protection. Going into the light was something all spirits needed to do. If they didn't, well, that was not a good scenario for anyone.

All this to say, I wanted to give Mort the opportunity to say goodbye, but it was looking like I would have to wait. He had his own schedule in mind, and I could see why finding answers surrounding the circumstances of his death might come first. Ghosts normally could hang around for at least a couple of weeks without suffering any ill effects, so there was time. But wondering about what Mort had planned for said time had me up past my bedtime.

I needed to do something. Burn off some energy. Favorite place in the world or not, I was far too angsty to stay cooped up in my loft any longer.

I pushed myself up from my armchair and walked over to the coatrack by my front door. I pulled on my red rain jacket and fastened it over the pajamas Izzy had recently bought me on a whim. They were a top and bottom set with a fluffy bunny print. Not my usual style, but they were quite cozy. I then slipped some sneakers onto to my bare feet and made for the door. I probably looked ridiculous. If Nora could see me, she would be horrified. But it was late. I wasn't likely to run into anyone; and besides, going full fashionista didn't seem necessary for a nighttime bike ride.

I stepped outside onto the landing and took a deep breath of the night air. The sky was clear and dotted with twinkling stairs. I trotted down the steps anchored to the side of the carriage house, smiling at the sweet chirp of spring peepers coming from the trees. I loved that sound. Definitely a harbinger of spring. I pulled open the large door on the lower level of the carriage house and grabbed my bike. Before I hopped on, I took off the wicker basket I normally kept clipped onto the front handlebars.

Tonight, I needed a little speed.

I swung my leg over the seat and pressed down on the pedals, launching myself toward the empty street. The turn of my bike's wheels sent the low-lying mist clinging to the road swirling. Countless fairy tales would have people believe that our kind only rode broomsticks, but this witch preferred her bike.

Evenfall was charming at any time of day, but at night, with its wrought iron streetlamps glowing softly under the towering trees that lined most every street, it was downright enchanting.

The town itself wasn't large by any stretch of the imagination, but it did have a long history. Once a pastoral village, Evenfall had done quite well during the industrial revolution and later on with the expansion of the railway. As a result, there were a number of beautiful old buildings from various time periods that were, for the most part, lovingly maintained. We had a couple of farmhouses stretching back to before the Revolutionary War, one or two Federal-style mansions, and a number of Queen Anne houses—Ivywood Hollow included—that made for quite the picturesque village. We even had a working railway from the nineteenth century that toured to neighboring towns. Unsurprisingly, perhaps, Evenfall had become a tourist hotspot. On top of the quaint architecture, we were surrounded by abundant greenery and waterways. You didn't have to go far to see the Catskill Mountains or, of course, the sea.

I leaned into the turn that would take me to the town square. Given the way my hair was trailing behind me, I was probably riding too fast, but I didn't have much fear of falling. Night rides tended to stir up my magic, and I knew a little bit of my charm was helping me along. Once or twice, when I had truly lost myself in a ride, the wheels of my bicycle had left the pavement completely. But I tried to stay on top of that. Sightings of flying bicycles were not something I wanted to encourage.

Just then, I felt a rush of air swoop over the top my head.

I smiled. I guess I wasn't the only one who couldn't sleep.

I turned my gaze up to the night sky. I could just barely make out the shape of the black bird soaring overhead. Dog.

Dog, the crow, just to be clear, had appeared one day in the window of my uncle Gideon's tower room at the B&B. Gideon, being the kind soul that he was, offered the bird a peanut, and they had been fast friends ever since. I would never refer to Dog as Gideon's pet though. He would not like that. And given that he could be a bit of trickster, I did not want to get on his bad side.

For a long time, we had thought of Dog as being a fairly ordinary bird. But not that long ago, he had shown us another side of his feathered nature when he'd helped pass along a message from our last ghostly visitor. Gideon had done some research, and it turned out that many believed crows were messengers for the dead.

I looked up at the sky, searching for the bird again. I finally caught sight of him by the glint of a shiny *something* clutched in his claw.

"Dog," I called out. "What have you got there?"

The crow made a few wide circles around me as I continued to glide down the street; then he picked up speed and shot out like an arrow headed for the park just off the town square.

Hmm, it seemed like somebody wanted to race. Well, I was more than willing.

I stood up on my pedals, pushing hard, enjoying the freedom that the night offered.

I tore after the bird, but it soon became clear I had no chance of winning this race. In fact, just as I truly got up to speed, I spotted Dog perched on the top peak of the town gazebo.

I slowed my pace as I pulled up to the quaint structure with gingerbread trim.

"Okay, you won," I said, panting and dropping one of my feet to the ground. "But I think I did a pretty good job keeping up." Suddenly the smile fell from my face.

There it was again! That feeling I had been telling my aunts about earlier.

The skin on my arms prickled as my gaze traveled over the sleepy trails of the park.

Not a soul in sight.

I stilled all my senses as the feeling continued to roll over me. *What was that?* It was like nothing I had ever experienced before. And I wasn't exactly frightened by it. No, if I had to pinpoint exactly what I was feeling, I would say it was like a sensation of nervousness stirring in my core. Or maybe excitement? It was like I was ten years old again, standing at the end of the high dive at the public pool for the first time.

I closed my eyes and turned all of my attention inward.

to focus more deeply. I could almost sense where it was coming from. I felt my magic twist and turn inside my chest, awakening to my need. I let it build then sent it out in all directions. I felt the extension of my senses ripple out over Evenfall, searching, until . . .

My eyes snapped open.

Got it!

Nora was right. We Warren women weren't the type to ignore funny feelings. It was time I followed whatever this was all the way to the source.

I turned my bike around.

Dog cawed behind me.

"I'll be right back. I just need to check something out."

He cawed again. This time the noise sounded a touch annoyed, but I wasn't going to let whatever this was get away from me now that I had it in my enchanted sights.

I pedaled slowly into town. It was hard to say how I knew where to go. I was working solely on my magical instincts, not wanting to overthink it. I somehow knew that was the key because whenever I had tried to focus directly on the feeling for too long in the past, it disappeared.

When I turned onto Main Street, glowing softly in the streetlamps, I found all the cozy little shops shuttered for the night. Nothing was stirring.

I got off my bike and closed my eyes again.

I was close, but not quite close enough. Whatever it was . . .

It was behind the shops!

I guided my bike across the street and up onto the sidewalk. I then ducked into the small alleyway beside Furry Tales Pet Shop.

I walked slowly down the narrow space between the brick walls, doing my best to ignore the slow drip coming from a drainage pipe and the overly loud sound of my footsteps on the pavement.

But again, I wasn't scared. Well, not really scared. I was a Warren witch, after all. I was more than capable of taking care of myself.

Suddenly, I pitched forward, stumbling in my footing.

Yes, I was completely capable of taking care of myself as long as I stayed on my feet.

When I got to the opening at the end of the alleyway, I peeked my head out and looked from one side to the other. There wasn't much to see. Just a few large garbage bins lined up against some fencing. Except . . .

I peered along the wall to my right. Farther down, I could almost swear there was something by the back door of one of the shops. I couldn't be sure though. It was very dark. Almost too dark? As a general rule, witches have good eyesight at night. I should have been able to at least make out something by that door. But it was shrouded in darkness. Perhaps it was because the light above it was out? Well, I could fix that.

A quick charm should do it.

I leaned my bike against my hip and rubbed my hands together. A second later I threw my palms out toward the light fixture, whispering, "Illuminate."

I could see the spell leave my mouth, curling through the mist into the darkness. For a moment, the bulb above the door flickered, but then it died out.

That wasn't right. The spell should take regardless of whether the lamp was in working order or not.

I tried it again.

Nothing. Not even a flicker this time.

I planted a fist on my hip. What was going on here? For a little while, not too long ago, I'd had some trouble with my magic after I had taken it for granted, but we were on very good terms now.

I threw out the spell again.

Still nothing.

Huh. I debated walking over, but following funny feelings into dark spaces didn't seem like the wisest move. And speaking of which, the funny feeling was gone. So gone, in fact, that I was doubting whether it had ever existed.

That wasn't right either.

Something had brought me out here. I hadn't imagined it. And why wasn't my spell working?

No, no, there was definitely something more going on here, and I was going to find out what it was, even if it took putting every last bit of power I had into the spell. I closed my eyes again and took a long slow breath, calling up the magic from the deepest depths of my being. Forces rolled through me like storm clouds. I dropped my hands to my sides, spreading my fingers wide, reveling in the sensation. I'd like to see any darkness stand up to this power.

When I was ready, I threw my hands out again. "Illumin—"

I cut myself off with a scream as a cloud of bright yellow sparkles exploded from my fingertips. I then whirled around to face the person who had tapped me on the shoulder.

"Nora!" Heat came to my face as my aunt watched the cloud of sparkles blink out around me. It was a little embarrassing to lose control of a spell in front of another witch. And the look on my aunt's face wasn't helping. "What are you doing here?"

"What am I doing here?" she asked with feigned lightness. "Oh, I was just out for a midnight stroll when I spotted my niece ducking into an alleyway. Given that's the case, I think the more appropriate question would be, what are you doing here?"

I dropped my hands to my sides, knocking several of my fingers against the handlebar of my bike. I flinched as my cheeks burned with embarrassment. "Well, I couldn't sleep, thinking about Mort, so I thought I would go for a bike ride. But then Dog wanted to race, and before I knew it, I was having that funny feeling again. So this time I tried to follow it, and it led me into the alley, but then it disappeared.

Once I got back here, though, I spotted a strange dark spot beneath a door, so I used a spell on that light over there." I pointed behind me. "But it didn't work. So then I thought I'd give it a little more power. *And* that's when you tapped me on the shoulder, scaring the magic right out of me. So really, that last part was your fault." I ended with a deep gasp for air.

"Are you referring to the fixture over there positively beaming with light?" Nora asked, looking behind me.

"No. Of course not. I told you it wasn't working." I looked over my shoulder. Except the light fixture was now beaming, glowing like a little yellow sun, and the entire area around it was perfectly illuminated, revealing nothing. Just a couple of steps with yet another garbage can. I whipped back around. "I swear it was completely dark. I tried the spell at least three times. It wasn't working." I frowned. "Stop looking at me like that."

"Like what?"

"Like you think I'm making this all up."

"Oh no, I don't think that at all. Something is clearly very wrong with you," Nora said. "Just look at how you're dressed."

I looked down at my rain jacket and pajama pants. "I will have you know Izzy bought these pj's for me. And they are very comfortable."

"I'm sure. Although perhaps they should have come with a warning label that reads *for indoor use only*."

"All right. All right," I said, giving her look.

"I think we should get you home."

"I can't. I kind of left Dog hanging back at the gazebo. I should probably go find him."

"I saw him swoop by. He's already on his way back to Ivywood Hollow."

Nora waved out a hand for me to take the lead back into the alleyway. We walked in silence awhile before she finally asked, "Are those fuzzy bunnies on your sleep-wear?"

"They are."

"We really need to find a cure for this spring fever of yours. The sooner the better."

Chapter 4

I WOKE UP THE next morning with my quilt bunched up around my face. I felt wonderful all cozy in bed. I had left the window open a crack, so the room was cool, but the warm morning sunlight streaming in had me warm and toasty.

It was the perfect day to spend a little extra time in bed. Especially given my late night. Except I couldn't do that at all. The memory of the previous day came flooding back. Mort Sweete. Dead. Murdered?

I got dressed in jeans and an ivory lace-trimmed shirt, splashed some water on my face, and gave my teeth a quick brush. I then dropped my messenger bag on my shoulder, put on sunglasses, and headed out the door in record time.

Birds twittered overhead as I walked down the drive toward the sidewalk. I probably didn't need to hurry. If Mr. Sweete needed something right away, he could simply materialize in front of me. But the fresh spring air had me invigorated with purpose. I was energized at the prospect of helping my recently deceased candymaker. The only problem was I needed to find him first.

It was a marvelous day. Morning dew sparkled on the grass and bright yellow daffodils had sprung up in more than a few of my neighbors' gardens along with a smattering of pink and red tulips. I scanned the trees overhead for Dog, but he was nowhere to be found.

As I got closer to town, I decided to head for the Sweetes' Shoppe. I didn't know exactly what Mort had planned, but it seemed like as good a place as any to start. When I was maybe two blocks away, I heard a familiar voice call out my name.

I flinched and ducked my head down into my shoulders.

Out of the corner of my eye, I caught sight of a woman in her early twenties scampering after me. She was positively glowing in the bright spring sunlight. And I do mean glowing. Her shiny neon pink ponytail was giving off a faint aura, but it was no match for the thousand-watt smile on her face. She was clearly very excited.

And that was just terrible.

Nixie had moved to town for college not too long ago, and when she wasn't in class, she could be found working her aunt and uncle's store, Charmed Treasures gift shop. Now, I liked Nixie. I really did. It was impossible not to. She just had one of those personalities. But not too long ago, she had asked me for something pretty specific, and she had been waiting not so patiently for an answer as to whether or not I would give it to her. Truth be told, I had been putting the whole thing off. I could easily give her what she wanted, that wasn't the issue, but I wasn't sure if it was the right thing to do.

I kept walking at a brisk pace as the young woman hurried up to my side.

"Hi, Nixie," I said quickly, not turning to make eye contact. "It's good to see you. I don't have time to chat though. I need to get to town."

"Oh no, you don't," she said, jumping into my path and planting her hands on her hips. She looked like an angry pixie dressed in her jeans short overalls, ponytail swinging side to side. "You promised to give me an answer by now."

I sighed.

"So? Are you going to be my fairy godmother and make all my dreams come true?"

I ducked around her. "I haven't decided yet."

And I was pretty sure what she was asking me would end with all her dreams being crushed, not coming true.

Nixie hopped over a planter filled with pansies to dart in my path again. "Come on, Brynn. You owe me more than that."

I stopped walking, but I still refused to meet her gaze. "I'm sorry. It's just that I've been really busy lately."

"Lie."

"And I haven't been able to give it much thought."

"Another lie."

"And the truth is I don't even know where to begin."

"Lie. Lie. And lie." Nixie dotted the air with the tip of her finger.

I grunted. "I'm not lying."

"You totally are," she said, folding her arms across her chest. "Witch hunter blood, remember?"

That's right. Witch hunter blood. The most annoying of all the bloods.

Several months back, Nixie had confronted me with being a witch. It turned out that her family had been in Evenfall as long as ours had, and she had heard some stories. It also turned out that her family was comprised of a long line of witch hunters. They had all stopped practicing more than a century ago, and none of her current family members believed there was any truth in their history, but that hadn't stopped Nixie. For a long time, I put off all of her *ridiculous* accusations, but it had gotten to a point where she had started questioning herself, and everything she knew to be true. I eventually decided the situation wasn't fair, and, as a result, I may have shown her the teensiest bit of magic just so she wouldn't doubt herself anymore. That was a big no-no in the witching community, and for good reason. By showing Nixie that tiny bit of magic, I had created a monster. A monster who apparently had been gifted with the ability to know when I was lying.

My gaze darted about, probably subconsciously looking for a means of escape. "Nixie, I—" Just then something on the inside of her wrist caught my eye. "Stars above, did you get a tattoo?"

"Stars above?" She raised her eyebrows and smiled. "You are adorable sometimes." She pulled up her sleeve to show me the designs underneath.

I gasped. "They're lovely, but could you maybe have started with just one?" I stared at the inside of Nixie's forearm; on it there were three pale brown tattoos, a sun-moon design, a goddess symbol, and an elaborate letter *N* done in calligraphy. Each one was beautiful in its own right, but lined up in a row, they didn't have much coherence.

"They're not permanent. It's henna. I'm just trying them out." She yanked her sleeve back down. "Now, stop trying to change the subject."

Had I been that obvious? I finally dared to look Nixie directly in her hopeful eyes.

"Please, Brynn. I promise if I can't do it, I'll let it go. I'll never ask you again. Just give me one." She stuck a finger in the air. "Just one spell."

And there it was. The thing Nixie wanted from me. After I had confirmed all her suspicions, my little witch-hunting friend had somehow gotten it in her head that with enough time, practice, and dedication, she, too, could wield magic.

"We've been over this. I don't want you to be disappointed. Humans can't do magic." That was the simple truth of it. While some humans did have a touch of magic to them, often manifesting in special talents and abilities, they certainly never had enough to do spell-work.

"Just give me a chance. I know I can do this."

"Nixie, it's impossible."

Her eyes widened. "Oh my God! You're lying! You're lying again!"

That witch hunter blood of hers really was annoying. And it was also the thing about her that was giving me the slightest bit of doubt. When Nora had first met Nixie, she had tried to spell her—repeatedly—when she realized how much she knew about us. But none of the spells had taken. There was definitely something different about the girl. But that didn't mean she could wield magic. My theory was that her witch hunter blood gave her some protection *against* magic. "I'm not lying *exactly*. I am almost positive you won't be able to do a spell."

"But not completely certain."

"The odds are infinitesimally low."

"But not nonexistent."

I fell silent. No, not nonexistent. The truth was I had put some thought into giving her a spell to try. I couldn't exactly see the harm. Well, there was the harm of her being disappointed, but that was going to happen one way or another regardless of whether I gave her a spell. And maybe it would be easier to accept if she came to that conclusion on her own. Besides, witches didn't own magic. We worked in partnership with it. It was up to the *powers that be* to decide whether or not they wanted to work with someone. It just never happened to be with humans.

So yes, I had put some thought into this. So much, in fact, I had a spell copied out in my bag. I had done it without really intending to actually give it to her. It was nothing too taxing, and certainly not dangerous. Just something that she could practice until she came to the conclusion herself that there was no point.

"Please," Nixie said, clutching her hands to her chest. "Just let me try."

I gave her one further look, then opened the flap of my messenger bag.

"No way! You're going to do it?" she squealed. "You're going to give me a spell?"

"Would you keep your voice down," I hissed. The street was fairly empty, but we couldn't be too cautious. "And yes, I'm going to give you something to try, but only on one condition."

"Name it. I'll do anything."

"You spend the next week doing more than just thinking about magic. Get outside. It's spring. You should be meeting some of the young people in this town. Make some friends, other than Nora." Nora did spend a fair bit of time over at Charmed Treasures. Nixie whipped up a number of homemade cosmetics and Nora seemed interested in helping her with the botanical components. I think she just loved the way Nixie worshipped her.

"Do you really think Nora considers me a friend?"

I rolled my eyes. "Probably. Yes. But don't tell her that."

"Do you think she'll practice the spell with me?"

"No!" I shouted. "Absolutely not. You cannot tell her about this."

"Why not?"

"Because she'll turn us both into toads!" I didn't know if that was true or not. Mainly because transmogrification spells were a lot of work. But I knew she wouldn't be pleased.

Nixie laughed. "Nora's so cool. But she won't turn me into a toad. My witch hunter blood will protect me."

How nice for her.

I passed her the spell and found myself buried in an ambush hug.

"You're the best, Brynn!" she shouted, rocking us back

and forth. "I can't tell you how much this means to me. Thank you so much!"

"Okay," I said, tapping the arm she had around my throat. "I think it's about time I got"—I cut myself off at the roar of a car engine—"going."

Suddenly a powder pink Cadillac convertible zoomed up the road behind us. As it roared past, I caught a glimpse of the woman in the driver's seat. She had a lime green silk scarf wrapped around her head and white framed sunglasses. In the small back seat there was a placard with a stake. I didn't have time to catch the words, but I was pretty sure it was a For Sale sign. If I wasn't mistaken, that was Cookie, wife of Les Sweete, part owner the Sweetes' Shoppe and Mort's cousin.

None of that mattered though. No, what I was concerned about was the ghost beside her in the passenger seat. Mort. And he wasn't in the passenger seat exactly. No, he was standing on top of it, waving his arms in the air to get my attention.

Well, he definitely had it.

He looked like he was about to shout something at me, but a low-hanging tree branch sliced right through his torso, leaving sparkles swirling in its wake.

"Brynn?" Nixie asked, releasing me from the hug. "Are you all right?"

I blinked. "I think so."

She gave me a sideways look.

I sighed. "Just another day in Evenfall."

Chapter 5

"ARE YOU SURE you're all right? 'Cause it kind of looks like you've seen a ghost."

That joke just never seemed to get old.

"You did! You saw a ghost, didn't you? That is amazing!"

While Nixie prattled on about the coolness of talking to ghosts, I hurried up the street. The pink Cadillac had parked right in front of the Sweetes' Shoppe. Cookie was already driving the stake of the sign that read *For Sale by Owner* into some earth beside a tree in the sidewalk. Circling around all that was a very angry ghost, shouting all sorts of unpleasant things.

"Is this about Mr. Sweete?" Nixie asked, skipping along beside me without taking her eyes off the spell. She was going to run right into a streetlamp if she wasn't careful. "I heard he had a heart attack."

I stopped. "Who told you that?"

She shrugged, dragging her eyes up from the paper I had given her to look at me. "I don't know. Everyone." Her gaze dropped back down.

"Did you get any details?"

"Not really."

I walked on.

"Just that he was found in the town gazebo," she called after me.

The town gazebo? Was that why Dog was trying to lead me to the park? But why? Maybe Mort was hanging out there? Ghost did often return to where they passed to help process things.

"No!" Nixie shouted. "Is that a For Sale sign?" I guess she had finally looked up from the spell long enough to register what was going on up ahead. "I can't believe this. I thought Cookie already had a buyer."

I glanced in Nixie's direction before hurrying on.

"It's just that my family's looking to buy another shop, and, well, it's complicated."

Normally I would have encouraged her to go on, but I couldn't help thinking Mort needed me more. He was trying to kick the sign out of Cookie's hands, his foot going right through it.

This time I was the one to dart in front of Nixie's path. "I hate to cut this short, but I really need to do this next thing alone."

"No problem," she said, waving me on, her eyes back on the spell. "Good luck with your thing."

I took a few backward steps. "But don't forget what I said."

She didn't answer, once again lost in the incantation I had given her.

"Nixie?"

"Yeah. Yeah," she said, not looking up. "Go outdoors! Meet people! Springtime! Yay!" She waved a shaky fist in the air.

"That's the spirit," I replied dryly.

I fast walked my way up the street, trying not to draw unnecessary attention to myself. This was one of the trickiest parts of being a witch of the other side. Trying not to react to ghosts—what they were saying, what they were doing—in public. For example, right now Mort was trying unsuccessfully to pick up a large rock. I think he wanted to drop it on the For Sale sign. At least I hoped it was the For Sale sign he wanted to drop it on.

I stood a good distance away from the melee and tried to get Mort's attention with a small wave. I didn't want to alert Cookie to my presence. Luckily, she was already placing the mallet back in her convertible. Once she had it tucked away, she turned back to look at the sign and wiped her hands together, completely oblivious to the ghost shouting in her ear.

"You can't do this, Cookie! You're going to kill him! Is that what you want?"

Cookie didn't react in the slightest.

"You've already killed one man. Why not make it two?!"

"Mort," I hissed. Ghosts usually had pretty good hearing. If it was hearing at all. I often thought they could simply sense when people were thinking of them.

The spirit's gaze snapped in my direction. "There you are!" He stomped toward me. Right through Cookie. Once he was through her, he stopped and shuddered. He really didn't have this whole ghost thing down yet. "What took you so long?"

"I'm afraid my teleportation skills aren't as good as yours," I whispered out of the corner of my mouth.

"Don't be cute. You almost missed her." He gestured back at Cookie, who was walking around the convertible to reach the driver's seat. "There she is. My murderer in the flesh."

I blinked.

"Do something!"

"What is it exactly that you'd like me to do?" I whispered.

"Go right up there and tell her to her face that you know

she killed me." The spirit swept his hand out. "Tell her. Tell everybody! Tell the world!"

Just then Cookie spotted me as she dropped herself into the driver's seat of the convertible. "Morning."

"Morning," I mumbled back.

"Morning? Morning! Why don't you just invite her over for tea?"

I tried very hard to keep my face still as Mort ranted, but even so, I probably looked strange standing on the sidewalk by myself, face devoid of all expression.

Thankfully the convertible roared to life.

"Quick. She's getting away!"

As Cookie drove off in her powder pink car, Mort's hands dropped to his sides, a defeated look sweeping over his face.

My heart broke for him. I knew how hard it could be for ghosts to witness the events in the world around them and not be able to interact. "Mort," I said gently, "why don't we have a seat?" I suggested moving toward the bench in front of the candy shop. "I really do want to help. I think it's time you told me everything."

Chapter 6

MORT FOLLOWED ME glumly to the bench.
It was such a lovely spring day. A day ripe with
new beginnings and fresh life. I could only imagine how it
must feel to be removed from it. But even more than that,
new beginnings were intrinsically linked with endings, one
always following the other. I knew even if Mort wasn't con-
sciously aware of it, at some level, being surrounded by all
this new life had to feel cruel. Many spirits did find comfort
in knowing that life would carry on after their passing, but
that was something that usually took time.

We didn't say anything for a while. Mort sat beside me
in silence, his elbows on his knees, his shoulders slumped.
Eventually he turned to look at the large stone urn beside
the bench and said, "We plant impatiens in there every
year, Les and me."

I nodded. "I've seen them. They're lovely."

"Les always picks bright colors. Fuchsia is his favorite.
He claimed it would make the customers think of candy.

I always joked it was the candy that made the customers think of candy." Mort looked over his shoulder through the plate glass window to the tiered display of boxed goodies on the other side. "I guess I'm candy for the flowers now."

I smiled sadly. "You're more than that. You're still you. Just in a different form."

"I don't much like this form."

"No, I imagine not."

He inhaled deeply, but I knew it was just habit. He wasn't taking in any air. Sparkles did swirl prettily about him though. "I had no idea I'd be so glittery." He held up his hands to look at them, then dropped them back into his lap. "As the kids like to say, this really sucks."

I chuckled. Unfortunately, it was right as Birdie Cline, head of the Women's Society, came upon us, pushing through her morning power walk. She gave me a funny look.

"Just remembered a joke," I said, composing myself.

She gave me an unimpressed nod while straightening the top of her pale yellow tracksuit. "It's a shame what happened," she said, looking up at the store. "I'm guessing you've heard."

I nodded, then glanced over at Mort. I knew what I was about to ask might upset him, but then again, it also might help fill in some of the blanks. "What exactly did happen to Mr. Sweete? Does anyone know?"

"Heart attack mostly likely," Birdie said, marching on the spot.

"Balderdash!" the ghost beside me shouted.

"He was found in the town gazebo early yesterday morning," Birdie went on. "Empty box of chocolates in his lap. He had diabetes, you know. And some sort of heart arrhythmia."

Mort jumped to his feet. "That's a lie! Not about the health stuff," he stammered angrily, "but I never would have had a box of chocolates in my lap."

Birdie and I exchanged parting remarks as Mort ranted on.

Once she was gone, he collapsed back onto the bench. "You can't believe a word that woman says."

I didn't answer.

"Did you hear the judgment in her voice? I'll have you know that she has a sweet tooth herself." He wagged a finger in the air. "Chocolate and peanut butter. That's her weakness. And I've been a veritable angel since I was diagnosed with diabetes. You can ask Angie. She'll tell you."

I perked up at the mention of his wife's name. It was the opening I'd been waiting for. "I'd actually love to speak with Angie. If you think it's the right time."

He wagged his finger at me. "I see what you did there."

I held up my hands. "You caught me. But, Mr. Sweete— I mean Mort—I've been in your wife's situation, and I can't tell you how much it would have meant to me had I had the opportunity to say goodbye to my husband."

"No. No. No." He shook his head in a big motion. "It's way too soon for all of that. It will only upset her." As he said the words, his form faded in and out. Again, that often happened to ghosts in the early days. They didn't have much control over where they manifested. Thinking of a loved one often sent them directly to that person. If I had to guess, Mort was about to pop home.

"Try to stay with me," I said quickly. "I know you want to be with Angie. But I really would like to discuss this. It's not my first time connecting loved ones, and I can tell you the experience can be quite comforting."

Mort's form solidified. "So, you want me to lie to my wife? Is that what you're saying?"

I straightened up. "What do you mean?"

"She's going to have all sorts of questions. Number one on that list? She'll want to know if I'm at peace, and like I've been trying to tell you, Ms. Warren—"

I shot him a look.

"Brynn," he corrected. "I am not at peace."

I took a sharp breath. "Right. Because you've been murdered."

He nodded.

"And you think Cookie's responsible."

He nodded again. "I know you don't believe me. But it's the truth." He studied my face. I guess he could see he wasn't making much headway because he added, "Just because I can't remember my death doesn't mean I don't know what I know. Something happened that night. I'm sure of it. And it wasn't a heart attack."

"I don't suppose you have any proof of this?"

"None."

"Motive then?" His form was wavering again.

He smiled grimly and directed my gaze back over to the For Sale sign.

"Cookie wanted to sell the shop?"

He nodded.

"But you wouldn't."

"I would not."

I bit the corner of my lip. "As far as motives go, it's not the strongest."

"You don't know Cookie. She's always been jealous of the time Les spent in the shop." Suddenly his eyes seemed distant. He was looking at something I couldn't see. "Oh, sweetheart," he whispered. "Please don't cry." His eyes snapped back to mine. "Sorry. That was for Angie." He was fading quickly now.

I nodded.

"I was murdered, Ms. Warren," Mort said, his voice sounding faraway. "And if you don't do something, I think Les could be next."

"What? Why would Les be next? You just said Cookie was jealous—"

There was no point finishing the question. Mort was gone.

I slumped back against the park bench.

Some ghosts sure knew how to make an exit.

A COOL, DELICIOUS NIGHT wind greeted me as I climbed the last step of the spiral staircase into the tower room of the attic. Ivywood Hollow had three main floors, but its turret made up a fourth, where my uncle Gideon lived and spent nearly all of his time.

Despite being in the attic, the room was warm and welcoming with its exposed brick walls and crisscrossed ceiling beams. There was a small porthole window for Dog's comings and goings on the front wall and a much larger window on the back that opened up to a small balconette that served as an observation deck. Gideon had built it himself. He could be quite handy when he chose to be.

"Ah, Brynn, there you are," my uncle said, not looking up from the papers on his desk.

I smiled. Of course, he had been expecting me.

He sat in the warm circle of light coming from his antique banker's lamp with green glass shade. "I wanted to show you something. I've been doing some writing and—" He stopped himself short as he gazed up at me. "By the expression on your face, it looks like you have something more pressing."

"It can wait. I'd love to hear your haikus."

A loud caw came from the window. Dog's talons scraped against the porthole frame as he found his footing. A second later he hopped over to his perch in the corner of the room.

"I think our feathered friend here would like you to go first." My uncle gestured for me to sit on his battered but sturdy leather sofa. "I'll make us some tea." He bustled over to his small kitchenette. He reached for the kettle, then turned to peer at me over his glasses. "Or is this more of a brandy-type conversation?"

A vision of Mort trying to kick down the For Sale sign popped in my mind. I rubbed a hand over my face. "Tempting, but I think the tea will be fine." I dropped onto the sofa, opting to sit on the end closest to the antique stove that heated the room. The spring air was sweet and fresh after the long winter, but still chilly.

A few minutes later, Gideon brought over two mugs and placed them on the coffee table. Once settled in the armchair across from me, he asked, "So does your troubled mind have anything to do with your recent visitor?"

I reached for my tea, its spicy scent swirling up to greet me. "It does. He thinks he's been murdered."

Gideon's eyebrows shot up his forehead. "Another murder in Evenfall? What has happened to our sweet little town?"

"I said he *thinks* he's been murdered. He's a very stubborn ghost. He won't even entertain other possibilities." I saw the corner of my uncle's mouth twitch. "What?"

"What, what?" he asked with a smile.

I frowned at him when I realized what was going on. "Izzy told you about the porch, didn't she? About how she thinks *I'm* being stubborn because I know I won't ever fall in love again."

My uncle's eyes twinkled. "She may have mentioned it."

"And do you have any thoughts on the subject?"

"Who me?" Gideon placed a hand on his chest. "Oh no. No opinions whatsoever."

"You are a smart man, Uncle."

"But your aunt did also say something about a funny feeling you've been experiencing?"

I told my uncle everything I could about my so-called funny feeling. Unfortunately, once again, it didn't amount to much. I wasn't as quick to dismiss it this time though. Something had drawn me into that alleyway, and I hadn't imagined that darkness surrounding the door.

"How curious," Gideon mused once I was through. "I'm not sure I've heard of anything like what you are describing. It has been some time since you've seen a ghost though. Do you think the two could be related?"

I shook my head. "Nora asked the same thing, but no, I don't see any connection. The funny feelings started a while ago; and while they are getting stronger now, I think the timing is just coincidental."

Gideon made a considering noise under his breath. "I've never been a big believer in coincidence, especially not in spring."

I tilted my head. "I'll bite. Why is it exactly you don't believe in coincidences in the spring?"

"It's a time of new beginnings and growth," he said with a small shrug. "The veil between us and the powers that be is at its thinnest during times of change."

I folded my arms over my chest. "So, what? You think the powers are trying to communicate with me through funny feelings and ghosts?"

"Possibly. Possibly."

As a witch, I had been raised to look for signs from the *powers that be.* It wasn't a foreign concept. Gideon had visions of the past and future, after all. But that was his gift. This idea that there were signs left around for the rest of us to follow like bread crumbs on some predetermined path was a little harder to believe. Sometimes things did just happen. Call it coincidence. Happenstance. Good luck. Bad luck. Whatever. If you started to look for signs to control those things, well, they were everywhere. And nowhere. It was an exercise in madness as far as I was concerned.

"It's just a thought," Gideon said, reading my skepticism. He raised his cup to take a sip. "But back to the topic at hand, am I to take it you don't believe your ghost has been murdered?"

"Everything I've heard points to natural causes. He's a

bit older—or was a bit older—and he had a heart condition and diabetes. He was also found with a box of chocolates on his lap. An empty box of chocolates."

"I see."

I pulled a throw blanket off the back of the sofa and wrapped it around my shoulders. "I've been giving it some thought, though, and I think there's actually something more going on with him."

My uncle waited as I gathered my thoughts.

"He's really adamant that I not talk to his wife."

"That's unusual, isn't it?"

"It is," I said with a slow nod. "Talking to loved ones is usually the only thing spirits want to do."

My uncle gave me a questioning look. "What do you think is going on? Were the two estranged?"

"No, just the opposite. I get the sense they were close. Not to play amateur psychologist, but I think he might be afraid of saying goodbye."

"Ah, so all this talk of murder is his way of avoiding the subject." My uncle looked pensively into his tea. "I can understand the motivation. Saying goodbye is painful."

"I can understand it, too, but he needs to get over it."

Gideon's eyes widened under his bushy eyebrows.

I grimaced. That had come out a touch harsher than I had intended. "I just mean that there isn't a lot of time for him to come to terms with what has happened, and I don't want him to miss his chance to say goodbye."

Time *was* limited.

Again, Mort had only so long to walk the mortal plane. A week or two at most. If ghosts stayed any longer than that, their spirits began to darken, and if they didn't hightail it over to the other side, eventually they lost themselves entirely and became specters. Nobody wanted that. Specters were scary. They were the ghostly creatures people tended to think of when it came to hauntings. Thankfully they were also pretty rare. The pull into the light was strong. All this to say, we didn't have months for Mort to get comfortable with saying goodbye.

"Well, my unasked-for advice is to be gentle with this ghost of yours. As you and I both know, what he is going through is incredibly difficult. Maybe denial is his only way to cope right now. But out of curiosity, does this spirit have a suspect in mind for his murder?"

"He does. He thinks his partner's wife did him in."

"Partner?" Gideon said, swiftly putting his mug down on the table. "Who exactly are we talking about?"

"Izzy didn't tell you who it was?"

"No, she did not," my uncle replied, looking quite serious.

"Mortimer Sweete from the Sweetes' Shoppe."

My uncle's face dropped.

"What? What is it?"

"Maybe I should have been the one to go first after all."

Chapter 7

GIDEON GOT UP from his seat and hurried over to his writing desk. He retrieved a few papers, then headed back over to me. "Have a look at these."

I reached for the sheets. I didn't read the words, but I could tell by the line groupings they were haikus. "Do you think these might be premonitions?"

"It's hard to be certain. This is all very new to me."

Again, witches usually had a key magical skill, a gift that stood out from all their other talents. For Gideon, though, his ability was at times more of a curse than a gift. Since he was quite young, he could see into both the past and the future. Unfortunately, he had no control over the content of his visions, and even worse, he could almost never change what he saw coming. Most tragically, my uncle had foreseen the death of his fiancée in a car crash, the accident that had also claimed the lives of my parents. He had raced to the scene, but it was too late to do anything but say goodbye. After that day, Gideon locked himself away in the attic. He never again wanted to experience knowing someone's future.

That being said, recently things had changed. A few months back I had gotten myself into a wee bit of trouble, magically speaking, and my uncle had rushed out into the night to save me. Actually, it wasn't me he was trying to save. It was the town. I had nearly burned it down. But, regardless, in that case, he hadn't had a full-blown vision. No, he had been tipped off to the fact that something may not be quite right in his poetry. The same fiery themes kept popping up. It had led him to speculate that maybe there was something he could do with his powers to help others if he could follow the clues leading up to the vision.

It was a significant breakthrough for him. The hope it brought had even managed to coax him into coming out of the attic once or twice when we didn't have guests.

I dropped my eyes to the page in my hand and read aloud the first poem. *"The magic of spring, quietly promises my heart, that rainbows will overwhelm me."* I looked up at my uncle. "I can see why you are concerned. Magic of spring? Quiet promises? Rainbows? Sounds terrifying."

My uncle folded his arms over his chest. "Keep going."

I shook the papers to straighten them out. *"Flowers bloom in spring, but bulbs stay buried below. Who dies? Who's reborn?"* I frowned. "Okay. That one is a little more ominous but not exactly concerning."

"And the last one," my uncle prodded.

I cleared my throat. *"Killed for a candy, on the first day of spring. Goodbye to sweete-ness."* The pages fell into my lap. "Gideon!"

My uncle grimaced.

"Why? Why did you write this?"

Gideon's grimace turned to a frown. "You have heard the expression about not shooting the messenger, yes?"

"Sorry. I didn't mean to blame you," I said sulkily. "But this last one, it sounds awfully murdery."

"It does, doesn't it?"

"And why did you write *sweetness* like that? With the extra *e*? Did you mean Mort Sweete?"

"I didn't mean anything," Gideon said, bringing a hand to his chest. "Again, just the messenger."

I sank back into the sofa. "I thought I had this all figured out. And then you had to go and throw a *haiku* in the works."

"Maybe not," my uncle said, wagging a finger. "I've been working under the presumption that these haikus of mine are hints of things to come. Not of things that have already passed. Mortimer has already died, so really this could have nothing to do with him at all."

"Except we both know that you can see into the future *and* the past, so maybe your haikus are also history." I frowned. I wasn't sure if that made any sense, but I think my uncle got my meaning. "And, if they are glimpses into the future and not the past, then that would mean someone else is about to be murdered!"

My uncle smiled weakly. "You're welcome?"

This was not good. Mort had mentioned something about his cousin being in danger, and they did share the last name Sweete. I brought my mug up to my lips just as Dog squawked. I jumped, spilling my tea. I threw the crow a look over my shoulder, but he was busy smoothing down an errant feather. Just then I remembered the adventure he had taken me on the night before. "Hey, Dog!"

He raised his gaze, looking a little put out. He probably didn't like me interrupting his grooming activities.

"What were you trying to show me the other night?"

Dog glared at me, then dropped his beak back into his feathers.

I sighed. He probably hadn't forgiven me for standing him up in the park. When I caught Gideon looking at me, I filled him in on the events of the night before. When I was through, he said, "Brynn Warren, are you trying to steal the affections of my bird?"

"I don't think you have anything to worry about on that front. But bird problems aside, I'm really confused about how to handle things going forward. I mean on the one hand, there is no concrete evidence of murder, but on the other, there's Mort and his very strong feelings on the subject. And now there's this." I gestured at the haikus on my lap. All of this uncertainty was driving me nuts. I knew, of course, that an autopsy could determine Mort's cause of death, but I was pretty sure Angie Sweete would have to push for it, and there was no way I was going to point her in that direction. Given Mort's concerns about me upsetting his wife, I felt fairly certain he would haunt me for the rest of my life if I took that particular course of action. "I just wish there was a way to know for sure what happened. Like a crystal ball or, or—Gideon?"

My uncle had jumped to his feet. "Crystal ball, no."

He hurried back over to his worktable, muttering under his breath. "What day is it? No, it can't be. What are the odds? The timing is remarkable. The stars won't be in this alignment for—what is it now? Seventy-three years? The luck. Or is it luck? Oh, ho, ho, ho. Serendipity at work!" He wagged his finger at the sky. "If I know the powers that be, this is no coincidence."

"Gideon, what is going on?"

My uncle whipped back around with a smile on his face that was equal parts delight and excitement. "Brynn, go find your aunts. Tell them to fire up the cauldron. The big one in the backyard. I have to check my charts, but if I'm right, there isn't a moment to spare."

"What moment? Right about what?"

Gideon's eyes twinkled in the lamplight. "My darling girl, there might just be a way to find out what happened to your Mr. Sweete after all."

Chapter 8

I RUSHED DOWN THE many flights of stairs to find my aunts. Gideon was too busy throwing around star charts to explain his plans any further, but given how excited he was, I wasn't going to take any chances by wasting more time. Once I was on the second floor, I stopped to listen in the direction of my aunts' rooms. They weren't there. I sensed it. Well, sensed it *and* I heard a pan clatter against the floor in the kitchen below.

I sped down the stairs. Faustus was stretched out on the bottom step, filling up the entire length. I jumped over him. I was so going to pay for that later.

"Izzy! Nora! Quick! I need your help." I raced toward the kitchen. "I just talked to Gideon about Mort and the fact he thinks he's been murdered and—"

As I slid through the threshold on my socked feet, my mouth snapped shut.

It may have had something to do with the fact that my aunts looked quite alarmed, along with our two guests, the newlyweds, Becca and Mark.

"Oh, hello," I said with a weak smile.

"Hello, darling," Izzy said, voice quavering.

"I was just . . ." I looked back and forth between my aunts for help.

"Discussing that television program we've been watching?" Nora gave me an unimpressed look from her chair by the small kitchen table. It was a good excuse, especially considering Nora had never watched a television program in her life. Which was also probably why she made it sound like something from the nineteen forties.

"Oh," Becca replied with a chuckle. "For a moment there I thought . . ." She exchanged an amused look with her husband. "I don't know what I thought."

"Right," Izzy said. "Now where were we before Brynn rushed in? Oh yes!" She hurried over to her double-door glass-front refrigerator. Yes, my aunt appreciated more traditional kitchen appliances—her original woodburning fireplace slash stove was evidence of that—but she liked her modern conveniences too. "I was just about to get you those chocolate-covered strawberries." She turned with a plate in her hand, then nearly dropped it. "Gideon!"

Gideon?

I whirled around to see my uncle standing at the threshold of the kitchen. He wasn't looking at me or his sisters though. No, his eyes were focused solely on the young couple. They were also filled with terror.

Mark extended his hand. "Hello."

"Oh no, no," Gideon said, backpedaling to the far side of the kitchen until he was pressed up against the wall. Actions like handshaking often triggered his visions. He clearly wasn't in the mood to be taking any chances.

Mark's hand dropped.

"He has a skin condition," Nora said in an overly loud whisper. "It's not contagious but very embarrassing."

Gideon gave his sister a stormy look but said nothing. He then nodded politely at Mark and edged his way along

the wall. When he arrived at the small table where Nora
was sitting, he placed a piece of paper in front of her, gave
it a pat, then backed away once more in the direction from
which he had come. Once he reached the threshold, he said,
"Enjoy your evening," then made a near run for the stairs.

"Well," Izzy said, cheeks flushed. "Here are your strawberries, and . . ." Her eyes darted around the kitchen. She
held up a finger for the couple to wait, then she scurried off.
I heard her footsteps thumping down the stairs to the base-
ment. The four of us smiled at one another awkwardly until
she returned a moment later, champagne bottle in hand.
"Please, take this," she said, struggling to catch her breath.
"On the house."

My aunt Nora's expression twisted in horror as her eyes
trailed over the label of the champagne bottle her sister had
just given away.

"Thank you so much," Becca said. "I mean, Mark here
is more of a beer guy"—Nora whimpered—"but I love
bubbles."

Izzy and I smiled as the couple left.

Once they were out of earshot, Nora spluttered, "Really,
Izzy? The 1985 Krug brut?"

Her sister's eyes widened in innocence much like they
had when we had been on the porch. "Is that what that was?"

Nora slapped the table, sending a few purple sparks flying out from underneath her hand. "I was saving that for a
special occasion."

"I'm sorry," Izzy said, "but we have a reputation to up-
hold. Besides, I think there's another bottle in the cellar."
She frowned. "And what kind of special occasion?"

"I don't know! A wedding? A significant birthday? A
birth of a child?" Her eyes slid over to me.

This time my eyes widened.

"A beer man," Nora said dejectedly, brushing away a
tiny purple spark smoldering in the paper Gideon had left

She flipped it over absentmindedly. In an instant, her expression changed from despondent to captivated. She was eyeing the paper like a cat might watch a mousehole.

"What is it?" I asked, regaining some excitement. "Gideon didn't have time to explain."

I hurried over to the table, Izzy following close behind.

Nora slid the paper over to us. The sheet was covered with hand-drawn constellations that didn't make much sense to me. I had perhaps been a touch negligent of my studies when it came to reading the stars. I could name most of the constellations on sight, but remembering when and where they would appear in the night sky was not my strong suit. It didn't come up a whole lot in my work with ghosts. Or really at all. Yes, there were some spells that could only be done when the stars were in a particular alignment, but those spells were rarely if ever used because they were so difficult to keep track of. Truth be told, knowing star dates was a dying art.

"Well, I'll be," Izzy whispered.

"Did you see this part?" Nora pointed at something on the page.

"Oh my, that would mean . . ." Izzy exchanged looks with her sister. "Do you think there's time?"

Of course, not knowing star dates could, on occasion, be annoying.

"It will be very tight," Nora said, "but yes."

"What are you two talking about?" I demanded.

Nora slid the paper closer to me. "Your uncle may have his foibles, but also he has his fortes." She pointed to the title at the top of the page.

I read the words, then looked up at my aunts. "A spell of re-creation? Does that mean what I think it does?"

"We have to hurry," Izzy said, rushing about in circles. "Look at the position of the stars!"

I cleared my throat. "I, uh, can't tell time by the stars."

"Neither can she." Nora rose to her feet. "But luckily your uncle can. Look at the time he's written at the top corner of the page."

"Eleven forty-eight until twelve oh-four? Six minutes?"

"That's our window to complete the spell," Izzy said. "So, let's get going! There's no time to lose."

I scanned the list of ingredients written in tiny letters under all the diagrams. There were *a lot* of ingredients.

Izzy slapped her hands together. "Nora, fire up the cauldron. Brynn, start pulling out the tools. I'll work on the ingredients."

Nora strode past me, her eyes suddenly glowing bright green. "This is going to be fun."

Chapter 9

IT TOOK SOME time to get a straight answer out of Izzy, but while we were rushing around gathering tools and ingredients—and avoiding the cat, who only ever seemed to want to be underfoot when we were busy—I was able to piece together exactly what it was we were doing. The spell's name was somewhat self-explanatory. If we were able to brew the ingredients together just right, then say the incantation at the exact moment the stars came into alignment, then we should be able to see—or re-create—the moment of Mr. Sweete's death in the vapors of the cauldron.

But my aunts were right. There wasn't a moment to spare. And, unfortunately, many of the ingredients had to be prepared in specific ways before they could be used.

"How's that mulled wine coming, Brynn?" Izzy shouted over the music filling the kitchen. My aunt liked to listen to the oldies station when she was cooking up spells. I was always amazed at just how many songs there were about magic. "I Put a Spell on You" was my favorite.

"I think it's done," I said, plucking a spoon out of the air.

Utensils often took on a life of their own when we were making potions. I gave the brew one last stir, then poured the warm liquid from the copper pot into a large mason jar, using a sieve to filter out all the cloves and cinnamon sticks.

Izzy wiped her hands on her apron and came over from the island, where she had been grinding herbs. She held the jar up to the light and turned it ever so slightly. "Well done, darling. It looks lovely." She then dropped it to her lips and took a long sip.

"What are you doing?" I asked, swatting her on the arm. "That's for the spell!"

Izzy let out a satisfied sigh. "I know. But these recipes always make extra. Every witch needs to sample her brew."

I folded my arms over my chest. "And how was the brew?"

"Wonderful. Now it's time to add the frog tears."

"Are you going to sample those too?"

"No, I am not," she said with a little hiccup. "Let's finish up. We need to get outside. It's almost time."

A few minutes later, we headed out, both of us laden down with heavy trays.

We walked slowly over the winding flagstone path to reach the back corner of the garden, Faustus trailing behind. The spot was surrounded by tall trees and gave the best cover for our magic work. As we approached, the loud crackle of the fire greeted us.

"There you two are," Nora said as Izzy and I came around the last bend. "It's almost time."

I smiled at my aunt. She was always something to behold while she was spellcasting, but with the fire lighting up her face, and her long red hair trailing behind her, she was almost terrifyingly beautiful. A giant cauldron hung above the flames, suspended from a tripod. Normally it was stored in the greenhouse. Thankfully we had a spell to roll it out here. It was too heavy to move otherwise.

"Did you put the barrier up?" Izzy asked.

Nora froze.

"Sister!" She whispered a charm under her breath. It would have been impossible for any human to sense, but I could feel the shield form a bubble around us. We had been a little slack with hiding some of our magical activities in past years. The trees did offer good cover, but ever since our new neighbor, Mr. Henderson, moved in, well, let's just say, we had to be extra careful. For his benefit as well as ours. Izzy had handled our last slipup, but I don't think she felt particularly good about *how* she handled it.

"There," Izzy, said placing her tray on the ground beside Nora. "I think we're ready to begin."

I bent down, following suit, and caught Faustus out of the corner of my eye pouncing at something underneath a bush. Toad most likely. We had quite a few. They were often attracted to witches. Thankfully, our furry friend never killed any of them. He just enjoyed playing with the small amphibians. It was hard to say if the feeling was mutual.

"All right," Izzy said, wiping her hands on her cherry print apron. "I'll read out the sequence. You two alternate putting the ingredients in the cauldron."

"No, no, Sister," Nora said, stepping forward to reach for the paper resting on the tray. "Allow me to read out the sequence."

Izzy snatched it up. "I've got it."

"No, really, I don't mind. You save your lovely voice." Nora smiled solicitously. It was very unlike her.

"My voice is fine. Thank you," Izzy said firmly.

Nora's smile dropped.

I had to suppress a giggle. Nora hated it when her sister read the sequence. When spellcasting, Izzy's voice tended to take on a much lower resonance. I guess to evoke the sacredness of the situation? It made Nora's nuts.

"Baneberry!"

I jolted and snapped my eyes over to Izzy. Apparently, we were getting started.

I grabbed the bowl of crimson berries from my tray and dropped them into the bubbling stew.

"Skullcap!"

My smile deepened. Izzy's voice had a gong-like vibration to it now. That was new. It could probably be attributed to the wine.

Nora rolled her eyes and tossed in the delicate stalk of small purple flowers.

We went on like this back and forth for a while until we came to the last ingredient.

"Mulled wine!"

Nora picked up the jar. "It feels light."

"Mulled wine!" Izzy commanded.

Nora poured the wine into the cauldron, raising her arm high in the air to create a dramatic cataract.

"There," Izzy said, wiping her hands once again on her apron. The three of us crept forward to peer into the swirling vapor rising from the brew.

Nora looked up at the stars, then her watch. "We should get started on the chant."

I nodded. "I really hope this works. Mr. Sweete deserves to know what happened to him."

"Did I hear someone say my name?"

Chapter 10

I YELPED AND CLUTCHED my chest. I think I could be excused for it though. Mr. Sweete had appeared in front of the cauldron, flames lighting up his translucent form, giving him an almost devilish appearance.

"Mr. Sweete!"

"Mort," he corrected.

"Mort." I took a shaky breath. "This really isn't a good time."

"The candymaker's here?" Nora asked. "Get rid of him. The clock is ticking."

"I'm not going anywhere until I know what's going on."

I couldn't see any reason not to tell him. He had asked for my help. The problem would be getting him to leave once he knew what we were up to. I gave him the quickest possible rundown of the spell, then finished with, "We're really hoping to get you all of the answers you're looking for, but we'll need to concentrate in order to pull this off, so if you could give us some privacy, that would be fantastic."

My voice had taken on a *pretty-please* tone, and I had m
hands clutched to my chest.

"No way am I leaving."

My hands dropped. I knew that wasn't going to work
"Look, Mort, I can understand you wanting to be here, bu
we do really need to concentrate and—"

"I won't make a peep," the ghost said, turning an imag
inary key over his lips.

"And," I said more forcefully, "have you considere
what it will be like to see your own death?" I didn't want t
put it so bluntly, but it needed to be said. I knew Mor
wanted answers, but wanting answers, and seeing firsthan
what actually happened, were two very different things.

"I'm a big boy," he said. "I can make my own decisions
And it's time you all saw what Cookie did to me."

"Brynn, darling," Izzy called over. "We don't reall
have time for debate."

I gave Mort another look.

"I'm not leaving," he said, meeting my gaze. "This is m
death we're talking about. I have a right to be here."

That was true. Besides, there was a chance he might b
able to lend insight into what it was we were about to see.
just hoped it wouldn't be too much for him.

I nodded and shifted my position to form a triangle wit
my aunts around the fire. Mort hovered behind me.

"Have we all memorized the chant?" Izzy asked, th
flames casting unfamiliar shadows over her face.

Nora and I nodded.

Oftentimes spells were long, involving several stanza
of rhyming couplets. In this case, though, it was just a fe
lines of prose, repeated like a chant. That actually made th
spell more difficult because it required all of us to visualiz
exactly what we wanted from the enchantment.

"Wait!" Nora hissed. "He died at the town gazebo
right?"

Which could result in some difficulties.

I nodded quickly.

"Got it." Nora straightened her shoulders as the waves of heat from the fire blew her hair back from her face.

Izzy raised her arms up to the sky. "Let us begin."

In an instant, my aunts' eyes flashed bright green. I knew mine had done the same. Mort squeaked behind me. I probably should have warned him about that.

"*Stars of night. Stars of night. Grant us the vision. Align our sight.*"

"I'm guessing Shakespeare didn't write these, huh?" Mort whispered at my back.

I shushed him.

Continuing the chant, we began to walk widdershins around the cauldron.

Mort followed close behind me, like a shadow. "Is this what you women have been getting up to back here all these years?"

I grunted. "It's not something we do every night. Now hush."

Once we had completed three revolutions, we headed back the other way, chanting the entire time.

"Nothing's happening," Mort observed.

I answered him by closing my eyes. Again, this spell required a great deal of focus. My aunts and I had discussed it beforehand and agreed to concentrate on three things in order to conjure the vison. Unless we sent out our intentions clearly, the enchantment wouldn't work.

Suddenly a force of magic clicked into place. The spell had locked in.

My aunts and I immediately stopped our circling of the cauldron and faced the steaming brew, now repeating aloud the agreed-upon symbols of re-creation.

"*Gazebo. Mort. Death.*"

"*Gazebo. Mort. Death.*"

The spirt behind me gasped.

The vapors above the cauldron, now purple and red,

parted, revealing a picture in the simmering potion underneath.

Sure, enough, it was the town gazebo. The park surrounding it was shrouded in darkness, but the distant horizon glowed with a thin yellow line.

"That's the gazebo, but where am I?" Mort asked, his voice right by my ear. "Can you adjust the view on this thing?"

I turned to face him. "Adjust the view on the cauldron?" I blinked. "No, we cannot."

He shrugged. "Just asking."

I turned my gaze back around.

"Maybe you guys got your stars aligned wrong because I don't see—"

"There," Nora said, her glowing eyes focused intently on something in the brew. "He's on the path."

Indeed, a still living Mort had entered the picture. And he certainly did look alive. Vital, even. Despite being a big man, he walked briskly, even hopping past the last step onto the floor of the gazebo.

"Look at me!" Mort shouted. "I'm the very picture of health."

I waved my hand for him to quiet down.

"But I don't get what I'm doing there. The sun's not even up. Les always handled the morning stuff."

"What's that he's holding?" Nora asked, leaning closer toward the hot potion. I touched her shoulder to stop her from toppling in.

"When are you going to see about getting glasses?" Izzy muttered. "Your vanity will be the death of you."

"I can see just fine. There are extra bubbles on this side of the— Oh, I think it's a box of chocolates."

"Hogwash!" Mort roared. He tried valiantly to push me aside so that he could get a better look, but his hand went right through my shoulder. I was just grateful he didn't try to go right through me. It was rather unnerving when ghosts did that. I shuffled to the side so that he could get in closer. "I don't recognize that box. It's not the kind we use in the store. It must be . . ."

Mort trailed off as he watched his still-living self take a seat on the bench that lined the inner walls of the gazebo. He placed the box on his lap and lifted off the lid.

"I'm sure they're delicious," Izzy muttered. "Everything made in the Sweetes' Shoppe is delicious, but don't do it, Mort!" She brought a tight fist to her mouth. "Remember your diabetes!"

Mort gave my aunt a withering look. One which she, of course, could not see. "I swear to you, I will not eat those chocolates." He looked back at his re-created living self. "I don't even sample our own recipes much anymore. Only when we want to try something new. I'm the customer relations guy."

Mort watched himself pluck one of the gold-foiled treats from the box and delicately unwrap it. The Mort in the vision looked at the chocolate carefully, then muttered in a voice that echoed from faraway, "*X, O.*"

"What does that mean?" I whispered. "Like hugs and kisses?"

The spirit shook his head.

The vision of Mort then brought the chocolate up to his nose and gave it a sniff. A strange look came over his living face. Confusion, maybe. When I looked over at ghost Mort, I found the exact same expression.

I darted my gaze back at the brew just in time to see the still living Mort pop the chocolate into his mouth. He chewed, then said, "Well, that's unexpected."

"What's unexpected?" Izzy asked the vision in the cauldron. She then looked up. "Mort, what's unexpected?" Unfortunately, she was looking at the wrong side of me.

"He's over here," I said, jerking my thumb.

"Oh." She adjusted her gaze. "Sorry."

Mort shook his head again.

"He doesn't know," I filled in.

"Everyone," Nora said softly, "I think it best if you all look away now."

Mort's expression fell. "Is it . . . *happening*?"

"I believe it is happening," Nora continued, unable to hear the ghost. "He's clutching his chest. There's no need for you to see this. For any of you. I'll keep watch."

Normally, despite the difficulty of witnessing such a thing, I would have stayed to see if there was any more to learn, but Mort looked so crestfallen, I knew where I was needed. I backed away from the fire, Mort floating beside me. "I don't understand any of this. I don't look like a man who's in fear for his life. Surely one or two chocolates wouldn't have triggered a heart attack."

"Maybe it wasn't the chocolates at all," I said gently. "You can't blame yourself. Death is inevitable for all of us. Maybe it was your time."

"Wait a minute," Nora called out.

"What's happened?" Izzy rushed back to the cauldron. "Surely, it's over by now."

"It certainly looks like it's over," Nora said. "And *somebody* has arrived to make sure."

"What do you mean somebody?" In a flash Mort disappeared from my side only to reappear a half second later at the cauldron. "Who is it?" he asked, dropping his head into the swirling steam.

I rushed back over to get my own look.

"No, no, no," Mort said. "This isn't right. I've been eavesdropping on all sorts of conversations around town, and I was found by Chief Walters on his way home from the fire station, and that," he said, sticking his finger right into the potion, "is not Chief Walters."

I couldn't argue with him. Chief Walters was a bear of a man and the silhouette of the figure approaching the gazebo was slender. The image was fuzzy though. I glanced at my watch. Twelve oh-three.

"The spell's fading!" Izzy said.

"Can't you stop it?" Mort shouted. "Look, whoever that is, they're coming toward me, dead me, I mean I'm dead me, but—" He grunted with frustration. "Whoever that is has to be my killer!"

I knew we couldn't draw that conclusion outright, but it didn't seem like the time to argue. Besides, the shadowy figure did look awfully suspicious. I would have expected a person in that situation to be calling emergency services or administering some sort of first aid, but this individual appeared calm, their movements slow and methodical. The vision was fading by the second, but the figure approaching the recently deceased Mort, was now reaching out a hand to check his pulse.

"Do you think that's Cookie?" I asked, not taking my eye from the potion.

Mort drifted back. He probably couldn't take any more.

"Are they trying to help him?" Izzy asked.

"I don't think so," Nora said. "I believe they are making sure the job is done."

"Oh! And look." Izzy gasped. "They're gathering up the rest of the chocolates!"

Just as the words had left my aunt's mouth, the vision disappeared.

We all straightened up and away from the cauldron.

Cold dread washed over me. "Mort, I am so sorry. You were right all along. I think those chocolates were poisoned."

I turned to face him, but found only Faustus seated on a tree stump, licking his paw.

Chapter 11

I WOKE TO A chilly room and the sound of raindrops hitting the windowpane above my bed. It was one of those heavy, drenching downpours that the spring plants love but is slightly dispiriting for the rest of us.

I didn't get much sleep. Casting big spells often left some residual magic flowing through the veins. But that wasn't my biggest barrier to rest. No, it was Mort. From the very beginning, he believed he had been murdered, but actually seeing it play out? I could only imagine what it was doing to him. Someone had wanted him dead. That was a lot to process. Coming to terms with an act of fate was something we all had to deal with at times, but Mort's life had been stolen from him, along with the time he had left with his wife.

And that was where I needed to start.

I got out of bed and dressed quickly. It was time I spoke to Mrs. Sweete. If anyone had in-depth knowledge into her husband's life, it would be her. I knew Mort had his reservations about my speaking to Angie, but I had no intention of letting her know that I had made any contact with her husband. I wouldn't do that until he was ready. And given how limited his time was, I wanted to get him answers fast. I believed it was the only way he would be willing to say goodbye to his wife, and I wasn't about to let that precious opportunity pass them both by.

Thankfully the rain had eased by the time I was ready to go. Just to be safe, though, I pulled on my red rain jacket, buttoning it to the top, and grabbed my umbrella on my way out the door. I stopped in at the B&B to pick up the breakfast casserole Izzy had promised to make. After the reenactment spell, she told me she had little hope of getting any sleep, and she had a few things she wanted to get ready for the following day anyway. Given what we had seen, she wanted to make something that would bring Angie a little comfort.

Despite the fact that I was being tortured by the delicious scents of sharp cheddar and ham wafting up from my basket, my spirits brightened considerably on the walk over to Mort's house. A quick check of the phone book had given me his address. I couldn't help but be cheered at the sight of all the spring flowers that had seemingly popped up overnight. And as if they weren't enough to lift my mood, I spotted a robin splashing around in a puddle. Judging by the water droplets flying through the air, the bath was long overdue.

Once on Mort's street, I tracked the house numbers to a tidy black-and-white cottage. I suppose *bungalow* would be the technical term, but with its charming white picket fence, black shutters, and climbing rosebush by the door, *cottage* certainly seemed more appropriate. It even had a cute sign that read *The Sweetes*. My heart pinched with sadness.

I checked my watch to make sure I wasn't too early to pay a call, then clicked open the gate and let myself inside. It was hard to gauge what sort of reception I would receive.

Angie and I were practically strangers, yet here I was about to knock on her door during what had to be the most difficult time of her life. I took a peek into the large window to the right of the door. There was a light shining farther into the house, but everything was still. It didn't look like any family members or friends had descended just yet.

I knocked lightly on the door.

Silence followed, but then a shadow moved inside. A moment later the door opened to reveal a small woman in a pale pink bathrobe with bloodshot eyes.

"Mrs. Sweete, my name is Brynn Warren. I'm so sorry to come to you under these circumstances, but I was hoping to talk to you."

"I know who you are," she said with a small smile. "Please. Please, come in."

A MINUTE OR TWO later, we were settled on the sofa in their living room.

While Angela Sweete clearly wasn't in her best state, Mort's wife was a truly beautiful woman. She had pretty pale blue eyes; silvery blond hair; and small, delicate features. More than any of that, though, she had gentle way about her that was quite endearing.

"I'm so sorry I'm not dressed," Angie said, tightening the belt of her robe. "I seem to have lost all track of time."

"Please don't give it a second thought. I should be the one apologizing for dropping by unexpected."

"I am so happy you did." She looked down at her hands fidgeting in her lap. It wasn't hard to guess what she was thinking, or rather what it was she was hoping for. I found myself wishing once again I had managed to convince Mort to speak to his wife. I knew he didn't want to tell her what we had learned about his death, but she was clearly suffering. I could only imagine that hearing from him would help. "Can I make you some tea? Or serve you some of the casserole you brought by?"

"I'm fine, really."

"It's nice not to have to think about food. Please thank your aunt. My neighbors have all been so kind." I followed her gaze over to an enormous bouquet by the window.

"My, that's stunning," I said, getting up to take a closer look. The large flowers in the bouquet had frilly white petals with pale yellow centers. I couldn't quite place them. They looked a little like peonies, or maybe carnations, but neither variety quite fit. "Are they gardenias?"

She smiled. "No, daffodils. Double daffodils. I think they're called Early Cheer. Elias Blumenthal sent them. Maybe you know him? He's the head of the gardening society here in Evenfall."

That gave me pause as I sat back down. I did not know Evenfall had a gardening society. What's more, I didn't know if Nora knew Evenfall had a gardening society. My aunt wasn't exactly a *society*-type person, but she was definitely the type who would expect an invitation from a society that specialized in her area of expertise. An invitation that she could then decline. That was a problem for another time though.

"He's been very kind. He lost his wife too. Many years ago."

We sat in silence a short time before I said, "Mrs. Sweete, I came by today to see if there's anything I can do to help." It wasn't a lie. Yes, I wanted to talk to Angie so that I could better understand what happened to Mort, but the ultimate goal was to help them both.

She cleared her throat. "If I'm honest, I was hoping to speak to you, Ms. Warren."

"Please call me Brynn."

"Brynn. And you must call me Angie. I've heard some stories around town," she said, her hands still fidgeting in her lap. "Is it true you can communicate with those who have passed?"

"It is."

Tears spilled down her cheeks. "Then you have a message for me? From my Morty? Is he here now?"

I gave her hand a squeeze. "He's not. I'm sorry. And I don't have a message for you right now. But I do expect to have one for you shortly." I said the words quickly, hoping to avoid having to elaborate. "In the meantime, I'd love to learn more about his life, about the type of man he was."

A heartbreaking smile spread across Angie's face. "Oh, where would I even begin? High school, I suppose. That's where we met. He was so shy back then."

"I'm sorry, Mort—I mean, Mr. Sweete—was shy?"

"Did you know him, dear?"

"Not well," I stammered. "Just from the candy shop. Every time I saw him, though, he seemed larger than life."

"That's Mort." The smile dropped from her face. "I mean, that *was* Mort. I guess I have to get used to saying that." She took a shuddering breath. "Back in high school, though, he was as timid as a mouse."

"Was it love at first sight?"

"Oh no," Angie said with a giggle. "Well, at least not for me. Mort always said it was for him. It wasn't until he started tutoring me that I saw him in a new light."

Angie must have caught surprise in my expression because she added, "I know. He doesn't seem like the bookish type, but my husband had hidden depths."

Again, the memory of Mort trying to kick down the For Sale sign with his ghostly foot flashed through my mind. It was difficult to reconcile that Mort with the young man she was describing.

"Anyway, it didn't take long after that for me to realize we were meant to be together, and we have been, ever since." Angie's voice shook as she brought a tissue to her eye. "I thought we'd have a good many years yet." She looked over at a box in the corner of the room. "We were starting to downsize, planning our next phase of life."

Mort hadn't mentioned anything along those lines. "Were you thinking of moving?"

"No, concrete plans. My daughter's husband is sick. They live in Florida. We were thinking of maybe moving down to help her with the kids, but Mort loved working with Les in the shop so much. I don't know if that ever would have happened."

"I am so sorry. This all must be such a shock."

"I can't even tell you." She pressed her fingers to her cheek. "I should have known something was wrong when Mort kissed me that morning. He left so early. Les was usually the one to open the shop. I was still half asleep when he got out of bed. I didn't even think to ask what he was doing. *See you soon, Sweetness.* That was the last thing he said to me." She dropped her hand. "That was his pet name for me. I always told him *Sweetness* Sweete was sugary even for him, but he'd always say it wasn't enough for me."

My throat tightened. I knew what Angie was feeling all too well. "I've heard that it was a heart attack?"

"The coroner seems to think so. Mort had a checkup not too long ago. He had some heart trouble, but everything was stable." She blinked some tears away. "But I suppose at our age things can change quickly. They told me they found him with an empty box of chocolates. The paramedics actually asked if I wanted to keep it." She shook her head. "I can't imagine why I'd want it."

"Everyone's different. Sometimes it's hard to let go of anything."

She nodded, then peeked up at me hopefully. "Do you really think you'll hear from Mort soon?"

As she asked the question, a prickle ran up the back of my neck. I glanced behind me, almost certain Mort would be there, but he wasn't. "I believe so. Yes."

"You'll tell me when you do?"

I needed to choose my words carefully. I didn't want to lie to this lovely woman. "As soon as Mort has a message for you, nothing will stop me from delivering it."

"I don't mean to push. It's just . . ." She cast a look over to the end table beside the sofa. "I need to tell him something." She rose to her feet, tightening her bathrobe again. "It's silly really. But I would feel better if he knew." She walked over to the table and picked up an envelope. "Mort and I never kept secrets, and I was going to tell him." Color filled her cheeks.

"What is it?"

"An anonymous love letter."

Chapter 12

ANGIE FIDDLED WITH the envelope like she was holding herself back from tearing it to pieces.

Out of all the things I had been expecting her to show me, an anonymous declaration of affection was not one of them. I scooted forward on the sofa, peering at the letter in Angie's hand. If I wasn't mistaken, *Angela* was typed on the front. Not printed from a computer but actually typed.

"It isn't right. I am a happily married woman. *Was* a happily married woman," she corrected.

"Are there any clues as to who sent it?" I really, really wanted to read the letter, but I didn't want to push too hard.

"None. There isn't even anything personal written inside. Just a few lines from love poems. Shakespeare. That kind of thing. The sentiments are beautiful, but so misplaced. I can't believe anyone would think I could return those feelings. I just wish I had told Mort before he . . ." She dropped the letter back on the table. "I know there's no reason to feel guilty, but still."

"If you don't mind my asking, why didn't you tell Mort right away?"

An impish smile came to the corner of her mouth as tears sparkled in her eyes. "If you knew my husband, you'd already know the answer to that."

I raised an eyebrow.

"The drama," she said, rolling her eyes to the ceiling. "I needed to prepare myself for the drama."

I laughed.

"What I'd give to hear him bluster now." Suddenly a strange look came over Angie's face. "Would you listen to me, carrying on like I'm the only widow in the world." She rushed back over to the sofa. "Have I been insensitive? You lost your husband too. And at such a young age."

Living in a small town meant everybody knew my story even if they didn't know me personally.

"No, you haven't been insensitive at all. Take it from someone who has been there. You need to be gentle with yourself right now. There will be time later to give back. And speaking of time, I have probably taken up enough of yours."

She sighed. "It's getting close to midday. The phone will start ringing soon."

I actually had a difficult time remembering the first few weeks after Adam's death, but I knew quite well from the experience of others that those first days could be over-whelmingly busy. Decisions. Arrangements. It's afterward that things get quiet. I rose to my feet.

"I can't tell you how grateful I am that you reached out to me, Brynn."

"Please. Think nothing of it."

"And . . . ?" She let the thought trail away, but there was no mistaking the hope in her eyes.

"And I'll be back as soon as I have something to tell you. I promise."

I TOOK MY TIME heading home. The rain had stopped, but the day was still gray.

I wasn't sure what to make of all that Angie had told me. The love letter loomed largest in my thoughts, but following close behind was the large bouquet of daffodils from her neighbor. Was it possible the two were related? It was something I needed to follow up on. Once I figured out how.

As I neared home, picking my way around puddles, I spotted my neighbor Mr. Henderson coming out from around the back of his house, holding a bundle of stakes under his arm.

Just the man I wanted to have a word with.

Truth be told, most days, I did my best to avoid him. For a number of reasons. It certainly wasn't because he was unfriendly. Just the opposite, in fact. He was quite neighborly. Maybe a bit too neighborly. You see, Mr. Henderson was the type of neighbor who couldn't resist peeking around his curtain to see what everyone else was up to; and when your neighbors are witches, that habit could be a bit of a problem. In his case it certainly had been. After checking in on us one particular evening and seeing something he definitely shouldn't have, Izzy performed a small memory-wiping spell on him. It was kind of funny. Nora was usually the one to spell first and ask questions later, but Izzy had jumped right in before anyone could object. Memory spells required careful planning. Without precautions, they could easily go wrong. Thankfully Izzy's spell hadn't, but in hindsight I wasn't sure she had made the best call. It was a long shot that Mr. Henderson would have been able to handle what he had seen, but perhaps he deserved the opportunity to try before Izzy stole his memory? It was difficult to say. Having others know our secret was risky. Humans didn't always play nicely with witches. But we should have at least discussed it.

All this to say, any other day, I might have ducked back the other way and taken the long route to Ivywood Hollow, but today was different.

"Good morning, Mr. Henderson!" I called out cheerily. "Are we expecting an invasion of vampires?"

He looked confused.

"All the stakes," I said, pointing to the bundle under his arm.

His eyes lit with understanding as he looked down at his collection. "Oh! Yes, I see. You were making a joke."

Apparently not a very funny one. I should have known better than to pick at this thread.

"You know it's not wise to make light of such things in Evenfall."

I nodded. I did know. He had told me several times. In fact, this particular topic of conversation was yet another one of the reasons why I usually avoided my neighbor.

He lowered the stakes onto his lawn. "In this town, any number of strange creatures could be lurking right underneath your nose."

I stepped to the side. I had been standing right underneath, well, his nose.

"I'm glad you're here though," he said, straightening his glasses and smoothing down his white hair, which always seemed to be standing on end. "I've been wanting to speak with you." He waved me in closer, which was funny considering there was absolutely no one around. "Did you hear about Mort Sweete's passing?"

I nodded.

My neighbor leaned even closer toward me. "I saw his spirit last night."

Oh dear.

I should have seen this coming.

As part of his self-imposed neighborhood watch duties, Mr. Henderson was perpetually on the lookout for supernatural activity. He was always seeing ghosts. In fact, if he was to be believed, he saw far more ghosts than I did. Haunting the woods. Hiding under bushes. Hanging out at local coffee shops. He saw them everywhere. To be fair, my neighbor usually did see something when he had these sightings. They just weren't ghosts.

"Really?" I tried to contort my expression into polite interest. "Where exactly did you see this spirit?"

"Well, I was going through my attic last night, looking for a box when . . ."

As Mr. Henderson went on, my eyes trailed up to the attic window in his Arts and Crafts bungalow.

It only took half a second to spot my neighbor's ghost. If I wasn't mistaken, his spirit had taken the form of a white plastic bag snagged on a tree branch, floating gently in the breeze.

I brought my attention back down just in time to hear, "Anyway, I went off to bed, but you can bet I left my table lamp on."

"Very wise," I said with a nod. "Thank you for telling me. I'll be sure to stay vigilant." Overall, that hadn't been too bad. Maybe I could shift the topic to *my* ghostly concerns. "Now that I have you, though, can I pick your brain about something else?" I didn't wait for him to answer. "Last time I was in your house, I noticed that you owned a vintage typewriter."

"Oh yes," he said, rocking on his feet. "It's a beauty, that one. Made in 1942."

"Do people actually use typewriters anymore? Or are they just for show?" Angie's anonymous love letter had me thrown. I couldn't remember the last time I had seen a typewritten page.

"Oh yes. They are very much still in use," Mr. Henderson said with authority. "They've gone through a big resurgence as of late. Young people love them. Hipsters and Hollywood types."

Huh. I had no idea. Maybe Nixie wasn't the only one who needed to get out more. "But can you get ink for them?"

"Sure can," he said with a big nod. "You just order the ribbon online. If you're interested, you should go talk to Simon at the antique shop."

Evenfall only had one antique shop. As Time Goes By. I had walked by it hundreds of times, but I couldn't recall ever having been inside. My aunts had certainly never suggested it. Ivywood Hollow already had so many antiques. Truth be told, most witches had a minor problem with *collecting*, so it was probably best we didn't go beyond window-shopping.

"Simon's got at least four or five for sale. He can tell you all about them. That man is a walking encyclopedia."

"I may do that. Thank you." I took a step toward the sidewalk. "I should probably let you get back to your *stakes*." I put a little inflection into the word, hoping he'd take that opening to fill in exactly what it was he was doing. While the stakes were most likely gardening related, I was suddenly a touch concerned that Izzy's spell may have had some side effects after all. Unfortunately, he didn't take my bait.

"You are very welcome, neighbor," he said, giving me a two-finger salute at the corner of his forehead. "Oh, and good luck today!"

I had already made it back to the sidewalk, but that stopped me in my tracks. "Good luck?" I backpedaled a few steps.

Mr. Henderson's eyes widened. "Did I say *good luck*?"

"You did."

He straightened his glasses, which had once again fallen askew. "Are you sure I didn't say good day? Maybe goodbye?"

"You most certainly said *good luck*." My eyes narrowed. "Good luck for what?"

"I don't think I was supposed to say anything," he said, his gaze darting about. "In fact, I'm certain of it. Besides you'll find out soon enough." He turned on his heel.

"Stop right there."

His shoulders popped up around his ears.

"What is going on?"

He turned slowly. "I ran into Izzy this morning. She was wondering if I had seen you head out."

I tapped my umbrella on the sidewalk, creating the sharp staccato beat of a ticking clock. "Why?"

He grimaced. "She was interested in figuring out when you were getting back. I think she might be planning a special lunch for you?"

A loud clang rang out from across the street, like someone had dropped the lid of a garbage can. When I turned back around, Mr. Henderson was halfway up his lawn.

"Got to skedaddle. Nice talking to you, Brynn!"

As I watched him flee in terror, I couldn't help but wonder what that had all been about. What kind of lunch could Izzy be planning?

It was possible Mr. Henderson was having another one of his flights of fancy, but somehow I didn't think so.

I took slow steps toward the B&B. As I neared, the clouds parted, and a beam of sunlight dropped directly onto the house.

I frowned.

My gaze trailed over the facade of Ivywood Hollow. It looked *different*. Maybe it was the sudden parting of the clouds? Or the sight of songbirds gathering above the roof, twittering and playing aerial tag? I had never seen birds gather there before. Hmm, and the large cherry tree on the front lawn was in full bloom when just this morning all of the pink buds were still tightly closed.

And . . . was that a rainbow?

I blinked. Yes, there was indeed a rainbow arcing from nowhere and landing on the tower peak of the house.

Stars above, what was going on?

Sometimes when my aunts and I were experiencing strong emotions, the atmosphere around the B&B changed, affecting wildlife, our neighbors, and even the weather. When my aunts were fighting, for example, a storm cloud often appeared directly above the house. That I was used to. But all this sunshine and rainbows? Somehow this was more disturbing.

As I crept up the drive, I noticed something else.

"You have to be kidding me," I whispered.

The outer walls of the B&B were sparkling. Literally sparkling. Like someone had painted all of Ivywood Hollow with a thin coat of glitter.

And I knew exactly the witch responsible.

I picked up my step and made a beeline for the carriage house. I was having none of *whatever* this was. If I was really careful, I could sneak up to the loft without anyone ever knowing I was there.

I hurried for the stairs, ignoring the delicious scent of— give me strength—quiche lorraine with roasted red pepper and smoked Gouda, floating on the breeze. Izzy made that so well, but even so, I knew it probably wasn't worth whatever it would cost me to go inside.

I had just planted my foot on the bottom step when I heard, "Oh, Brynn!"

I jolted. Maybe I could pretend not to hear her? I could at least give it a try. I took another step and felt the tiniest magical swat at the back of my neck. I guess my aunt was in no mood to be ignored.

I turned around. Izzy was practically beaming from the threshold of the front door. She looked lovely in yet another frilly dress.

"There's someone I want you to meet. Come over, darling."

Someone she wanted me to meet?

I shook my head.

"Don't be silly. We're waiting."

I moved slowly toward the B&B, valiantly attempting to come up with reassuring thoughts. I was an adult. I could meet people. My aunt couldn't drag me into anything I didn't want to be dragged into.

I walked up the porch steps.

"There you are," Izzy said happily. She stepped out of the way to reveal a tall handsome man standing behind her. "Brynn, I'd like you to meet Jacob." The man stepped aside to reveal two others. "And his brother Thomas. And their friend Michael. I probably should have said I have a few *someones* I'd like you to meet." She laughed merrily. "They've all stopped by for brunch. Why don't you join us?"

Again, my aunt couldn't drag me into anything I didn't want to be dragged into—except maybe a thrown-together version of *The Dating Game, Witches Edition*.

I struggled to think of an excuse to leave. I knew I only had a second to come up with a suitable lie. Any longer and it would be horribly obvious that I was making it up.

"I . . ." I had nothing. That's what I had.

"Come along," Izzy said, looking quite pleased with herself.

As I passed my aunt on the threshold, I whispered, "You are so dead."

She batted a hand at me.

"And that quiche had better be good."

Chapter 13

"SO, HOW LONG do you plan to stay mad at Izzy?"

"I'm not mad."

The following day had turned back to glorious sunshine and fresh spring air. Nora strode down the sidewalk with me trailing behind, struggling to keep up. How my aunt could walk so quickly in her four-inch spike-heel boots was beyond me. She did, however, look fabulous in her black fitted pants and dark fuchsia turtleneck. Not every redhead could pull off pink, but Nora, of course, wasn't just any redhead. She had her hair pulled back in a severe ponytail and was wearing her signature oversized black sunglasses. We were on our way to Elias Blumenthal's house.

After giving it some thought, I decided on this particular path forward. Nora was a gardening expert, after all, and Elias was head of Evenfall's gardening society. Surely, that was reason enough for the two to meet; and once that got us in the door, then I could maybe throw in a few questions of my own. I hadn't gotten around to telling Nora about the whole society thing. I thought that might hurt my chances of securing her support in this endeavor. I figured I could deal with that situation when it came out. Besides, maybe it wouldn't bother her that the town had a club devoted to her area of expertise and hadn't thought to invite her, even though Ivywood Hollow's gardens were award winning and quite famous on the Eastern Seaboard. It was possible. Not likely. But possible.

Really, none of that was important right now. I had bigger issues. I hadn't seen hide nor sparkly hair of Mort since we had performed the reenactment spell. I knew it hadn't been a good idea for him to witness his own death.

"If you're not angry, why didn't you come over for dinner last night?" Nora asked.

"Brunch was quite filling." Not that I was angry about it. A touch frustrated maybe. Slightly annoyed. The teensiest bit miffed.

"Well, by all means, stay angry as long as you wish," Nora said, clicking along the sidewalk. "Izzy always does come up with the most delicious recipes when she feels guilty."

"I'm not angry."

Nora whirled around on her heel. "But you might want to keep one thing in mind."

I jerked to a stop.

"Your aunt did have the very best of intentions. And there are worse things than sharing a meal with three charming warlocks."

I grunted. There may very well be worse things, but I doubted there were any more awkward.

Stars above, it had been a disaster. There had been more cringeworthy moments than I could count with Izzy and me sitting on one side of the dining table, the three warlocks on the other, the five of us making small talk. I think Izzy had recognized pretty quickly that she had miscalculated her chances of success with her little plan. I had never

heard her talk so much, trying to fill in the many silences
and I didn't do much to help her out.

And yes, they were all lovely men from good witching
families. Any woman would be lucky to catch their collec-
tive eye, so to speak. Just not this woman. Once they had
left, I escaped back up to my loft, saying nary a word to my
aunt. She knew what she'd done. The quiche was excellent
though.

I hurried my steps to catch up to Nora, who had resumed
her punishing march. "Whose side are you on anyway? I
thought I made my feelings on the subject of *love*"—I said
the word with an implied eye roll—"clear. To the both
of you."

"Pardon me." Nora brought a hand to her chest. "I most
certainly had nothing to do with Izzy's ill-advised plan."

"I guess I'm just so used to you being the one who—" I
cut myself short.

"Me being the one who does what?"

Doesn't listen? Crosses boundaries? Sometimes ignores
other people's feelings? There were so many options.
"Never mind."

"I will have you know, dear niece, that I tried to dis-
suade my sister from her matchmaking shenanigans, but
she's got it in her head that you believe in the Warren family
curse when it comes to love, and that's what is holding you
back. And while I know this a difficult time of year for
you," she said, voice softening, "it is also a tricky one
for your aunt. You need to cut her some slack."

Wait, what? Yes, spring was difficult for me. How could
it not be? The anniversary of Adam's death had passed not
too long ago. In a strange way all the beauty of the season
increased the loss, the pain of his absence. But I was staying on top of it. All that being said, though, since when was
spring a tricky time for Izzy? She loved this time of year.
She had made that abundantly clear. "Why is spring difficult for Izzy?"

Nora's step faltered, but she recovered a split second later. "I never said spring was tricky for Izzy."

"Yes, you did. You just said it."

"I most certainly did not."

"You most certainly did."

"Nonsense. You misheard," she said, refusing to meet my eyes. "It's that spring fever of yours. It's affected your hearing."

I was almost running now, trying to keep up with my aunt. She had quickened her pace to a ridiculous degree. But she wasn't getting away that easily. "My hearing is just fine. You said—"

"I said spring was tricky for *Gideon*." Nora spun around again. I had to skid to a stop to avoid running into her. "Speaking of which, have you ever heard the story of when your uncle Gideon first fell in love with Lydia?"

"No."

"Forget Izzy." She raised a mischievous eyebrow. "His story is much more fun."

Chapter 14

IT WAS CLEAR Nora was trying to derail me. She obviously had alluded to something she shouldn't have when it came to her sister—something I really wanted to know—but now I wanted to hear Gideon's story too! Lydia was my uncle Gideon's one great love. The one he lost in the accident that had also killed my parents. Usually, when the topic of her came up, everyone was sad; but if the death of my husband had taught me anything, it was that memories should be cherished and embraced. Death can't take those away.

"It was back in his senior year of high school," Nora said, launching into the story, not waiting to hear any objections on my part about her having changed the subject. "Gideon had quite the following of girls back then. He was always wearing dark-colored turtlenecks and writing poetry. The ninnies couldn't get enough. But even though he had his pick of the troop, he never really seemed to show much interest. Then one day the strangest thing happened."

"What?"

"He tripped." She gave me a playful smile, then turned to head back down the sidewalk.

"He tripped?" I scampered after her. "Why is that strange?"

"Well, it wasn't. If he had tripped only once." She gave me a quick look. "But he didn't. He tripped again. And then again and again. Walking to school. Rambling the halls. Running track. He couldn't stay on his feet. He was turning black and blue all over."

I frowned. "This doesn't sound like a happy story so far."

She laughed. "Oh no. We were very concerned. Mother thought about taking him to see a doctor to get some testing done; but as you well know, medical equipment doesn't always behave around witches, so you can imagine how desperate she was to even suggest it. But then we noticed a pattern." She paused as a jogger loped by. Even though the man made sure to give us plenty of space by leaving the sidewalk and running on the road, Nora still gave him an imperious look. My aunt did not appreciate people sweating in her vicinity. Once he was gone, she continued. "Where was I? Oh yes, the pattern. Well, Gideon's difficulties staying upright never happened at home. Only at school. At first, we thought maybe there was another witch around who might be toying with him for some reason, but it wasn't a witch at all."

"It was Lydia." My voice had taken on a squealy tone. I cleared my throat and tried again. "It was Lydia, wasn't it?"

"It was. Whenever that girl got within a few hundred yards of Gideon, he would just fall all over himself."

I made another excited sound low in my throat.

"That's when we knew."

"Knew what?" I already guessed the answer, but I wanted to hear her say it.

"Gideon had fallen in love. That's the way it happens for some witches. When they are hit with Cupid's arrow, they literally fall head over heels."

"That is so cute."

"It was and Gideon was so embarrassed. It didn't stop until he got up the nerve to talk to her."

"Aw," I said, drawing out the sound. "Now, going back to Izzy and—"

"Never mind all that. What exactly are we doing today? You said you needed my expertise?"

Clearly, I wasn't going to get any answers out of her right now.

"We are going to introduce ourselves to Elias Blumenthal."

Not only had I not told Nora about the gardening society, I hadn't really told her much of anything at all. Just that I had a problem, and she was the *only* one who could help me. Making my aunt feel special was usually the best way to ensure her help. I filled her in on the enormous bouquet I saw at Angie's house and the anonymous love letter that had turned up in her mailbox.

"Oh, how exciting," Nora said. "I can think of no better way to spend a morning than conversing with a suspected killer."

I blinked but didn't answer. I hadn't exactly said he was a suspected killer. That seemed a bit premature, and I could think of at least a few better ways to spend a morning, but to each their own, I guess.

"I imagine I will be quite good at this."

"At what exactly?"

"Sleuthing."

I smiled. It must be nice to have my aunt's confidence. "Okay, but remember, no magic." We'd had some trouble in the past with Nora using her magical abilities to get the truth out of people.

"You are absolutely no fun," my aunt said with a sniff.

I wouldn't have said *absolutely*.

"But you have no cause for worry, my lovely, unkempt niece," she went on, eyeing my jeans. Nora was not a fan of jeans. Even if they were an attractive dark wash and looked quite nice with my cozy light knit sweater. "I will get all the answers you seek without the help of any magic."

And here I had thought I just brought her along as a botanical icebreaker. "Well, good, but I thought I might take this lead on this."

"Whatever for?"

"I have had experience with this type of thing."

"She solves one murder, and she thinks she's Poirot."

"I do not think I'm—" I cut myself off. We were getting off track. "You know what? It doesn't really matter which one of us does the questioning as long as we stay focused on finding out two things. Mr. Blumenthal's feelings toward Angie, and whether or not he has an alibi for late Tuesday night, early Wednesday morning." It was hard to say exactly how or when the killer got the chocolates to Mort, but I reasoned that time frame was a good place to start.

"Should be easy enough," Nora said. "Is this the house?"

I stopped at the stone path that led up from the sidewalk to a tidy white clapboard dwelling covered in ivy. There were flower beds lining the walls on either side of the front door; and, although it was hard to see from our vantage point, it looked like the backyard might be teeming with plants, given the large fronds draped over the fence.

"I believe so."

Nora strode up the path, saying to me over her shoulder, "Well then, let's meet our killer."

"Suspected killer," I hissed back.

"Technicalities," she trilled, swirling her fingers in the air before bringing them down onto the brass knocker and giving it a resounding whack.

Chapter 15

ELIAS BLUMENTHAL WAS not at all what I had expected.

Going in, all I really knew about him was that he was a gardener and that he had lost his wife at a young age. For some reason that had led me to picture a sweet older man who like to putter around in his backyard.

That was not Elias.

No, when the gardener in question opened his front door, I'm embarrassed to say, the phrase that popped into my mind was *stone-cold fox*. He was tall, maybe in his late fifties, and had the broad shoulders and lean build of a much younger man. He had strong, patrician features and an elegant smile that looked like it had taken several years of practice to get just right. He was wearing a sweater over a button-down shirt—a little like something Mr. Rogers might wear—but somehow, he made the look appear as though he should be brunching by a lake nestled in the Alps, not talking to puppets.

I may have been getting carried away, but I could tell

Nora was also floored by his good looks. It showed up in the tiniest of frowns between her eyebrows. If I had to guess, she was a touch put out, given that she was used to being the most attractive person in any grouping.

"Good morning, ladies," he said. "How may I help you?"

I resisted the urge to titter. His voice held the faintest trace of a German accent, which may not be known as the sexiest of accents but it did give him a certain air of . . . something.

"Hello," I said, getting a hold of myself. "My name is Brynn Warren, and this is my aunt Evanora."

"Evanora Warren?" Elias repeated. "From Ivywood Hollow?"

"Yes," Nora replied suspiciously.

He held out a hand to her.

She slowly reached toward it, looking at him like the gesture might be a trap.

"I am honored to meet you. I have heard the most wonderful things about your garden."

"Really?" she replied. "I have heard nothing of yours."

Sometimes I couldn't help but think my aunt should be banned from going out in public. "Until recently, is what she means," I said quickly. "That is why we are here."

Both looked over to me.

"I believe you know Angela Sweete? She mentioned that you were the president of Evenfall's gardening society. We had to see what you've been up to."

He brought his hand to his chest. "I would be delighted to show you. It is still early in the season, but I would be happy to give you a tour. Please, follow me."

I made a move to follow Elias into his house, but Nora didn't budge. "Are you coming?"

"I'm sorry, did you just say Evenfall's gardening society?"

Uh-oh.

"Evenfall has a gardening society?"

"I . . . oh . . ." I rushed inside.

Yes, bringing Nora probably hadn't been the best idea after all.

I TOOK THE BRIEF walk through Elias's home as an opportunity to get a better sense of who the man was. From what I could see, the small house was immaculately tidy. The kitchen we passed was so clean it almost looked unused. Unfortunately, the only other room I was able to catch a peek of was his office. All the walls had built-in bookshelves, and the room was devoid of furniture except for a desk. There was no computer resting on it, only a rotary phone and stack of books. One of the tomes was as thick as the four or five resting on top of it. I had just enough time to catch the name *Shakespeare* printed on the spine. Hadn't Angie said the love poems in her anonymous letter were by Shakespeare? It wasn't exactly a smoking gun, but it was something.

I must have hesitated too long at the doorway of the office because I felt sharp poke into my shoulder blade. I guess Nora had deigned to come inside after all.

I hurried after our host.

Entering Elias Blumenthal's back garden was like stepping into another world. It was only postage-stamp-sized, but he had used every square inch to fill with plants. There was so much *green* I found my gaze bouncing around, unable to choose a spot to land. While a number of the plants were, of course, in the many beds covering what had once been a lawn, many others were potted, and quite a few had cages over them. Maybe to keep animals out? The species ranged from large tropical varieties that gave the space an almost jungle-type feel to small delicate flowers that looked as though they might wilt if you stared at them for too long. If I had to guess, the closeness of the plants had raised the temperature of the yard by at least a few degrees, which probably explained why his flowers were a little further along in terms of the season.

"This is quite remarkable, Mr. Blumenthal," I said breathlessly. "Who knew you had this treasure hidden away in your backyard?"

"Apparently quite a few people," Nora quipped under her breath. "An entire society, you might say."

I smiled brightly.

"Please call me Elias," the handsome gardener said. "And thank you for your kind words."

"Angie was the one with the kind words," I said, hoping that had sounded more subtle than it felt.

"Have you spoken to Angela recently?" he asked. "I have been quite worried. Such a difficult thing to lose a loved one."

He seemed genuinely concerned about Angie's well-being. I didn't know him well enough to read anything more into his expression though. His concern might simply be that of a neighbor or friend, but I couldn't be certain. Also interesting was the fact that he used Angie's full name. I wondered if other people used it or if he was the only one. It was of note, given the long form was written on the envelope of the anonymous love letter she had received.

"She is doing as well as one might expect," I said, watching Nora disappear behind a tall bush, trailing her fingers over a waxy leaf twice the size of her hand. I knew she was put out at the thought that Evenfall had a gardening society, and its members hadn't thought to anoint her as its queen; but there was nothing better than a collection of plants to mollify her ruffled sensibilities.

"I hope I have not offended your aunt," Elias said quietly.

"Why would you think that?"

"Naturally, all of our society's members are aware

of Ivywood Hollow's superior gardens. We would have reached out to her, given our shared interests; but when it comes to your aunt, some of our members are—" He paused. "What is the word I am looking for?"

"Intimidated?"

"Ah yes, thank you, some of our members are intimidated by your aunt's superior skills."

I suppressed a smile. Somehow, I doubted it was just her skills they were intimidated by.

"I completely understand," I said. "Don't give it a second thought. I'm sure Nora is fine. Actually, I think she might be in heaven." Again, gardens were my aunt's happy place. "So, did you know Mort well?" I tried to keep the grimace from my face. That transition definitely hadn't been subtle. Nora was right. I was a good ways from achieving Poirot status yet.

"Not very," Elias said. If he had been nonplussed by my asking, he certainly didn't show it. "Angie and I have become good friends through our shared botanical curiosities. Mort wasn't interested in plants though." An amused smile touched the corner of his mouth.

I raised an eyebrow.

"Oh, I was just remembering the tour I once gave Angie, Cookie, and their respective husbands. The women were quite receptive—they are both society members—but, well, as the saying goes, I believe the men could not wait to get out of here."

"It's hard to imagine anyone wanting to leave this garden," I said with a sigh before catching myself. It almost sounded like I was flirting with Elias Blumenthal. And while I had no romantic interest in this much older gentleman, he really was a handsome specimen with a beautiful garden. It was a good thing Izzy wasn't here. She'd probably try to set me up with him too.

Elias smiled. "You are too kind."

I almost replied but something caught my eye.

The back wall of Elias's house was mainly windows, presumably so that the view of the garden could be enjoyed from the inside, but that didn't much matter. No, it was what I had spotted inside Elias's office that caught my interest. I hadn't been able to see it before because of the large stack of books on his desk, but from this view, it was plain.

A typewriter.

"Ms. Warren, is something the matter?"

I met Elias's inquiring eye, not quite sure what to say. Thankfully, I didn't have to say anything at all.

"So, this potting club of yours," Nora interrupted, appearing from behind a veil of leaves. "When does it meet?"

Elias looked over, momentarily flustered by the transition. "The third week of each month?"

Nora planted a hand on her hip and tilted her head to the side. "Next week, then."

"Why yes," Elias said, recovering his composure and gifting us all with a solicitous smile. "If you would like to join us, we were planning to meet at Birdie Cline's house."

"Cancel that." Nora swatted the idea away with her free hand. "Ivywood Hollow must host your next meeting."

"Oh, Ms. Warren, we would be most honored," Elias said with a bow. I kind of loved this man. Very Captain von Trapp. "But it's such short notice. We would not want to put you out."

"You know, we'll do more than just host the meeting. Let's make it a grand affair. Dinner too. My sister will be more than happy to whip something up."

Elias looked uncertain. "We do have seventeen regularly attending members."

"Seventeen," Nora repeated with a somewhat scary chuckle. "And not one had the nerve to invite—"

I cut her off with a look.

"I assure you, Izzy won't mind," she said with an almost genuine-looking smile. "I'll treat you all to a lecture. In my greenhouse."

That caught my attention. Nora rarely let people into her greenhouse.

"Now that you have shown me yours," she said, "it's only right that I show you mine."

I cringed at the unfortunate phrasing. From anyone else that would have come off as quite the flirtatious statement, but from Nora it sounded almost like a threat. Not that I had ever really seen my aunt flirt before. Maybe it always came across as threatening.

"I will have to speak to the other members. I wouldn't want Birdie to be offended."

Nora scoffed. "I will handle Birdie. We are great friends."

Great friends? That was not how I would put it. Archnemeses might be more appropriate. Given that both were alpha females, it was difficult for them to coexist in small spaces. Truth be told, I think Nora envied Birdie's ease with inserting herself in the community; and Birdie perhaps envied, well, all that was Nora.

"What night did you say it was that you held your meetings?" my aunt went on.

"Wednesdays?"

"Not Tuesdays? I've always found Tuesday to be the night most clubs choose to meet."

"No, I usually spend Tuesday nights in," he said, flustered at the speed at which things were progressing. "There's a gardening show I enjoy before heading off to sleep."

"Next Wednesday it is, then." Nora finished by shooting me a satisfied look.

I had to hand it to her. Her comment about Tuesdays had been fairly nonsensical. I didn't think there was a *usual* night for clubs to meet, but she had been talking so quickly, Mr. Blumenthal had revealed—maybe without realizing it—that he most likely did not have an alibi for the hours leading up to Mort's death.

Suddenly Elias's rotary phone rang out, reaching us through the open window of his office.

"We should let you get that," I said quickly.

"I am expecting a call from my brother." He cast a look over his shoulder. "But I can certainly call him back."

"Nonsense," Nora and I both said.

"If you're sure . . . ?"

"We insist." Nora gestured over to the gate. "We'll show ourselves out."

"It was a pleasure to meet you both. Please be sure to fasten the latch behind you. Some of the plants—"

"I am well aware of what some of the plants are," Nora said darkly. "I'll be in touch with the details for the meeting."

Once Elias had stepped back inside, Nora grabbed my arm. "Quick we need to split up. Who knows how much time we'll have."

I heard Elias's cheery voice answering the phone in German. I couldn't see him in the office. He must have picked up an extension in some other room. "How much time for what?"

"To mentally catalog the plants," she said as though it were obvious. "This is clearly no ordinary garden."

"What do you mean it's not an ordinary garden? What kind of garden is it?"

"A poison one, my dear niece," Nora replied with a slow smile. "Mr. Elias Blumenthal has created a magnificent poison garden."

Chapter 16

M Y EYES TRAILED over the backyard, seeing the
magnificent greenery in a disturbing new light.

"Now, you take that side," my aunt commanded. "I'll
take this one. We need to identify as many plants as possible to narrow down the most likely candidates. Some are
entirely inappropriate for making chocolates."

I would have thought all poisonous plants would be inappropriate for making chocolates, but who was I to quib-
ble? "Wait, you want *me* to identify the plants?"

Nora tilted her head back, seemingly gaining a few
inches in height. "My darling niece, any witch worth her
salt knows how to identify poison plants. Are you telling
me all those hours I spent teaching you botanical identify-
ing features were wasted?"

"No." I mean not when she phrased it like that.

"Then go." She shooed me away with her fingertips.
"Oh! And while I shouldn't have to say it, do not touch any
of the plants in cages."

My arms suddenly wrapped themselves in close to my chest.

Nora gave me a withering look, then rushed away.

I turned slowly, eyeing the dangerous-looking wall of plants confronting me. Now, I was no slouch when it came to plant identification—I did know more than most—but Nora had very high standards. I searched through my memory for all the tidbits she had given me over the years. All I could remember was that there had been a lot of Latin involved and counting of leaves.

Okay, focus, Brynn.

What did I remember? Hmm, I knew there was a story involving monks and poison. Monkshood? Or was it wolfsbane? Wait, weren't they the same thing?

I chewed the corner of my thumbnail. Sorting through memories clearly wasn't the best approach. Maybe if I wandered through the plants, something would hit me. Hopefully, not literally, given that this was a poison garden.

A faint slithering sound came up from the ground, making me jump. My eyes searched for the source and spotted the tail of snake disappearing around a terra-cotta pot. Great. Snakes. I mean it seemed only right this garden had snakes. Why stop at poison?

I moved hesitantly around a tall pot filled with what looked to be stinging nettle. Certainly not the most attractive of plants with its dandelion-shaped leaves and covering of hairy spikes, but I did know it had its charms. Nora used it frequently in spells *and* hair care products. She claimed it made her locks shiny.

I eyed a cluster of bright red flowers with bluish-black pistils. Poppies. They, of course, could be used to make opium. But somehow, I didn't think they would be the flower of choice for a poison confection. It would be difficult to get the amount right to ensure an overdose. Regardless, I tucked the plant away in memory.

I made my way around the potted nettle to eye another plant with towering, delicate stalks. I knew it would be a couple of months before it bloomed. Belladonna, if I wasn't mistaken. I leaned in, then jumped back as something caught my sleeve. I whirled around to face my botanical attacker.

The bush that had grabbed me looked innocent enough with its fresh pink buds, but there was something about it that triggered a faint memory of danger. Now, what was it? I studied its branches from a distance, not quite ready to step closer. I knew this plant. I just couldn't remember its name.

Suddenly an icy cold sensation ran through my veins. Some of the plant's branches had been slashed. I would have used the word *pruned*, but no, these were not clean cuts. They were jagged breaks. That was wrong. Elias was obviously an expert gardener. I couldn't imagine him carelessly hacking his plants.

Where was Nora? She'd be able to identify this bush in an instant.

I almost called out her name, but I didn't want to alert Elias. I frantically looked around the garden trying to spot my aunt's pink top through the foliage, but she had disappeared.

What *was* this plant's name? I almost had it. It was right on the tip of my—

"Mort!"

Chapter 17

"I WOULD LIKE TO have a word with you, Ghostie."

I stared wide-eyed at the spirit suddenly standing in front me, his arms crossed over his chest. The look on his face suggested he was taking enormous pains to remain calm. It was disconcerting, considering he was still dressed like a member of a barbershop quartet.

And, *Ghostie*?

"I'd like to have a word with you too. But not right now. I'm kind of in the middle of something." He certainly did have a habit of popping in and out at the most inconvenient times.

I tried to peer through my ghost friend's chest to the bush behind him, but he was having none of it. He stooped to catch my eye. "You went to see Angie. I thought I made my feelings clear on that subject."

Those words sounded familiar. Actually, it was possible I had said something just like that when I had been talking to Nora earlier about Izzy's ambush brunch.

"I told you I didn't want you speaking to my wife," Mort went on. "But you did it anyway."

I put my hands up. "I can explain." I had, of course, wanted to explain things before I spoke to Angie, but Mort had not exactly been making himself available. That being said, I could hardly blame him after what he had seen in the cauldron. I needed to be sensitive to what he was going through. And patient.

"I don't want to hear your explanations."

Even if he wasn't exactly making it easy.

"I thought I could trust you."

"I . . . you can." Mort's words stung, but I had to stay focused. I looked over my shoulder to see if Nora had reappeared. Hopefully she was making better progress than I was. "And you don't have to worry. I didn't tell Angie I had actually seen you."

The spirit's eyes bulged. "That doesn't make a lick of difference. She knows your reputation. She would have had hopes the minute she saw you on our doorstep."

Mort seemed to have a pretty good visual of my meeting with Angie. How did he know I had visited his wife? Had he been eavesdropping?

I tilted my head toward the house. I could still hear Elias's voice coming from inside, so that was one good thing at least. "Listen, I understand where you are coming from, but we both want the same thing here. I don't want to upset Angie. I want to find out what happened to you, so that you feel comfortable saying goodbye to her. It's what I do. And I think you know time is limited."

Mort floated back from me. "You mean the light?"

"I know you feel its pull. We don't have all the time in the world here. Angie could help us find the answers you need."

"It's not worth it if it upsets her."

"She's already upset." I hadn't meant to put it so bluntly,

but maybe it needed to be said. This clearly wasn't the best time to be having this conversation, but given Mort's schedule, it might very well be the only time. "Your wife is grieving. She's trying to process what happened and speaking to you might help."

"No," the ghost said, scissoring his hands in the air. "I won't lie to her, and the truth is we don't know what happened to me. We don't even know if I really was murdered!"

My jaw dropped open, but no words came out.

"That's right. You heard me." Mort refolded his arms over his chest. "We don't know anything for sure."

I blinked. "I'm a little confused here. What do you mean—"

"Brynn," Nora hissed at my shoulder. "We need to go. Elias is saying *Auf Wiedersehen*."

I peeked over at the house. "Okay, but—"

By the time I had turned back around, Mort was gone. Again.

"Why are you just standing there? Let's go!"

My aunt grabbed my arm, and I stumbled after her. In my attempt to keep my balance, my hand brushed over a leaf peeking through the bars of a cage.

Nora's eyes widened. "What did I tell you about the plants in the cages?"

I grimaced. "Not to touch them?"

"Not to touch them," she repeated, dragging me through the latched gate, clicking it shut behind us.

A FTER NORA HAD given my hand a thorough once-over to make sure I had not in fact poisoned myself, she let me go my own way into town. She wanted to get started on making a list of all the plants she had observed. I tried to describe to her the bush I had seen, but when I couldn't tell her if the leaf pattern was opposite, alternate, or whorled, well, that pretty much ended our conversation for the time being.

It was probably for the best. I was having trouble concentrating.

I couldn't have heard Mort correctly. Here, I had thought we were both finally on the same page. But now *he* wasn't sure if it had been murder after all?

It made no sense. He was the one who came to me, claiming he had been murdered, and we had both seen the vision of his death. Granted, it wasn't as though we saw his killer pull a trigger so to speak, but someone had been there when he died. Someone who did not offer any aid when he was in distress. Someone who checked to see if he was dead!

This ghost was going to be the death of me.

I needed to talk to him. Find out what he was thinking. But once again, it looked like I would have to wait until he was ready. Mort was a regular Houdini when it came to sudden appearances and disappearances.

As I headed into town, I tried to put Mort's declaration out of my mind and process all that Nora and I had learned. All handsomeness aside, Elias Blumenthal was presenting as a possible candidate for our killer. After the re-creation spell, I felt fairly certain that the chocolate Mort had eaten was poisonous—even if Mort didn't—but had that poison come from Elias's garden? And what about the typewriter? Had he been the one to write Angie those anonymous love letters? Of course, the person who wrote those letters wasn't necessarily the murderer, but the timing of both, while possibly coincidental, was strange.

I needed to find out more about all the personalities involved, and I knew just the person who could fill in some of the blanks.

The sun was high and shining brightly as I walked into the center of town. Members of Evenfall's business association were busy hanging flower baskets from the wrought iron lampposts that lined either side of the street as tourists languorously strolled the sidewalks.

As I passed by Charmed Treasures, I took a peek inside. Nixie sat behind the counter, staring intently at a sheet of paper resting on its surface. Her fingers danced in the air as she mumbled some words. Hopefully she hadn't been practicing the enchantment nonstop. But, again, some lessons had to be learned the hard way.

A small smile returned to my face when I spotted my destination in the distance. It was a lovely historic royal blue building with large plate glass display windows. The gold letters spelling out the store's name glinted in the sunlight. Lovely Leaves. Tea and bookshop. My old place of work.

I opened the door. Bells tinkled above me.

Much of the upset I had been feeling drained away as I stepped inside. I loved everything about this place, from the towering mazes of bookshelves to the creaking floors to the small café area with its heavy wooden tables and stools. Oh! And the smell. I took a deep breath, inhaling the signature scent of old books, Earl Grey tea, orange peel, and cloves. I definitely loved that too.

Everything was just as I had expected except for the fact that there was a young woman behind the counter. Right where I used to stand. She looked quite pleasant, smiling and chatting away with customers, and she had the most adorable dimples at the corners of her mouth. I instantly disliked her.

Well, maybe not really. It was hard to be replaced.

Now where could Theo be?

I wandered into the first corridor of shelves and the many stories closed in around me. I could almost feel the fictional worlds and characters rubbing up against me like a cat.

I trailed my fingertips against the spines lined up neatly on the closest ledge. Gideon would never dare to do such a thing. He might have visions of all the people who had ever read the books, but I was only able to pick up on the faintest emotions left by past readers. Thrills and chills. Romance and sorrow. They were very gentle sensations. The slightest tingles.

Ouch!

Or not.

I brought my fingertips up to my lips. "What in the world?"

Apparently, some of the books had a bit more of a bite.

I read the title of the little green monster I had touched. *The History of Dressage.* I frowned. I did not know much about horse dancing, and I could honestly say I never really had a desire to learn.

"Did you shock me?" I glanced side to side. Like it wasn't bad enough I was talking to spirits on the street? Now I was talking to books?

I poked its spine.

Nothing.

I gave it another poke just to be sure.

Nothing at all.

I tipped it out of its slot. The weighty little tome didn't zap me again, but I suddenly had the strangest feeling that I was supposed to have this book.

Great. Yet another strange feeling.

This was Gideon's fault. That zap had probably been static electricity, but all of his talk of signs and there not being coincidences had me second-guessing myself. Again, that was the problem with the whole concept. You could read something into anything.

I glanced suspiciously down at the text. "Do you have something further you'd like to say?"

The book didn't answer.

"You wouldn't happen to know anything about some funny feelings I've been having lately?"

Still nothing.

"Maybe some information about a recently deceased candymaker?"

Silence.

I frowned at the book, then jumped as a voice whispered at my back, "Who are we talking to?"

Chapter 18

"THEO!"

I smiled at my former boss.

Theo was in her mid-sixties but had the energy of a twenty-year-old. While her hair was always a little wild, and the round lenses of her glasses gave her a slightly bug-eyed look, the kindness and intelligence in her gaze won over everyone who met her. In truth, Theo's face was one of my favorite faces in the whole world. Despite the fact that she looked amused for having caught me talking to a book.

"Are you two chitchatting?" she asked. "Or is this a serious discussion?"

"We were just getting to know each other," I said with an embarrassed smile.

"I have always found books to be the best conversationalists."

I nodded. "That being said, I was hoping to have a word with you."

"Brynn, you know, I'm always happy to talk with my favorite ex-employee."

I made a face. "Even if it's about Mortimer Sweete?"

"Oh my, that does take some of the fun away, doesn't it?"

"Do you mind if I ask you a few questions about him?"

Theo gave me an assessing look. Of course, she knew all the rumors about my ability to speak to ghosts, and I knew she suspected a great deal more about my family, but she saved me the awkwardness of having to make up any stories. "Certainly. Come sit. Let me take care of a few customers, then we can have a cup of tea together. I'm not sure how much help I'll be, but I'll do my best."

ABOUT TEN MINUTES later, Theo and I were seated across from each other, at one of the tall bistro-style tables near the counter, each of us with a cup of tea and a slice of lemon poppy seed cake.

"This is delicious." I dabbed my mouth with a napkin.

"It should be," she said with a big smile. "Your aunt gave me the recipe. Cassandra made it though." She looked over to the young woman behind the counter.

"Oh, Cassandra, is it?"

Theo smiled. "My niece. She's helping out. You'd like her."

I made a noncommittal noise.

"Brynn Warren, are you jealous?"

I smiled, dropping the act. "Maybe a little." Theo and I both knew how much I loved my time working at the bookstore. But as much as I missed it, for the time being at least, I had my hands full dealing with ghostly problems.

"So," my former boss said, holding her teacup delicately in front of her, "what can I tell you about Mort?"

"I'm not exactly sure." This wasn't the first time I had come to Theo to ask her about people I only knew in passing. Perhaps it had something to do with her love of books, but Theo was quite good at character assessment. I trusted her judgment unreservedly when it came to human nature.

"I met up with his wife, Angie. I'd love to help her during this difficult time, but I know almost nothing about Mort other than hearing he could be a bit of a . . ."

"A blowhard?" Theo offered with a wry smile.

I nodded gratefully.

"Well, that's true. Mort could be opinionated. And loud. But it was mainly bluster. Deep down the man was a sweetheart."

"His wife told me as much." I lifted my cup, catching the delicate scents of citrus rising from the tea.

"We all went to high school together," Theo said. "Nobody thought Mort stood a chance with Angie. She was the homecoming queen and just as sweet as could be. But Mort, well, adolescence wasn't the kindest to him. He grew so tall so fast. I swear he couldn't enter a room without knocking something over. He always tried to act like a tough guy, but when Angie was around? It was all cow eyes."

"Cow eyes?"

"You haven't heard that expression?" Theo asked. "I must be getting old. It means he was smitten. Infatuated."

I smiled. "And what did Angie think of these cow eyes?"

"Oh, I don't think she paid much mind to it at first. She was used to attention from boys. But Mort was devoted. She could do no wrong. That being said, I don't think he ever really considered the possibility she'd return his affections. But, eventually, I guess Angie decided she could do worse than to attach herself to a man who thought she was wonderful."

"I can see how that might hold some appeal."

"And you know, their devotion to each other never changed," Theo said thoughtfully. "Whenever those two were together, they had the look of a couple who had won the lottery. They were definitely a love match. I don't know how she's going to cope without him."

"She does seem to have some caring neighbors," I said over my teacup. "Elias Blumenthal for one dropped off a stunning flower arrangement."

A strange look came over Theo's face. If I didn't know better, I'd say it was almost salacious. "I wish Elias Blumenthal would take care of me."

"Theo!"

She chuckled. "Of course, I'm teasing. But he is one handsome man. Terrible tragedy losing his wife so young. I heard she drowned in the bathtub."

I blinked. A poison garden, a typewriter, and a tragically deceased wife? Again, I didn't want to think of Elias as a suspect for Mort's murder, but the circumstances weren't making it easy. "What about Mort's cousin, Les? Did the two of them get along?"

"Oh yes, they were more than cousins. They've been best friends since grade school. I'm sure Les is devastated." She sighed. "I'm guessing he'll retire now."

"I did see Cookie putting a For Sale sign up at the store."

"She didn't waste any time. Not that I'm surprised. She and Les always had a bumpy relationship. Rumor has it, she resented the amount of time he spent at the shop."

"I don't really know Cookie, but I've heard some less than flattering things."

Theo shook her head. "I'm not sure it's all fair. Everybody accuses Cookie of being domineering, but I think that's why Les married her. He wanted someone to tell him what to do. Then he resented her for doing it. But I've always believed no one can ever really know for sure what goes on in a marriage except for the people in it."

I turned my teacup in its saucer, weighing how to approach my next question. I trusted Theo wholeheartedly, but I wasn't sure it was a good idea to let slip any of my suspicions about Mort's death. I wanted to ask her if he had any enemies or past grudges, but that didn't seem appropriate, so I went with, "Can you remember anything in Mort's life standing out?"

"What do you mean?"

"Anything out of the ordinary? Something he was known for?"

Theo studied me, probably wondering why I would want to know such a thing; but in the end, she decided against asking for an explanation. She understood that there were some topics I'd prefer not to discuss. "There is one thing. I seem to recall Mort having a brush with death once before." She looked off toward the window. "Now what was it?" She tapped her chin. "I believe it was fairly serious. I remember him being in the hospital."

"A car accident?"

"No, no, not that." My former boss sighed. "I can't remember. But surely someone at the memorial will know." When Theo caught my expression, she added, "Les and Cookie have arranged for a public one to take place in the park tomorrow morning. Mort was a town fixture, after all. I'm sure many will attend. If you're looking for answers, that's where they will be. I'm sorry I couldn't be of more help."

"No, you've helped a great deal." I absentmindedly patted the book I had resting on the table.

"You're not thinking of paying for that, are you?"

I smiled. "Well, I wasn't going to steal it."

"Just take it," she said, waving a hand. "I know you will be shocked to hear this, but I don't have all that many requests for books on *horse dancing*."

"It's a new interest."

Just then the front door of the bookshop opened. The bells above the entryway tinkled, and the newlywed couple staying at Ivywood Hollow stepped in, smiling and reaching for each other's hand.

"Aren't they sweet?" Theo mused in a dreamy voice.

I caught her regarding me with the same hopeful expression Izzy had had back on the porch. "Why are you looking at me like that?"

Theo shrugged and brought her tea to her lips.

"Have you been talking to Izzy about more than just cake?"

She put her cup down. "Would you like some more?"

Chapter 19

I PULLED MY GRANDMOTHER'S afghan onto my lap
and curled up in the aubergine-colored armchair by the
fireplace in my loft.

It had been a day.

Poison gardens. Angry ghosts. Zapping books.

I rubbed my forehead with one hand and gently threw
out the other in the direction of the hearth. Small flames
leapt up around the logs. Soon it would be too warm for
fires, but another spring storm had rolled in late in the af-
ternoon, bringing a chill with it. I closed my eyes, enjoying
the sound of the rain hitting the windowpanes.

After the bookstore, I spent the rest of the day at loose
ends, hoping Mort would pop up. I was fairly certain he
knew I wanted to speak with him. Again, ghosts had an
uncanny ability to sense when others were thinking of
them. But, unfortunately for me, he was being as evasive as
ever.

As the hours passed by, my frustration waned, only to

be replaced by guilt. The same words kept running through my mind.

I thought I could trust you.

Whether I wanted to admit or not, I *had* betrayed Mort's trust. I knew he didn't want me speaking to Angie, but I had done it anyway. I still believed it was the right thing to do, but that didn't change the fact that I had crossed a line.

Maybe that was why he had done an about-face when it came to the circumstances of his death. Maybe he didn't trust me to handle the situation delicately enough.

The flames danced and curled around the logs in the hearth.

I had meant well, but there may have been more behind my actions.

I brought my gaze up from the flames to the framed picture on the mantel.

Adam.

He was smiling and full of life in the shot, his hair falling into his eyes the way it always had.

For a long time, I hadn't been able to look at any pictures of my husband, but now the sight of him brought me comfort, especially on cold, rainy nights when I was feeling a bit lonely.

I had experienced what Mort was going through now. I knew what it was like to lose a spouse. And I could deeply relate to what Angie was suffering by losing Mort so suddenly.

The day I lost Adam there had been no warning at all.

We were supposed to meet in the park for lunch, and I had only just spotted him when it happened. He had raised his hand in the air to greet me and then he fell to the grass.

I can't remember what happened after that. I know I tried to bring him back. I almost tore myself apart trying to bring him back. I used every bit of power I possessed. But nothing worked. He was gone.

The doctors told me afterward it had been an undiagnosed heart defect. A widow-maker. There was nothing
anyone could have done.

In the days that followed, the only thing that kept me going was the thought that I would be able to hear from him
again. Not directly. I knew as a witch of the dead I couldn'
see or talk to him, but Adam and I had agreed when he had
still been alive that he would hang around on the mortal plane
as long as he could to pass on his final words to another spirit
so that I could hear from him one last time. But people did
pass in Evenfall, and I couldn't see any of them. My grief had
been so all-consuming, I temporarily lost my gift. It wasn'
until almost a year and a half later that I was able to see a
ghost again. It had been an incredibly rewarding experience.
I hadn't realized in my grief how much I missed helping spirits. Even if some spirits really were easier to help than others.

Regardless, I eventually did get to hear Adam's final
words. One ghost after another had passed on his message
until I was able to connect with the other side again. Hearing those words—regaining that *connection*—it had been
beyond precious.

More than anything, I didn't want Mort to miss that opportunity. And I didn't want Angie to miss it, either, because
her husband was waiting for some perfect time that might
not ever come.

Of course, there was only one way they would get that
opportunity.

Mort and I needed to work together.

I pulled the handmade afghan closer to my chest. My
grandmother had been a master with her needlework. She
infused each and every stitch with magic and love. This
afghan had grown with me since the time I was small, its
fibers always fresh and comforting.

Once I was settled, I grabbed *The History of Dressage*
from my messenger bag resting on the floor. Just because

Mort didn't want to talk right now, that didn't mean there was nothing for me to do. I could read a book on a topic I had very little interest in, in a foolhardy attempt to find meaning in static electricity.

I turned page after page, struggling my way through the instructional text. But aside from learning the difference between passage and piaffe exercises, I didn't glean much of anything from it.

After about an hour or so, my eyelids drooped. Sleep *had* been elusive lately. Maybe a tiny catnap was in order.

Just as I began to drift away to dreamland, a sharp *Tap! Tap! Tap!* sounded behind me.

I jolted fully awake but didn't move from my spot.

The noise had definitely come from the window, but it hadn't sounded like rain.

I stayed frozen, ears perked. I knew as a witch I was supposed to be the thing that people were afraid would go bump in the night, but I was definitely the one who was frightened right now.

It was possible I had imagined it. I had almost been asleep.

Tap! Tap! Tap!

This time I whirled around in my chair to face the noise.

The window behind me glittered with raindrops, but I couldn't see anything beyond the pane.

The afghan dropped from my lap as I slowly rose to my feet. I crept toward the window with catlike steps, ready at any moment to jump back. The tapping had stopped. The only thing I could hear now was the soft crackling of the fire and the gentle patter of rain.

I eyed the window, debating whether to open it. I really didn't want to, but I knew if I didn't at least take a peek outside, I'd be thinking all night about what had made the sound. I reached for the handle at the bottom of the frame.

Tap! Tap! Tap!

I hopped straight up in the air, then rushed over to the window and yanked it up.

"Dog! What are you doing here?"

I barely managed to get out of the way as the drenched bird took the opportunity of the open window to swoop inside. Once I had recovered from my fright, I pushed the window shut and faced my unexpected guest.

"Let me guess," I said to the large crow standing in the middle of room, dripping water onto the floor. "Gideon sent you to check up on me."

Dog gave himself a good shake, much like, well, a dog would.

"Make yourself at home, why don't you." I walked over to my kitchenette to grab a towel. "And, sorry for your trouble, but you can tell Gideon I'm fine."

Dog squawked skeptically.

"I am." I padded back over, then dropped to my knees to wipe the water sprayed across the wood planks. "I mean, yes, I am still annoyed with Izzy, but I'll forgive her. Eventually. And while I do have ghost problems, I'm managing."

Dog said nothing. Just stood there. Staring at me.

"What? Is this about the gazebo the other night?"

Silence.

"I am sorry, okay? I got distracted." I reached toward him with the towel. "Do you want me to wipe you down while I'm at it?"

The bird hopped a few paces to the side, looking down his beak at me.

"You might like it," I coaxed.

His skeptical expression remained, but he didn't move at my approach.

I ran the cloth slowly down his back.

At first, he felt quite tense, but eventually he pushed up into my hand.

"Told you."

I stroked Dog with the cloth for a minute or two, admiring the shine of his regal black feathers.

"There. I think you're dry, and the rain sounds like it's eased. Do you want me to open the window, so you can go?"

Dog cawed. Loudly. So loudly it echoed through the confines of the loft.

"Inside voices, please." I rocked back up to standing. It was too bad Gideon hadn't made friends with a songbird. "Do you want a treat? Is that it?"

Dog fell back to silence.

"I'll see what I have." I shuffled over to the kitchen cabinet. "If I had known I was going to have guests, I would have prepared better." I grabbed a peanut from the bottom of a plastic bag. "It may be stale." I tossed the nut onto the floor. Dog cracked the shell and ate the contents in a flash, leaving another mess behind.

"Right then." I walked over to the window. "Well, good night."

The bird cawed again before pecking at something under his wing.

"What is it? That was my last nut. It can't be that you want to sleep here."

Dog looked up at me briefly, then returned to sorting out his feathers.

"You don't want to sleep here. I've given you a snack. So, what do you want?" I asked the question more to myself than Dog, who was still ignoring me. This was ridiculous. Clearly, he wanted to communicate something. There had to be a way to figure out what that was. "Okay, I'm going to ask you some questions, and if the answer is yes, you caw. If it's no, say nothing."

Dog brought his beak up from under his wing.

"I'll take that to mean you're game."

The crow screeched and hopped in the air.

I waved my hands out. "Not game! Definitely not game!

Sorry. I did not mean that in the hunting sense. Unfortunate bit of wordplay there."

The crow settled down.

"Ready to play?" I tilted my head side to side and rolled my shoulders. It was habit. I could be pretty competitive when it came to charades. "Okay, did Gideon send you?"

Silence.

"So, this was your idea?"

Dog didn't caw but made another burbling noise. I took that to mean *kind of*.

I scratched my chin. "Do you . . . want me to do something?"

Loud caw.

I hopped with excitement, then bit the side of my thumbnail. "Okay, you want me to do something. What could it be?"

He didn't reply.

"Sorry. Not helpful. Yes or no questions only." I squeezed my forehead, studying the bird. "Can I do this thing you want me to do here?"

Silence.

I made a face. I didn't like the sound—or lack of sound—of that, at all. "So, we have to go outside?"

Loud caw.

"Seriously?" I whined.

Another loud caw.

"That was rhetorical."

I planted my hands on my hips and gave the bird a sideways look. "So, what you're telling me is that there is something you want me to do outside, and you're going to lead me to it?"

Another caw.

I took a sharp breath. This next question was the big one. "This thing you want me to do. This outside thing." I squeezed my eyes shut. "Does it have to be done right now?"

Silence.

I peeked one eye open.

Loud caw. Screeching even.

"Oh, come on."

Caw!

"Are you sure it can't wait until morning?"

Caw! Caw!

"Why are you being so stubborn?"

Caw*! Caw! Caw!*

"Dog!" I shut my mouth after that. Mainly because it sounded like we were both cawing.

We warred gazes before I finally shook my head in defeat. "I'll get my coat," I muttered, heading for the rack by the door. I glanced down at what I was wearing. Izzy had bought me a two-pack pajama set. This time I was wearing a baby chick print. Hopefully Nora wasn't in the mood for any late-night walks.

Once I had buttoned up my red rain jacket, put on some shoes, slipped on some thin gloves, and dumped my messenger bag over my shoulder, I opened the door, peering down at the crow by my feet. Much to my surprise he had something in his beak. "Where did that come from? You did not have that a second ago."

The crow dropped his catch onto the floor.

A ribbon.

"Is that what you were holding the other night? Where did you get this?" I asked, dropping down to the bird's level. "It kind of looks like a ribbon a candy maker might use to tie around a box."

I had been hoping for some sort of answer, but Dog just waddled past me, out the door, and into the night.

Chapter 20

I COULD BARELY MAKE out the crow's soaring silhouette against the black sky.

"Slow down! I can't pedal any faster."

Either Dog couldn't hear me, or he just didn't care. My
money was on the latter. He looked joyous, riding the night
winds.

Thankfully the rain had softened to a drizzle, but it was
still cold and damp. This bird had better know what he was
cawing about or there would be no more peanuts from me.

It didn't take long to figure out where we were headed.
Dog's flight path had me riding directly for town. I probably should have followed up on what he had been trying to
show me sooner, but live and learn. From now on, the crow
would be obeyed. When we reached the park, Dog circled
the town gazebo.

I swung my leg over my bike and walked the path lit up
by the park lanterns. Silver sparkles floated out from the
pavilion, emanating from the ghost seated inside. He had
an unearthly loveliness to him, but he also looked sad. His

hands were folded in his lap; his shoulders were slumped; and his face was downcast, staring at nothing that could be seen.

I guided my bike over the crunchy gravel, but the spirit didn't take any notice of me until I was climbing the steps to join him.

"Hey, look who the crow dragged in."

He was obviously teasing, but Mort's voice held a note of pure dejection. I think I would have preferred it if he were still angry.

Dog swooped down to perch on the deep pink crab apple tree on the other side of the railing where Mort was seated. The ghost glanced at him. "He a friend of yours?"

"You could say that."

"He's been following me around."

I smiled, sitting on the bench. "He has a special connection with those who have passed."

"Well, that's me."

"Maybe he thought you could use some company."

The ghost nodded. "I could probably use a friend even if I don't deserve one." He looked me in the eye. "I came off pretty strong back at Blumenthal's, didn't I?"

"It's forgotten. And I should be the one apologizing. I'm sorry I broke your trust."

"I knew what I was getting into. I remember you coming into the shop when you were little. You were fierce even then."

My smile deepened. "Your shop was probably my favorite place in the world back in those days. You made a lot of kids happy over the years."

Mort clasped his hands together. "I sure hope so."

I tried to meet the spirit's gaze, but he was back to looking down at the floor. I hated seeing him this way. But he was entitled to experiencing all the feelings that came with his transition. That being said, there was something we needed to discuss. "Mort, about what we saw in the cauldron. I know that couldn't have been easy, bearing witness to your own death, but what did you mean earlier when you said that maybe you weren't . . ." I still couldn't quite bring myself to say the word.

"Murdered?"

"Yes."

He shrugged but kept his eyes averted. "I meant just that. Maybe I wasn't murdered. We don't know anything for sure. Maybe whoever was there had their reasons for not helping."

There weren't many good ones I could think of. But clearly Mort wanted to believe otherwise. It wasn't that surprising. The idea of another living soul wanting you dead was no small thing. "Wouldn't you like to know for sure?"

He finally met my eye. "Doesn't make much difference, does it?"

"Mort!"

"What?"

"Of course it makes a difference. How could you ever say that?"

He threw his hands up. "I'll still be dead, won't I?"

"Balderdash!"

Mort dropped his chin into his chest. "Balderdash?"

"Yes, balderdash," I said loud enough to send some nearby creature scurrying off into a bush. "Not to the part about you still being dead but to the other part. It most certainly does matter."

"Balderdash." He chuckled.

"What's wrong with balderdash? You said it earlier. I thought I might give it a try."

He peeked at me out of the corner of his eye. "It sound funny when you say it."

I knew Mort still had some life to him, so to speak. "I will have you know, Mortimer Sweete, that we are not giving up. You deserve answers, and I'm going to help you find them. But in order for that to happen, we need to get a few things straight."

He frowned.

"If we're going to get anywhere with this investigation, we have to work together." I surprised myself by using the word *investigation*, but it felt right. That's what this was. I may never have intended to become an amateur detective, but it had always been my calling to help ghosts. I would do whatever needed to be done to help Mort. Because of my gift, I was the only one who could. "I'm proposing we make a deal."

Mort's frown deepened. "What kind of deal?"

I placed my hand on my chest. "I promise I won't speak to Angie behind your back. If you promise to stop with all your sudden appearances and disappearances."

His mouth twitched with a smile. "I don't know what to tell you, Ghostie. I don't have this whole afterlife thing down yet."

I squinted. "That may have been the case a couple of days ago, but I think you know exactly what you're do-ing now."

He chuckled again.

"And *Ghostie*?"

"It was either that or Glinda the Good Witch. You not a fan of nicknames?"

"Actually," I said, giving him a considering look, "it might be growing on me."

We fell into silence, listening to the last drops of rain hitting the gazebo roof.

"So," I said after a minute or two had passed, "do we have a deal?"

Mort took another phantom inhale. "I know you mean well, and I appreciate everything you've tried to do, but you said it yourself. Time is limited. And we don't have much to go on. I think maybe I need to accept what's what."

I didn't answer. Not because I didn't have anything to say, but because Dog had caught my eye from the crab apple tree. He certainly had gone to a fair bit of trouble to get me out here. Was it just to console Mort?

An idea was taking shape beneath the surface of my consciousness. I couldn't quite reach it though. Regardless, I found myself pulling the ribbon Dog had given me out from my pocket. "Do you recognize this?"

"Looks like a ribbon."

I gave Mort a withering look. "I know it's a ribbon, but do you use this specific type of ribbon at the shop?"

"Not exactly like that. Ours is thicker, and we don't use that shade of red. Why?"

"Dog brought it to me." I was definitely missing something. An insight I couldn't quite grasp. Or maybe an opportunity?

"Dog?"

"Sorry," I said, snapping my attention back to Mort. "That's the crow's name. I can't remember seeing the ribbon in the cauldron, but I think maybe it came from the box of chocolates you had that night. He probably found it somewhere around here."

Wait a minute. Somewhere around here.

Probably right around here.

"What is it?" Mort asked. "You got a funny look on your face."

I jumped up to my feet, looking in all directions. "Mort! Everyone thinks you died of natural causes."

"Right," he said, stretching out the word.

"So, they never would have done a search of the crime scene." I cringed at the term, but I was too excited to filter.

"Hypothetical crime scene," he drawled, but I caught him scanning the floor too. "You can't possibly think there's some sort of clue here? After all this wind and rain?"

"There's only one way to find out." There was nothing

on the floor as far as I could see, but it was hard to get a good look under the benches that ran along the inner walls of the gazebo. I dropped my messenger bag and got down on my hands and knees.

"You're wasting your time," the ghost said, but at least his voice held more vigor.

Just then Dog swooped down to the gazebo floor by Mort's feet.

"I think someone may have already done a search."

Mort scoffed. "I don't see anything."

"Move your feet," I commanded.

"But there's nothing there."

"Humor me."

The ghost shook his head and shuffled to the side.

I took the glove off my right hand and swirled my fingers. A tiny fire sprung up in my palm.

"Jiminy Cricket!"

"That one always gets the crowd." I lowered my hand under the bench, bringing the light of the flames close to where Dog was standing. A tiny glint of gold flashed up in a crack between two boards.

"What do we have here?" I asked, prying a bit of cellophane out, pinching it between the gloved fingers of my left hand.

"Is that what I think it is?" Mort asked.

"A candy wrapper." I curled my fingers into a fist, extinguishing the flames, before dragging my messenger bag across the floor. I pulled out a plastic bag filled with folded tissues. I dumped them out and then carefully placed the wrapper inside, sealing it shut. I wasn't ready to go to the police with any of this—they would ask a lot of questions I couldn't answer—but it was probably best to preserve the evidence. If that was indeed what this was. I then smoothed the bag over the wrapper. "There's something written on the foil."

"What?"

I squinted at the faint white script. "It says Naff? What's Naff?"

"He's, I mean, *it's* a candy supplies company. They make wrappers and boxes. That sort of thing. We use them, but ours have our name. Branding." Mort leaned toward me. "Let me see that. Bring it closer."

I brought the wrapper up so that he could get a better look.

"Turn it around. Let me see the other side."

The outer foil of the wrapper was gold colored, but the inner was white.

The ghost stared at it much longer than I would have expected. When he was through, he leaned back and shook his head. "It's got some smudges of chocolate, but that's about it."

I flipped it back around, studying the marks made by the chocolate the wrapper once held. They didn't look like random smudges to me. More like an imprint left from some sort of inscription on top of the sweet. "*X, O.* Remember? You said *X, O* when . . ."

I didn't have to finish. We both knew when he had said it.

"What do you think it means?" I asked.

The spirit shrugged. "No clue."

I rose to my feet, staring at the innocuous-looking wrapper.

Mort was wrong. Maybe we didn't know what the letters stood for, but we most certainly had a clue.

Chapter 21

SOMETIMES THERE IS not enough coffee in the world. That's how I woke up feeling the next morning, but, once again, I couldn't stay in bed recovering from any missed hours of sleep. There were things I needed to do. And I was already behind schedule.

After the excitement of finding the wrapper had died down, I realized we still didn't have a lot to go on, and I was in a tricky situation ethically speaking. The wrapper *was* evidence. There were traces of chocolate on it, most likely poisonous chocolate, and the police would be able to do far more with it than I could. But how could I possibly approach them? Angie would have to be the one requesting answers, but I couldn't go to her yet. I needed more evidence. Something concrete. I suspected saying *I witnessed your husband's death in the vapors of a cauldron* was a little more than she could take right now.

And then there was Mort. He was not as happy as I would have expected him to be, given our find last night. Maybe happiness wasn't a fair expectation though. The

change in him since the reenactment spell had been significant. It was like he had lost all heart in finding justice.
But he was still here. That was something. He hadn't yet
gone into the light, which told me he still had hope. It also
meant I needed to work harder.

And I needed to getting going.

Mort's memorial service was today, and if I didn't hurry,
I was going to be late.

I was hoping I might find someone who could tell me
about Mort's past brush with death. I couldn't believe it, but
I had forgotten to ask him about it the night before. In fairness, the wrapper had been distracting. Ideally, I would get
the chance to ask him about it today, but I didn't know if he
would show up. Much like witnessing your own death, attending your own memorial service was no small deal.

I headed over the B&B, noting the steel-colored Jeep in
the drive. A new guest had obviously arrived.

I opened the front door slowly, hoping to avoid any creaks.
Izzy should have finished serving breakfast by now. She'd be
in the kitchen, tidying up. We still hadn't spoken. I knew we
needed to. I didn't want her to think I was deeply angry with
her. Even if I was still miffed. But it would have to wait.
Time was short. I was really just looking for a quick jolt of
my aunt's coffee before I headed out, and I knew there was a
good chance I would find some still brewing in the dining
room. Izzy made the best coffee. I didn't even bother trying
to make my own anymore. It was too sad in comparison.

I tiptoed inside, meaning to head directly for the caf-
feine, but as I passed the tall counter we used for check-ins,
something caught my eye. I leaned over to get a better look
at the ledger. My gaze trailed down the list of visitors until
it settled on the last name.

Fredrick Naff.

Naff. Just like the name on the label I had found last
night.

That could not be a coincidence.

Given that this Fredrick Naff had only checked in yesterday and the memorial was today, I suspected there was a good chance I'd run into our newest guest at the service. I glanced at my watch. Speaking of which, I really, really needed to get going.

Once I had some coffee.

I hurried toward the dining room but was waylaid again by the sound of voices coming from the kitchen.

"Oh no, Sister," Nora's voice called out, sounding unnaturally loud. "You don't have to worry. I'm sure Brynn will be here for dinner."

I froze, ears perked for Izzy's response, but despite my effort, I only heard mumbling.

Luckily for me, however, Nora was still speaking at a deafening pitch. "I'm sure you're wrong. Our niece loves a good apology dinner." The word *apology* was enunciated with great precision.

More mumbling followed on Izzy's part.

"You don't have to worry," Nora went on. She was practically shouting now. "Brynn will be here. At seven o'clock. Only an incredibly *stubborn* person would not show up."

I rolled my eyes.

"Besides, she's already missed this morning's coffee. I know she wouldn't want to lose out on what you've dreamed up for supper."

No coffee?

My shoulders slumped.

A moment later I stepped out into the sunshine, shutting the door noisily behind me.

On the bright side, Izzy did make the best apology dinners.

I RODE MY BIKE into town. The spring air was luxuriously cool, but I didn't have any time to enjoy it.

A few people gave me funny looks as I sped by Main

Street's storefronts, but I couldn't worry about that. If I hurried, I would still have plenty of time before the memorial started to get the lay of the land, so to speak. Given that was the case, I surprised myself by skidding to stop a good block and half away from the park.

As Time Goes By. Evenfall's one and only antique shop.

An elegant rolltop desk stood displayed in the front window, but that wasn't what had caught my attention. It was the table farther into the store. It was covered in typewriters. Someone had been writing Angie letters on a typewriter. Maybe the answer to figuring out who that was lay with the typewriter itself. And if I could find out more about typewriter forensics—if there even was such a thing—maybe I could get Angie to give me her letter. I wasn't sure exactly how I would do that since I promised Mort I wouldn't talk to her, but that was a bridge I could figure out how to cross another time.

I looked at my watch again. I did have a bit of time.

Bells jangled as I entered the shop, lit only with the morning sun. I clutched my hands together as I walked by a set of shelves loaded with china and glassware. It's funny I knew very well it wasn't wise to go into a shop filled with old treasures and start touching things, but every time I was around antiques, that's exactly what I wanted to do.

"Well, hello there."

I yanked my hand to my side. Despite my best efforts my wayward fingers had been reaching for a lovely blue glass vase.

A cheery woman greeted me. She was short, plump, and wore a friendly smile. "Brynn Warren. For a moment I thought you were a tourist, but that beautiful black hair of yours always stands out in a crowd."

I self-consciously brought a hand up to smooth my hair down. It felt windblown after my ride. "You're very kind. It's Marjorie, isn't it?" I was sure we had met on at least a few occasions, town socials and the like.

She nodded. "What can I do for you today? Are you looking for something for the B&B? From what I've heard, Ivywood Hollow already has an impressive collection of antiques."

"Actually, no, I mean, yes, we have our fair share, but it was the typewriters that brought me in." I moved toward the table. "They caught my eye from the window."

"Oh yes," she answered, following me over. "They are going through a revival lately."

I ran my fingers over the keys of one of the machines. "I can't remember the last time I saw one in real life. Though, just last week, I watched a movie centered on them. A murder mystery. The killer was caught from evidence involving a typewritten letter." I had to stop myself from smiling. That wasn't bad. Much better than the transitions I had made with Elias Blumenthal.

"Keyed Up for Death," a new voice said.

I whipped around to face a man hidden in shadow at the back of the shop.

"Simon Davies," Marjorie scolded, "you are going to scare all of our customers away if you keep creeping up on them. And where were you this morning?" The woman smiled at the man I assumed to be her husband. He wore a plaid shirt buttoned all the way to the top and jeans that were too big, his belt working overtime. His unkempt hair was sticking out in more than a few directions—not that I was one to talk—and while he was missing the lab coat, I couldn't help but think he had a mad scientist vibe to him.

"I had a few errands to run," he said, giving his wife a chastened look. "I wanted to get out before all the tourists start clogging up the streets."

"Those tourists pay our bills," Marjorie chided but not unkindly. "Now what was it you were trying to say?"

"The movie," he said, looking at me, "it's called *Keyed Up for Death.*"

"That's it." I snapped my fingers. That really wasn't it. I

hadn't watched any movies about typewriters. And I hated lying to people. But it was for a good cause. "It was quite well done."

The man frowned.

"Or maybe not well done?" Hmm, my efforts in deceit clearly still needed some work. "But I did find the typewriter forensics fascinating. If there is such a thing."

"There most certainly is," Simon said, stepping into the light.

The woman leaned in and whispered, "Oh boy, you're in trouble now. You've stumbled onto one of his pet interests."

"You can tell a great deal from a typed note," he went on, ignoring his wife's teasing. "Kidnappers in the early days often used typewriters to compose their ransom notes, thinking it would grant them anonymity, but, of course, that wasn't the case."

"Oh, of course not," I said, matching his serious tone. I had no idea what I was saying.

"Just like modern-day printers, typewriters often leave distinguishing marks. While most manufacturers use pica or elite typefaces, there is a wealth of information that can be garnered about the size, shape, and style of the letters, making it easy for an expert to determine the exact model of the machine."

"But would it be possible to determine whether a particular letter came from a specific machine?"

"You did watch the entire movie, didn't you?"

I scratched my temple. "I may have fallen asleep briefly."

"The short answer is yes. Most machines do have a misaligned letter or two, or abnormal spacing. It isn't always easy to spot, but an expert would be able to identify a match."

"How fascinating." I really needed to get my hands on Angie's letter.

The man nodded, then abruptly retreated back into the shadows.

"Don't mind Simon," Marjorie said, patting my arm. "He loves talking about antiques, but people generally scare him."

I chuckled. "Do you know of any other typewriter aficionados in town?"

She tilted her head in question.

"I just wondered perhaps if there is a secret club for collectors. I know my neighbor Mr. Henderson would probably enjoy meeting others interested in them. Like maybe Elias Blumenthal?"

And I was back to square one with my subtlety.

Fortunately, Marjorie didn't seem to notice. "Elias Blumenthal," she said in a breathy voice. "Speaking of fascinating." She leaned in, whispering, "He's so handsome. But no, he's certainly never bought any of our typewriters. I would have remembered that." She sighed. "It's such a tragedy what happened to his wife."

This time I leaned in. "What *did* happen to his wife?"

She shook her head. "I don't think anyone knows for sure, but I heard it was a parachuting accident."

My jaw dropped. But not because of what Marjorie said. Although that was very shocking. No, it was because of what I saw out the front window of the shop. Now I wasn't one to speak of the devil, but it seemed he wasn't the only one to appear if you said his name aloud. As if we had conjured him with our words, Elias Blumenthal appeared on the other side of the glass. With Angie Sweete. His hand on her elbow.

"I'm sorry. Did I upset you?" Marjorie asked.

"No, not at all. There's just somewhere I need to be."

Chapter 22

DESPITE MY BEST efforts, I hadn't been able to catch up to the perturbing duo I had spotted from inside the antique shop. The sidewalks were packed with Evenfall citizens on their way to honor Mort, forcing me to take my time.

Now, it was entirely possible that Elias was just being a good friend and neighbor, and that's why he had been supporting Angie's elbow on the way to her husband's memorial; but given the anonymous love letter, poison garden, and previous wife's death, I think I could be excused for my suspicions. What's more, I had grown pretty fond of Mort. I considered him a friend. I didn't relish the thought of another man—Captain von Trapp or not—moving in on Mort's wife. Stars above, his spirit hadn't even lost its sparkle yet!

As I finally made my way into the park, I couldn't help but note that Cookie and Les had done a wonderful job setting up the service on such short notice. Rows of white chairs sat lined up on the lawn beside by the gazebo, and overflowing baskets of flowers hung from the trees. In many respects it looked more like a wedding than a memorial. The only clue to the contrary was the blown-up picture of Mort on an easel beside the podium in front of the chairs. He was laughing in the shot, head thrown back, eyes twinkling. He looked so joyful. I couldn't help but smile.

Given how late I was, there were only a few seats remaining at the back of the grouping. I was about to grab one when I heard, "Les, leave it. The table is fine. Go practice your eulogy if you need something to do."

The voice came from a woman with steel-colored hair and a conspicuous floral print dress, straightening confectionary boxes on the refreshment table. She didn't bother to look up as the man she scolded slunk away.

Les and Cookie Sweete.

Maybe I had arrived just in time after all.

I gathered my nerves as I moved toward the table. I didn't know Cookie all that well, but Mort had certainly made me think she didn't have the most endearing of personalities. In fact, if he was to be believed, Cookie was a downright terrible person.

"Brynn Warren," she said, looking up from her busywork. "How lovely to see you here."

Who was maybe really good at hiding her terribleness?

She rushed up and enveloped my hand with both of hers. "I'm sorry if I was brusque on the street the other day. I was still in shock." She gave me a warm smile. "I know we've only met once or twice, but I feel like I know you."

I raised my brow.

"Because of Adam."

A wave of emotion washed over me. Hearing Adam's name, especially when I wasn't prepared, still hurt.

"Oh, no. I've taken you off guard," she said with a tsking sound. "I should explain. Adam grew up across the street from Les and me. He was very dear to us. We were there for all the firsts. First steps. First time riding a bike. First couple of times he brought you home to meet his parents. We were devastated when he passed."

I forced a breath through the tightness in my chest.

"Les and I weren't blessed with a family," she went on, carrying the conversation for us both. "We lived vicariously through Adam. He had such a wonderful spirit about him. A zest for life."

I smiled. As much as it hurt, I loved seeing Adam through other people's eyes. There was something comforting in the knowledge that I wasn't the only one keeping his memory alive. "He did have a passion for life. That is certainly true."

"And here we are meeting up again after another death. Did you know Mort well?"

"Only a little, but it's hard to imagine Evenfall without him."

"There's no denying that," she said. If I wasn't mistaken, her tone had a touch of wryness to it.

"How is Les holding up?"

She sighed. "Truth be told, I've never seen him like this. He's insisted on doing a eulogy. At first, I didn't think it was a good idea. Too difficult. But Les rarely insists on anything."

There was something in her expression I couldn't quite read. Maybe she had some awareness of the rumors that she dominated her husband?

"Anyway, I should probably get back to him. We need to get started." She patted my arm.

"If there's anything I can do, please let me know." I meant the words innocently, but Cookie stiffened, her gaze sharpening.

Again, I had a reputation around town. A reputation I was suddenly sure Cookie was aware of.

Now, it wasn't so unusual to be known as a medium for ghosts. There were plenty of people claiming to have the ability on TV. And while I never asserted my gift, I was convinced there were those in town who thought I was a fraud. Was Cookie's sudden coldness a result of her believing I was some sort of con artist? Or was she worried about what I might know? As much as I was trying to read her thoughts, I knew she was trying to read mine. She could very well be the person responsible for Mort's death; and if she was a believer in my abilities, I could only imagine what she was thinking about my offer of help.

"Don't worry. I'll get my husband through this," she said, stone-faced. "He's stood by me in hard times. It's my turn now."

THE MEMORIAL WAS sweet and touching, tender and sad. After Les's eulogy there hadn't been a dry eye in the house. He did have some trouble getting through it. Cookie had been right about that. He broke down several times, especially when he talked of the fun he and Mort had working together in the shop, but in the end, Les managed to give all in attendance a portrait of a man who was both a fiercely loyal friend and a devoted husband.

I just wished Mort had been there to hear it.

That's right. He hadn't shown up.

I couldn't blame him. It would have been a lot for anyone to take. Still, it might have done him good to hear how much he was loved.

Speaking of which, I kept my eye on Angie for most of the memorial, and on the man seated beside her. There was no more inappropriate elbow touching on Elias's part, but that didn't make me any less suspicious.

One of the few times I did look away, I noticed another man I was certain I had never seen before. Granted, I didn't know everyone in Evenfall. Simon back at the antique store proved that. But I did recognize most; and, unlike Simon, this man didn't seem the type to shy away from attention. He was fair-haired, in his early sixties, and wore an exquisitely tailored pale gray seersucker suit with a yellow tie. He also had a mustache that twirled at the edges and a thin cane with a silver handle. And while *I* may not have known the man, it appeared Les did. Once the service was over and everyone got to their feet, I witnessed the two sharing a long hug.

I needed to find out who that was.

I moved to do just that when someone tapped me on the shoulder. Angela Sweete.

"Brynn, I'm sorry if I startled you. Could I talk to you a moment?"

"Of course." There were no obvious signs of tears, but Mort's widow looked absolutely exhausted. I held out a hand, and we walked away from the crowd. Once we were far enough not to be overhead, I asked, "Is there something I can do for you?"

"You haven't"—she dropped her voice to a whisper— "heard from Mort?"

I looked around the park, hoping to spot the wayward spirit, but he was nowhere I could see. "I am so sorry. haven't."

She let go of a shuddering breath. "I was really hoping could speak to him. Through you, I mean."

I gave her hand a squeeze. "I know how hard this day must be."

"It's not just that," she said, unclasping her purse and reaching inside. "I've received another love letter."

"What?!"

Unfortunately, I wasn't the one who had shouted. In fact, I hadn't said anything at all.

No, that *what* had been all Mort.

Chapter 23

DID I JUST hear my wife say *love letter*?"

Of all the times to appear.

Although maybe the timing wasn't coincidental. I had come to suspect my ghost friend was a bit of an eavesdropper. I could understand him wanting to lie low during the service. It would have been tough to hide his emotions, given how lovingly Les had spoken of him. That being said, he was making little to no effort to hide his feelings now. He was the angriest-looking man in suspenders and a bow tie I had ever seen. I did my best to focus on Angie, but it was difficult, given the fact that as Mort blustered, he also appeared to be swelling in size, much like a balloon. "That must have been very upsetting for you."

"I don't understand it." Angie clutched the envelope in her trembling hands. "Why would someone do this to me? Now, of all times?"

"I'll kill him! Anonymous, my shoe! I'd bet my afterlife it was Elias Blumenthal. He's always making up excuses to talk to my wife!"

"Angie," I pressed on, "I realize what I'm about to ask may sound strange, but could I have the letter?"

Mort's wife gave me a funny look. Her delicate eyebrows peaked in confusion.

"I've been learning a little about typewriters," I filled in. "Maybe I can figure out something about where it came from."

Angie thrust the envelope at me. "Take it. I don't want it."

Mort looked at the letter like it might be radioactive.

"Thank you for trusting me with it. I'll do my best."

"No, thank you," Angie said softly. She looked back over to the crowd. "I should get going. Elias is going to walk me home. He's been so kind. It's nice to have good neighbors." She gave me a weak smile and walked away. And not a moment too soon because I couldn't ignore Mort any longer. He had swollen to an alarming degree.

"Mort," I hissed under my breath. "Try to calm down. This can't be good for you. And we need to talk. I forgot to ask you something last night."

"What? Ask me?" Given the expression on his face, he was having difficulty processing the words I was saying.

"Try to focus. It may help you *shrink*." I cringed at his still growing size. "And don't you disappear on me! We talked about that."

"We also talked about you not talking to my wife!"

"She came to me!" I pinched my lips together. I was getting a little loud. "Forget all that for now. Focus. Have you ever had a near-death experience?"

Mort's gaze locked on mine. "What?"

"A near-death experience? Something that put you in the hospital?"

"No, no. Nothing like that. Now where's Elias and that stupid handsome face of his?"

I held up my hands in what I hoped was a calming gesture but dropped them quickly when I caught Birdie Cline giving me a funny look. How did that woman always manage to catch me at the worst possible times? "I'm sure Elias was just being neighborly," I whispered between my teeth. At least I hoped he was.

"Neighborly! I'm going to kill him!" Mort boomed. "Or haunt him! How do I do that? You know how these things work."

"Even if I did know, I wouldn't tell you. Listen, I understand you're upset. You have every right to be, but if it makes you feel any better, Elias Blumenthal is already on my radar so—"

"On your radar?" The spirit glared at me. "Wait a minute, Angie said another letter. You knew! You knew Elias was sending my wife letters and you didn't tell me!"

"I knew no such thing. All I said was that he was on my radar."

"I don't believe this!" Mort's ghostly form swelled to an even greater size.

"Mort, please. You need to calm—"

Mort exploded. Literally. He burst out in every direction, sending cascading waves of sparkles flying, like ripples in a pond. It was a very unpleasant sensation. And I wasn't the only one who felt it. A number of people shuddered as Mort rippled over them.

I sighed and planted my hands on my hips. This new understanding of ours was clearly off to a wonderful start.

A FTER THE MEMORIAL I headed back to the B&B. There wasn't much else I could do.

Mort had not rematerialized after his explosion. I mean, of course he hadn't. Why would he? Dramatic exits were his thing. And short of breaking into Elias's house and stealing his typewriter, I was at a loss for what to do next.

So, I opted to make myself a cup of tea, have a look at the letter Angie had given me, and then *maybe* take another stab at the horse dancing book.

The day had clouded over with more spring rain, so I clicked on a lamp to warm the gloom and sat cross-legged on the quilt on my bed, my messenger bag laid flat in front of me. I slipped on a pair of thin gloves and pulled out the envelope.

The letter was quite simple. All it said was, *I can't say what I want to, but this poem comes close.* Then underneath, the sender had typed out Shakespeare's sonnet 116, "Let me not to the marriage of true minds."

I couldn't help but feel a twinge of disappointment. There wasn't much I could read into the poem choice. And yes, Elias had had a big book of Shakespeare on his desk, but I was guessing more than a few people had the Bard's work lying around. Not to mention the fact that this sonnet had to be one of the most popular poem choices ever to express love. I personally had heard it read at least a half-dozen times at weddings.

The words were still lovely though.

I read the sonnet silently, turning each stanza in my mind.

One of the beautiful things about poetry was that you could read the same words over again and again and still find new meaning in them. This time I couldn't help but savor two couplets in particular.

Love's not Time's fool, though rosy lips and cheeks
Within his bending sickle's compass come;
Love alters not with his brief hours and weeks,
But bears it out even to the edge of doom.

My heart ached. Those words held the sentiment I had been trying to express to my aunts. My love for Adam hadn't changed. Death may have separated us, but the love could never be taken away. The thought was comforting. Life on this mortal plane was constantly marked by change. There was no way to stop it. But love had eternal life.

That being said, even comforting thoughts couldn't dispel all the loneliness I'd felt since Adam's passing. I loved Izzy for wanting to take that longing away, but it wasn't that simple.

I let myself sit in the feeling for a while. Burying my emotions had not proved to be a healthy coping mechanism for me in the past. My magic certainly didn't approve.

After a while, my thoughts drifted back to the letter in my hand. If the poem didn't offer any insight into the sender, maybe the physical aspects of it could.

I tilted the sheet toward the light. The paper itself was basic. White. No stains. No smudges. It certainly hadn't been read often. Angie had probably only looked at it for a second before tucking it away. I studied the individual letters next, using the information Simon had given me. It wasn't easy going at first. The type looked unremarkable. But after a few more passes, I did notice something. If I wasn't mistaken, the letter *d*, in all of its instances, was a tiny bit out of alignment. I took the envelope the letter had come in and lined its straight edge underneath the word *doom*. Sure enough, all the letters sat on its straight edge except for the letter *d*, which was just a touch higher.

That was something.

As I mulled over what to do with this information, my eyelids grew heavy. I still hadn't managed to get much sleep, and the soft patter of rain against the windowpane was very relaxing.

I had only meant to rest a moment. Maybe twenty minutes. Half an hour tops. But when I finally blinked my eyes open, the sun had gone down completely.

"Oh no."

Izzy's apology dinner!

I shot up in bed. What time was it? I squinted at my watch. Quarter to eleven!

I rolled out of bed and hobbled up to my feet. Yes, I had been annoyed with my aunt. But it wasn't as though I wasn't talking to her. Or eating her food! I peeked out the window behind my bed. Soft lamplight spilled through Izzy's bedroom window. Thank the stars. I needed to get over there to apologize.

I stumbled over to the door, then hopped on one foot to get my shoe on. I was actually kind of surprised that Nora hadn't come over and dragged me out by the ear. I switched hopping feet and pulled on my other shoe. But maybe they really were worried about how upset I was. They probably thought they had dredged up all sorts of feelings, and I was an emotional mess hiding myself away. But I was no mess! I took a quick peek in the mirror. I just looked like one. The mascara I had put on for Mort's memorial was smeared down one cheek.

This was terrible.

I hurried out my front door, rubbing the side of face. I almost ran down the stairs but stopped short when I saw how wet they were.

I looked around, then did a quick finger charm to dry them. Not that anyone would be able to see much of anything aside from steam rising. But we couldn't be too careful with Mr. Henderson always on the lookout. *The powers that be* would not be impressed if we spelled him again, of that I was quite certain. The steps dried in an instant. I raced down to the drive, then hurried across to the B&B. I slipped through the front door, gently clicking it shut behind me.

I only managed to make it a few steps before a distinct scent hit me, a faint whiff of dinner still hanging in the air. No . . .

I knew that smell. *Poulet en fricassee au vin de champagne.* One of my favorites. I tiptoed toward the kitchen and peeked in the threshold to find Faustus licking his chops. A near empty casserole dish lay on the floor, a single white grape left behind. Gone. It was all gone. An empty bottle of brut champagne sat on the counter. The one reserved for special occasions. Oh, this was heartbreaking.

Faustus, reading my thoughts, once again licked his lips. "Enjoyed it, did you?"

A rumbling purr reached my ears.

I sighed and left the kitchen, headed for the stairs. I couldn't help but think my empty stomach was just punishment for missing dinner. Actually no, it was excessive. Excessive punishment. I grasped the newel post, letting my chin drop to my chest. Ironically, I was about to eat *something*. Crow. That was another figure of speech I had to make sure I never used around Dog. He would not see the humor in that at all. I placed my foot on the bottom step of the grand old staircase, then froze to the spot.

There it was again. The funny feeling I had been experiencing as of late. Except it was different this time. Stronger. Like whatever was causing it was coming from inside the house.

I knew I hadn't imagined it! Actually, that wasn't true. I had been pretty certain at times that I had in fact imagined it, which was odd in and of itself, but I knew I wasn't imagining it now.

I climbed the stairs as quickly and quietly as I could, straining to hear or see anything unusual, but the house was almost unnaturally quiet. So quiet that I could hear the tick of the clock all the way from the parlor below.

I reached the landing of the second floor and turned left solely on instinct. I knew the newlyweds were in the Rosewater room, and while that was down this hallway, that wasn't where I was headed. No, I had my eye on the door marked *Cherrywood*.

Despite my best efforts to keep my step light and careful, as I approached the door, some hidden danger played havoc with my footing. I careened forward but, thankfully was able to right myself before I went all the way down.

I glanced at the cat by my feet. Faustus blinked innocently. What was it about felines that gave them the urge to trip people up at the most inopportune times?

"Do you think you could watch where you're going?" I whispered. "I'm trying to sneak up on someone here." Or some*thing*. It was hard to be sure.

I crept another step toward the door, Faustus still curling around my legs. If I reached out, I would be able to touch its glossy surface with my fingertips. I almost did just that, but then cocked my head to listen for any telltale sounds.

"Who are we spying on?"

I yelped and spun around.

"Gideon?"

Chapter 24

PEOPLE REALLY NEEDED to stop sneaking up on me.
"You scared me," I hissed, backing away toward the
steps. "What are you doing down here?"

Gideon placed a hand on his chest. "I thought I might
test my boundaries, spend some more time out of the attic.
I had no idea you were busy spying on the guests."

"I wasn't spying on the guests. I was . . ." I didn't know
what it was I was doing because once again the feeling had
disappeared. Actually, not just disappeared. It felt like it
had never existed at all. Like I had dreamed it maybe? Suddenly a large part of me was absolutely sure I had imagined
the whole thing. This was really strange. I considered myself to be a witch who knew her own mind. "I'm not sure
what I was doing." I scratched my temple. "Looking for
answers?"

"Come," my uncle whispered. "I know where you might
find some."

* * *

A MINUTE OR TWO later, we were seated on the small observation deck Gideon had created at the back of the tower. There was only enough room for two chairs, but it offered a fabulous view of the stars.

Viewing the night sky was a magical experience for me. I always felt that dueling sensation of being both relieved and awed by the immensity of the universe. Relieved in that it put my mundane worries in perspective and awed in the sense that there was so much I didn't understand.

"Cookie?"

I reached into the tin Gideon had held out to me. Chocolate chip. Excellent. Who needed answers—universal or otherwise—when there were cookies to be eaten? I took a bite. Crumbly and chewy. Sweet and rich. My only complaint was that they were bite-sized. They also had Izzy's name written all over them.

Seemingly reading my thoughts, my uncle said, "I heard you missed your aunt's dinner."

I swallowed hard. "I was on my way to apologize, but I got waylaid by my funny feeling." I knew I still needed to follow up on said feeling, but I figured I could go out of my way to meet the mysterious Mr. Naff at breakfast. Maybe I could see if the funny feeling was coming from him over pancakes. "And I didn't mean to miss Izzy's dinner. I fell asleep."

My uncle didn't answer.

"I did. I'm telling the truth. All of this business with Mort has led to some pretty late nights."

Gideon nodded, but he didn't look convinced.

"I'm not mad at Izzy if that's what you're thinking. I mean she did cross a line, but given how badly brunch went, I think she's learned her lesson."

My uncle looked at me, his eyes both kind and sad. "That wasn't what I was thinking."

"What were you thinking, then?"

He looked up to the night sky. "You are a compassionate person, Brynn, and your aunt went to a lot of trouble, so your falling asleep has me perplexed."

Heat flooded my cheeks. "I made a mistake. Am I not allowed to make a mistake?"

"Cookie?" my uncle offered, again holding out the tin.

I almost snapped that I didn't want another cookie. But who was I kidding? I grabbed one but did not thank him for it.

"No, if I'm being honest, I don't think your falling asleep was a mistake," Gideon went on. "I think it was a form of self-defense."

"Self-defense?" I said, struggling to keep my voice even. "Why would I need to defend myself? I didn't do anything wrong. It was Izzy who—"

"It's not your actions that need defense. I think you're trying to protect yourself against the possibilities your aunt tried to raise."

I leaned back against my chair and closed my eyes. "*Et tu*, Gideon?"

My uncle chuckled. "Name the Shakespeare play you took that from, and I'll give you another cookie."

The corner of my mouth twitched. "*Julius Caesar*. He says it to Brutus after he gets stabbed in the back." I slid my eyes over to my uncle, giving him a fairly *cutting* look of my own.

Gideon's smile deepened, but he did hand me the entire tin of cookies.

"You know, that's the second time Shakespeare has popped up for me this week."

"Perhaps it's a sign," my uncle said knowingly.

I groaned. "Are you about to give me another lecture on meaningful coincidences?"

"I was considering it."

I shot him a look.

"I have a feeling that this is a special time for you, Brynn. I can't explain it, and I haven't had any visions, but . . ." He frowned at the stars. "There are times in life when the universe opens up to us. Offers us paths or maybe opportunities that can change the course of our fates. I think this may be one of those turning points for you. If you choose to take it."

I hugged my knees to my chest, resting the cookie tin on the top of them. This was so not the conversation I had come out here for. "Well, you are entitled to your opinion, Uncle, but I know what I know. I fell asleep tonight because I was overtired. That's all. I'm not avoiding any *possibilities* that really aren't possibilities, because again, I know what I know. And I am perfectly happy with my life."

"Such certainty. Such conviction," my uncle mused, shaking his fist in the air.

My jaw dropped. Was he mocking me?

I opted to let it slide. Mainly because he had given me cookies, and I remembered something else I wanted to ask him. "I do, however, think there is more to read into Izzy's behavior. Nora alluded to something the other day. Something in Izzy's past that would explain why she's so desperate for me to find love?"

My uncle rolled his head against his chair to look at me. "Did she now?"

"She went a little light on the details though."

Gideon nodded, then turned away.

"What? You're not going to tell me either?"

"It's not my story to tell."

"Nora had no trouble telling me *your* story. The one where you were tripping all over yourself when you first fell in love with Lydia?"

Gideon's eyes snapped back to mine, his irises flashing bright green. "Did she now?"

"She did. And she didn't spare a single embarrassing

detail." I felt a little bad. It had been a while since I had played my familial guardians off one another.

But not bad enough not to do it.

I could see some furious goings-on happening behind my uncle's eyes. "Well, I may not be able to tell you Izzy's story, but I do have one to share about Nora. Would you like to hear that?"

Chapter 25

I GRABBED ANOTHER COOKIE and threw it into my mouth like I would a piece of popcorn. "Of course, I want to hear it," I mumbled. I probably should have said that first and eaten the cookie second. But this was very exciting.

"Then let's begin." My uncle waggled his eyebrows. "Once upon a time, there was a lovely but *prickly* young witch attending junior high."

I let out an excited gabble and waved my hand in the air. I had forgotten all about Nora's junior high year where *absolutely nothing happened.*

My uncle sat up to peer down to the garden below. "Just making sure your aunt isn't around. She has the hearing of a bat." Once satisfied, he leaned back in his chair. "Now, this witch was not very happy while attending school. She felt quite different from all the other young students. And this unhappiness manifested in a somewhat stormy temperament."

I chuckled. "Nora's hardly the first teenager to have a stormy temperament."

"Ah yes, but she was one of the few able to direct thunderbolts at her siblings."

I pinned my lips shut.

"But then one day the strangest thing happened. It was like a spell had fallen over her." My uncle waved his hands out like he was parting clouds. "The signs were subtle at first, but uncharacteristic."

"What signs?"

Delight lit up my uncle's face. "Well, for one, the young witch started whistling to herself while doing chores." His eyes widened at the marvel of it. "And then she started singing in the shower, loud enough for the neighbors to hear. Once she was even spotted skipping through the hallways of this very house with white daisies woven into her hair."

"Come on," I said, grabbing another cookie. That did not at all sound like the Nora I knew.

"After that, the signs became even more apparent. Every morning, when she traveled to school, the fair enchantress walked a path of sunshine. Quite literally. It could be the cloudiest of cloudy days, but every patch of pavement her foot touched lit up with beaming rays."

"Really?"

"Oh yes. And when she was digging in the back garden? Two lovebirds could often be spotted flying in circles above her head. Twittering away. *And* she would smile."

"No!" I knew she liked the sound of birds twittering. Everybody likes that sound.

"It was quite disconcerting for her family, to say the least. But it was the eldest sister who figured out what was happening." He gave me a warm smile. The eldest sister was, of course my mother. "The young witch was in love."

"So, what happened? She obviously didn't stay in that state forever."

My uncle's face fell, all his previous delight vanishing in an instant. "No. She did not." He sighed heavily. "I love remembering your aunt in those early days of infatuation. Over the years, I've pushed the ending aside."

"Gideon?"

"When people talk of young love and first breakups, they treat it so lightly."

I hugged my knees more tightly to my chest.

"We knew the exact day it had all gone wrong. Your aunt wouldn't say what had transpired, but . . ."

"You had a vision."

"Not of the usual sort," he mused, pyramiding his fingers beneath his chin. "I had a glimpse at the memory of another."

I nodded. I had experienced something similar once while looking at a photograph. For a brief time, I was the person in the picture, reliving the moment as though the memories were my own.

"Nora had come home in a terrible state. She flew through the door, threw off her belongings, and raced up the stairs to lock herself in her room. Your mother and Izzy ran after her while I stood in the foyer stunned, completely unsure what to do. Eventually I picked up her backpack to put it away. There was a sweater peeking out of the top I didn't recognize. When I touched it, I was transported. I could see Nora through someone else's eyes. We were at school, in the courtyard, and Nora was walking toward me, or rather the me who held the memory." Gideon placed his hand on his chest. "I was a torrent of emotion, overwhelmed with intense feelings of puppy love, I suppose, and . . ."

"And what?"

"Embarrassment."

I straightened in my seat. "What do you mean embarrassment?" Izzy had told me Nora had had a difficult time in school, so I should have been prepared for where this story seemed headed, but I wasn't. Not in the least.

My uncle stared out at the memory only he could see. "There were classmates all around us, jeering and heckling your aunt. Shouting all the horrible things kids do when they're faced with someone different. *You're not actually friends with her, are you? It's Nora.*" My uncle's face twisted into the ugly sneer of the kids in the memory before transforming back into something much more pained. But it wasn't his pain. It was the pain of the memory's keeper. "The look on Nora's face. She was so vulnerable. And beautiful. Her long red hair was like waves of fire in the sunlight. I wasn't worthy of her. I knew she was waiting for *me* to say something. Anything. For me to defend her. To acknowledge our connection. But I said nothing."

My throat tightened.

"The shame I felt, or rather Nora's young paramour felt, was horrific, but still they said nothing. The jeering continued and eventually your aunt just ran." Gideon slumped back against the chair. "Dark storm clouds rolled in from the sea that evening. It rained for eight straight days. Eventually your grandmother and great-grandmother had to intervene before Nora flooded the town. They went into her room—although she tried to keep them out—and they stayed in there for hours. When they came out, all Mother said was *It will be all right now.*"

"Not long after, I tried to talk to Nora about what I had seen. I couldn't help but think knowing what her crush, for lack of a better term, was thinking might provide some comfort, but she would have none of it. She wanted everyone to pretend like it had never happened."

I swallowed hard against tightness in my throat. "I hate that for her. I mean everyone gets their heart broken at one time or another, but not like that."

My uncle gave me a serious look. "It is different for everyone. And you would do well to remember that when it comes to both your aunts."

My eyebrows shot up my forehead.

"I think that's enough storytelling for one night."

"Gideon!"

"No, I have already shared more than I should have." A bewildered look came over my uncle's face. "Although I will admit Izzy is behaving a touch out of character." He peeked over at me. "Earlier, she was talking about the possibility of setting you up with our guest."

"What? You can't be serious." Apparently, my aunt had not learned her lesson after all.

"Not to worry. Nora objected. She was adamantly against it."

I huffed a breath. "Well, at least she understands where I'm coming from."

"I wouldn't go that far." Gideon squinted. "I think she simply disagreed with Izzy's choice. She seemed open to considering other possibilities."

"Unbelievable," I said. "Well, it's not going to work. They can try to set me up with every soul on the planet. It won't change how I feel." Stars above, I hoped my aunts got over this fixation on love soon. Despite what Gideon thought, it wasn't so upsetting for me that I'd miss any more dinners, but it was annoying. I was happy with my life the way it was. Why couldn't they see that? I stared back at the sky, once again allowing the vastness of the universe to seep into my soul.

We sat in silence a good long time before Gideon finally asked, "So, do you see any answers up there to your many questions?"

"Nope." I grabbed another cookie. I didn't put it in my mouth though. They were starting to lose their appeal now that I had eaten half the tin.

"Well then, perhaps you have an answer for what's going on down there?" My uncle pointed over to Mr. Henderson's house. Granted we didn't have the best angle, but I could see him coming out his side door with an armful of *pillows*?

An armful of pillows that he was now placing in various spots around his lawn.

"We need to have a family meeting about Mr. Henderson."

Gideon sniffed. "I'm sure that could be arranged if you think you can stay awake long enough."

I threw my cookie at him.

T HE NEXT MORNING, I stepped inside the B&B bright and early. The sweetest of morning scents greeted me. Coffee. I smelled coffee. I really didn't think I could go another day without it. And coffee wasn't all I smelled. There was also a rich, buttery scent hanging heavily in the air. I may have missed Izzy's special apology dinner, but her French toast was a wonderful consolation prize.

I followed my nose to the large dining room we used to serve our guests breakfast instead of to the kitchen. Despite everything, I still wasn't ready to face my aunt. A bounty of food welcomed me. There were serving platters stacked with French toast, bowls overflowing with berries, plates teeming with bacon and sausage, and towering tiered trays near ready to topple over with the weight of muffins and croissants. Izzy tended to go overboard when she was upset.

While all the food did vie my for attention, I stayed focused to my ultimate ambition.

Our guest.

Just as I suspected, seated at one of the small dining tables was the smartly dressed man I had spotted at the memorial.

His faded blond hair was swooped to the side and his thick mustache was once again twirled at the ends. Today, he wore a navy suit with a bright rose-colored cravat. His cane with the silver handle rested stylishly against a chair.

And now that I was at a much closer distance, I could

also see the man was in his sixties. Something I only took note of because of Izzy's belief that he was a suitable bachelor for me.

Not quite sure what to make of that.

And that wasn't the only thing I was uncertain about. Despite having my magical senses on high alert, I was unable to pick up on even the slightest glimmering of the funny feeling I had experienced the night before. I had been so sure it was emanating from our guest's room, but now I wasn't so certain.

Funny feelings aside, though, for Mort's sake, I needed to speak to our newest patron.

I headed over to the table of food, mulling how I might approach Mr. Fredrick Naff, but he did all the work for me.

"Ah, another diner," he said warmly. "I was beginning to feel lonely in here all by myself." He dabbed the corners of his mouth with his napkin, even though he didn't seem to be the messy eater type. "I'm sorry to say I drank the last of the coffee."

I froze, coffee mug in my hand.

"But may I recommend the French toast? It is quite remarkable."

I forced a smile, even though part of me felt like crying. "I'm glad you think so. Ivywood Hollow is actually my family's bed and breakfast."

"You must be Brynn, then," he replied. "Your aunt has told me all about you."

I just bet she had.

"Would you care to join me for breakfast?"

I had to admit I enjoyed his stylish mannerisms.

"I would be delighted." I served myself up some of the French toast. It had been a while since I'd had it. The way Izzy made it, well, it was definitely a once in a while treat. And given that I had yet again missed her coffee, I felt I was owed an extra swirl of maple syrup.

Once I had myself settled at the table, I asked, "So what brings you to Ivywood Hollow. It's Mr. Naff, isn't it?"

"Please call me Fredrick," he said, again dabbing the corner of his mouth with his napkin. "I booked my stay for business, but now, unfortunately, I'm here to say goodbye to an old friend."

"Mort Sweete?"

He nodded, eyes a touch sad. "Yes, Mortimer. I was quite shocked to hear of his passing."

I cut a square of French toast, being sure to keep my eyes on my plate. I didn't want Fredrick to read anything in them. "Did you know him well?"

"At one time. I grew up with Mortimer. We went to school together." He must have caught something in my downcast expression because he added, "He hated me calling him Mortimer. When I really wanted to bother him, I'd throw in his middle name for good measure."

"Which was?"

"Mortimer Wayne." A devilish twinkle came to Fredrick's eye. "I used it sparingly but to great effect."

I chuckled. *Mortimer Wayne.* I'd have to try that out the next time Mort was on the verge of ghostly combustion. "It does sound like you two were close back then."

"Actually, I was closer with Les," Fredrick replied, looking thoughtful. "He was my best friend, although he would have said Mort was his. We were both misfits back then. Mort felt responsible for keeping the bullies away from Les, and I got a bit of that protection by extension, much to Mortimer Wayne's chagrin." There was that devilish twinkle again.

"Did you all lose touch after high school?"

"Not entirely. I'm in the candy business too, you see." He pulled out a business card from a silver case and passed it to me. "I manufacture candy-making supplies. My family was always in production, and it pays remarkably well, but

I would have much rather been in the shop with Les making confectionaries."

"Was that ever an option?" The question came out before I had a chance to realize how impertinent it might sound. "I'm sorry. I'm prying."

"I'll attribute your curiosity to my masterful storytelling ability. But no, despite what I wanted to believe, I don't think it was ever a real possibility."

I waited.

He plucked the napkin from his lap and placed it gently on the table. "It's true what they say. Three is a crowd."

I wanted to ask him to elaborate, but even I had some shame about how far I was willing to push, and besides, I suspected I already knew. Mort and Les were family. To use yet another cliché, blood is thicker than water.

It raised some interesting questions. If Mort didn't want Fredrick being part of the business, maybe he pushed him out all those years ago? I knew how Mort could be. And if that were the case, did Fredrick resent him for it? I also couldn't help but wonder how often Cookie felt like a third wheel when it came to her husband's bond with his cousin.

"And then, of course, there were all the creative differences," Fredrick added.

I sat up in my chair. "Do tell."

"I, for one, love the occasional treat filled with liquor."

"And Mort didn't?"

"Mortimer thought it was *a waste of both good liquor and chocolate*," Fredrick said in a voice that sounded remarkably like Mort's.

I smiled.

"But really, all modesty aside, I think he was jealous of my superior talents. Les loved my chocolates. He brought all my creations home. Even the liquor-filled ones." Fredrick put a hand on his chest and gave me a nod that looked like a bow.

I raised an eyebrow. "Now, I have tasted the chocolates

over at the Sweetes' Shoppe, so you must be quite talented if, modesty aside, your skills are superior."

"Oh well," Fredrick said, "perhaps I didn't exceed Les and Mort's creations every time in terms of taste, but when it comes to hand stringing, I had Mort beat, *hands* down." Fredrick popped his eyebrows saucily.

"Hand stringing?"

"My dear girl, have you never heard of it?"

"I'm ashamed to say I have not."

"In that case, I'll have to give you a lesson."

Chapter 26

FREDRICK NAFF LOOKED down at his plate. It was empty of food, but it did have his used cutlery resting across it. He scooped up the fork and knife with the grace of a dancer and handed them to me. "Take these. I wouldn' want to stain the linens."

I smiled to myself. We did make a habit of washing the linens and were quite used to stains, but I could tell Fredrick was the fastidious sort.

"Now," he said, lifting a small stainless steel pitcher of maple syrup. "We'll need a touch of this." He poured a small puddle onto his plate.

I looked at him in question.

"I will admit hand stringing is a bit of a lost art. It's now mainly done by machine." He rolled his eyes with disgust. "But any chocolatier worth his salt still does it by hand." He deftly stripped off his jacket and took some pains to hang it neatly on the back of his chair. He then removed his cuff links, placed them on the table, then rolled up his sleeves.

"Have you ever noticed, Ms. Warren, the lines or shapes on the tops of chocolates?"

I frowned. "I have."

"Well, those lines aren't random. They are put there so that you know what type of chocolate you are eating."

"Really? I've never given it much thought." At least not until recently.

"Oh yes, in chocolates, made from scratch—and with love—you will find letters, shapes, and symbols that are all created by hand." He held up a finger, then dipped it into the center of the maple syrup. It only rested there a moment before he quickly pulled it back up, trailing maple syrup behind. His hand then danced in the air with a good deal of flourish.

"Did you just draw a letter *B*?"

He gave me a single nod. "For my charming breakfast companion. Now maple syrup certainly doesn't work as well as melted chocolate, but you get the idea." He picked up his napkin and wiped his hand.

I leaned back in my chair. "How fascinating."

"I'm glad you enjoyed my demonstration. There was a time when chocolatiers had a standard alphabet. The letter *C* might be used for cherry, for example. But over the years, the letters and symbols became personalized." He pointed his now clean finger back up in the air. "And you can always identify a chocolatier by their hand stringing. Think of it like a signature."

Like a signature. I thought about the candy wrapper I had tucked away in my messenger bag. "What about *X, O*? Do those letters stand for anything in chocolate making?"

"Aside from hugs and kisses, I've certainly never heard of that combination."

Hmm, was it possible Mort's killer had been trying to send him some sort of twisted message? I was half tempted to pull out the wrapper and show it to Fredrick to see if he could pinpoint the signature, so to speak. But as charmed as I was by this gentleman, I wasn't ready to rule him out as a suspect.

"I'm sorry, Ms. Warren. Did I say something wrong?"

"Not at all," I replied, brightening my smile. "Thank you so much for the lesson in chocolate making. You do seem talented. It's too bad the three of you weren't able to make it work."

"Well, not all hope is lost," Fredrick replied, rolling down his sleeves. "In terms of following my dreams to become a confectioner, that is."

"Sorry?"

"That was the business that originally brought me to town." He picked his cuff links up off the table. "Mort sent me an email. It must have been mere hours before he passed. He was looking to sell his stake in the shop. He was wondering if I might be interested. I dropped everything to get here. I didn't hear about his death until I arrived."

A cold shiver ran over me. Mort had never mentioned that. Although it was possible he didn't remember. "And are you?" I asked Fredrick. "Interested in buying the shop?"

"I am, but as the old saying goes, fool me once." He wagged his finger in the air.

I gave him a sideways look.

"I shouldn't go telling tales out of school. I know how small a town Evenfall is. But suffice it to say, Mort's email wasn't the first time I had been made an offer. And I don't enjoy being toyed with." For a moment he looked almost angry. "Ideally, I would have liked to run the shop with Les. I need a partner at my age. But given Mort's passing, I don't think he'll be up for it. I can figure all that out later though. If the sale goes through. The deal I've offered Les and Angie now has a time limit. It expires Thursday. At midnight we all turn into pumpkins."

Someone had offered to sell him the Sweetes' Shoppe before? I wanted to press the point, but I didn't see how. If

Fredrick Naff really was Mort's killer, I didn't want to tip him off to the fact that I was looking at him as a suspect.

"Now, I should be off," he said, pushing his chair back. "I have a neighboring auntie I must visit before I stop in to see Les." He rose to his feet. "It was delightful to meet you, Ms. Warren, and please tell *your* auntie that the French toast was magnificent." He finished with a chef's kiss in the air.

Mr. Naff strolled toward the door. As he reached the threshold, I called out to him. "Before you go."

Fredrick turned with a smile.

"The B&B is hosting a dinner for Evenfall's gardening society the day after tomorrow. You are most welcome to attend. If you think my aunt's breakfasts are good, you have to try her dinners." The idea of inviting him had just come to me. I needed to ensure I had another opportunity to speak to him as I tried to put all the pieces together.

"The gardening society," Fredrick said, a funny expression coming over his face. "I believe I met its president the last time I visited Evenfall. A devastatingly handsome man."

"Elias Blumenthal?" I offered.

"The very one. My aunt tells me his wife died a most tragic death. Attacked by a lion on safari."

I stifled a laugh. It certainly wasn't funny, but all these stories were getting ridiculous.

"I would be honored to attend the dinner, Ms. Warren," he said with a half bow.

"Well then, I'll see you there."

He tipped his cane in my direction. "It's a date."

B IRDSONG RANG OUT from the trees, the large magnolia at the corner of the street was in full bloom, and yet another bunny caught my eye as I walked toward town, but I barely registered any of it. My mind was full.

Well, I did notice Mr. Henderson's lawn. It was filled

with stakes and pillows. But that problem would have to wait. I had enough on my plate.

First and foremost on my mind was what Fredrick had said about Mort contacting him with an offer to sell his share of the shop. Mort seemed adamant against selling. I had to find out what changed his mind.

I would have liked to ask Mort directly, but he, of course, was nowhere to be found. Hopefully, he hadn't exploded himself into oblivion.

I adjusted the strap of my messenger bag and threw back my shoulders, channeling some of Nora's confidence. She was always expounding on the virtues of good posture. Once on Main Street, I cast a glance over to Charmed Treasures, but I couldn't see past the plate glass window reflecting the light of the morning sun. At some point I needed to check in with Nixie. Hopefully, she had taken at least a bit of what I said about finding balance into consideration, but somehow, I doubted it.

Again, a problem for another time.

There was only one person I wanted to talk to at the moment.

Fredrick had said he was planning to meet up with Les later, and I was hoping the location of their meetup might just be the Sweetes' Shoppe.

I was pleased to discover that when I pulled the brass handle of the front door, it swung open easily.

The Sweetes' Shoppe was most every child's dream. In the diffuse morning light, its faint watermelon pink walls gave off a warm, almost dreamy, glow. While the cousins had focused on selling their handmade chocolates and confectioneries displayed under two large domed counters on either side of the cash register, the walls were covered with shelves, filled with what looked to be every candy ever created.

As an adult, I obviously had far more restraint than I did as a child, but now that I was here, I didn't see what it could hurt to buy a small box of *something*. I'd have to wait my turn though. Minnie Abernathy and Birdie Cline were ahead of me in line, waiting for their orders to be fulfilled. They hadn't noticed me. I would have thought that the tinkling bells would have tipped them off, but they were deep in conversation.

"So," Minnie said conspiratorially, "are you going to the meeting at Ivywood Hollow?"

"Of course I am," Birdie replied. "You know I wouldn't miss any opportunity to see Elias Blumenthal."

My eyes rolled.

"I know," Minnie said with a giggle. "And I can't wait to see, or rather taste, what Izzy cooks up for us. I once ordered a Valentine's dinner from her for me and Ralph, and, I kid you not, the very next day, that husband of mine bought me a pair of diamond solitaire earrings I'd been hinting at for years. It was that good. I still dream about that meal."

I smiled. That sounded about right.

"She's such a sweet woman too," Birdie said. "Not that I can say the same for her sist—"

I cleared my throat. Loudly.

"Brynn," Birdie said whirling around. "I didn't see you there. We were just talking about the dinner being held at the B&B." An instant rosiness came to her cheeks.

I smiled coolly. "We are all very excited about it."

"Sorry about the wait," a man interrupted, coming out from the back of the store, holding a candy box.

Les Sweete was dressed the way he usually was at work with the striped collared shirt, sleeve garters, bow tie, and suspenders, but the cheeriness of the outfit did nothing to hide the fact that the man who stood behind the counter was in the firm grip of grief. I hadn't been able to see him up close at the memorial, but standing before him now, it was apparent that he had the look of someone who had aged overnight, his posture bowed, his eyes flat. I also couldn't help but note his resemblance to Mort. He was much smaller in stature, but the two men presented more like brothers than cousins.

"Les," Minnie said, "I can only imagine what a difficult time this is for you, but please tell us you're not seriously thinking of selling the shop."

"That's what the sign says." He looked bleakly out the window.

"We know that's all Cookie," Birdie said tightly. Her tone held an undercurrent of meaning. If I had to guess, she was yet another believer that Cookie was controlling when it came to Les. Birdie must have realized the harshness to her words, so she tempered them with, "I can understand her wanting you all to herself though."

"But where are we supposed to get our Monday morning fudge?" Minnie asked, holding up the box.

Les smiled, but it didn't reach his eyes. "There has been some interest already. Two potential buyers, in fact. Both seem pretty interested in keeping the shop going, so I don't think you'll be without fudge for long."

Birdie frowned. "I'm sure it won't be as good as yours."

Les gave both ladies a sad nod, and they took their leave.

I stepped up to the counter.

"Brynn Warren, it's been a long time since I've seen you in the shop, but you're a hard one to forget."

"I'm sorry?"

A flicker of life came to his eye. "It's just I remember you once tearing in here to buy a lollipop that had to be as big as your head. Your aunt rushed in a few seconds later, declaring in no uncertain terms that if I sold you that lollipop, it would be the last thing I ever did. Apparently, you had bought one before and got it tangled up in your hair. It was one of the funniest things Mort and I had ever seen, you and your aunt facing off with your arms crossed over your chests. I wasn't sure any of us would make it out alive."

I had no memory of that whatsoever.

"Your poor aunt. I remember lending her a hanky so that she could dab the sweat from her brow when you weren't looking."

I smiled. That couldn't have been long after my mother and father passed away. From what I'd heard, instant parenthood had been a shock for Nora.

"So, what can I get you?" Les asked. "Your choices are limited, I'm afraid. I'm selling off what's left before we close up shop."

I wrapped one arm around my waist and brought my hand up to my chin as I surveyed the options in the glass display. After my conversation with Fredrick that morning, I was seeing the samples with fresh eyes. It was impossible not to notice all the lines and patterns on the chocolates. Actually, everything about the treats suddenly seemed interesting. I pointed at a tray. "What are those?" I asked, looking up at Les. "Is there a reason they have a different wrapper?" Most of the chocolates had paper liners, but the ones I had indicated were resting in foil cups.

"What a good eye," Les remarked. "Yes, those are a bit different. They have a caramel center. The foil is there in case any of it leaks out."

"Sounds delicious. And what about that one? It looks like it has the letter *C* written on the top of it."

He nodded and rested his hands on the counter. "The *C* stands for coconut."

"Right. I should have read the label. What other letters do you use?"

"All sorts. Is there a particular type of chocolate you're looking for?"

"Yes, my friend had one just the other day. I think it had an *X*—"

"I've been looking for you all over town!" A voice shouted in my ear.

"Mort!"

Chapter 27

MS. WARREN, ARE you all right?"

I was fine. Technically. I mean my heart had practically jumped out of my chest at Mort yelling in my ear, but, in fairness, I should be getting used to that by now.

"What are you doing here?" Mort went on, completely unperturbed at having startled me. "I hope you're not upsetting Les now."

It was good to see my ghostly friend was back in fighting form.

"I'm so sorry," I said to the other Mr. Sweete. "I just realized I never offered my condolences for the passing of your partner." I cut a look to the ghost beside me. Maybe he didn't care if the entire town thought I was off my rocker, but I did.

"I saw you at the memorial. It would have tickled Mort that you came."

Mort didn't appear very tickled. "Your eulogy was lovely. Everyone was touched."

"It is hard losing someone you love, but you know that better than most."

I nodded.

"And I hope I did do right by Mort with the eulogy. He wouldn't have been comfortable with me saying how much I loved him. We're men of a certain age, you know." Les half-heartedly puffed out his chest. "But I did love him. He was my best friend."

"He was mine too," Mort added quietly.

I looked at the ghost with question. He seemed to understand what was on my mind because he said, "No, you cannot tell him that."

I pressed my lips together, then smiled at Les. "Well, I'm afraid I can't decide, so I think I'll take one of your sampler boxes. Can you surprise me?"

"Of course."

Just then something caught my eye on the counter. A business card identical to the one Fredrick Naff had given me. I pointed to it. "Mr. Naff is staying with us at the B&B. He mentioned you were old friends."

Mort grunted. "Oh boy, that piece of work is staying with you? He—"

"Freddie and I go way back," Les said, successfully cutting Mort off in a way I never would have been able to. "He's one of the interested buyers I was talking about. He actually wanted to run the shop with Mort and me back in the day. But Mort wouldn't hear of it."

The ghost folded his arms over his chest. "Ever heard the expression too many cooks in the kitchen?"

"They didn't get along." Les smiled as he delicately placed a chocolate in a paper box. "I think Mort was jealous of Freddie's talent, and maybe my attention."

"That is not true! Not on either front!"

Mort swelled slightly beside me. I really hoped he wasn't about to explode again. Once had truly been enough.

"It never would've worked," Les said, expertly tying a ribbon around the box. "I felt bad about it though. Freddie would have loved it here. But, I guess, now he might get the chance to have it all to himself."

"It doesn't sound like you really want to sell."

Les held me level in his gaze. "This shop has been my lifeline. If I didn't have it, I don't know what I would have done all these years. Things at home were—" He cut himself short. "I'm sorry. I haven't had a lot of sleep."

I shook my head. "No, I'm sorry. I shouldn't have pried."

"It's the shock of the thing. Somehow, I always thought I'd be the one to go before Mort. He was my anchor." Les let go of a shaky breath. "Now with him gone, I'm not sure I see the point in any of it."

"What does that mean?" Mort boomed.

I couldn't help but wonder the same thing. Les sounded so sad, so dejected. "Mr. Sweete, I know it's not my place, but sometimes it's a good idea to talk to someone in these situations. A professional maybe?"

He made a dismissive sound. "Nah, I've got Cookie."

"Cookie!" Mort shouted. "She won't help!"

"I'm a man of a certain age, remember." He handed me the box of chocolates over the counter.

I reached for my messenger bag with my free hand. "How much do I owe you?"

"It's on the house."

"I couldn't possibly."

"Really," Les persisted. "It doesn't matter."

Normally I would have accepted the generous gift without question, but again, the sound of his voice left me feeling like nothing much at all mattered to him.

"If you're sure." I struggled to find something more useful to say but came up blank. I backed away from the counter. I hated to leave this way. I wanted to make things better for Les, but I didn't see how I could do that without, once again, betraying Mort's trust. I gave the spirit one last pleading look, but he refused to meet my eye. Never had I met a ghost so infernally stubborn. I held up a hand to Les. "Please do take care of yourself."

He forced a smile. "I'm sure my wife will do that for me."

I headed for the door, assuming Mort would follow. When I looked back, he said, "I'm going to stay. I want to spend some time with Les even if he doesn't know I'm here."

I stepped outside. The sun was full and bright, but I couldn't feel any of its warmth.

I was disappointed that I wasn't able to speak to Mort alone. I needed to ask him about his contacting Naff with the offer to sell his stake in the shop, but his being with Les seemed more important right now.

I sighed and placed the small box of chocolates in my bag, spotting Naff's business card once again. The way this card kept popping up, Gideon would probably say *the powers that be* were trying to tell me something.

I took the card out and gave it a good look in the bright sunshine.

It was beautifully done. It personified all of Naff's grace and elegance. The script he used to write his name was the same as that on the candy wrapper, and it was no regular font. My guess was that he designed it himself then had it digitized. It was that lovely. The *N* in *Naff* in particular, with its curlicues and whorls, was gorgeous.

Wait a minute. I had seen this script before, and not on any candy wrapper.

My gaze darted about the street. It could be a coincidence, but something about all this suddenly felt quite serendipitous.

Chapter 28

I HAD TO WAIT an agonizingly long time to get the chance to talk to Nixie.

Immediately after I realized I needed to talk to her, I went to Charmed Treasures. Unfortunately, she wasn't there. Her aunt was at the counter, and she hadn't seemed particularly thrilled to meet me. Given that I didn't believe I normally put people off at first sight, I couldn't help but wonder if her witch hunter's blood had her on edge. Either way, she told me Nixie was in class and usually didn't get back until at least nine. She suggested I text her. When I told her I didn't have a phone, I think that only made matters worse. Everybody has a phone these days. I did, too, until recently. Phones, along with other electronic devices, didn't always play well with witches. The truth of it was they often went haywire. I thought I had it beat with my last phone. It did last five months, which was a record; but then, unfortunately, about two weeks ago it started ringing endlessly at three o'clock in the morning. I tried to fix it—I had been working on a spell that would provide it some protection from, well, magic—but Nora with her bat-like hearing had heard it from the B&B. She came over and put it out of its misery before I could stop her. She hadn't even bothered to use magic. She beat it to death with a fire poker on my stone hearth. I was planning on getting another phone. I just wanted to be certain I could ensure its safety before bringing it home.

All this to say, I did not think I had made a good impression on Nixie's aunt when I spoke to her, so when I arrived at their home later that night, after speeding across town on my bike, I opted not to knock on the front door. I was hoping I might find another way to get my young friend's attention.

Nixie's aunt and uncle lived in another one of Evenfall's beautiful old homes. It wasn't overly large, but it had an appealingly simple structure with its three stories that went straight up into a peaked roof.

I leaned my bike against a fence, then looked up to the window on the top floor. I knew that was Nixie's room. She had told me several times she liked having the top floor all to herself. I took a step back onto the road, straining to see inside. I hopped a few times to get a better view—I wasn't about to perform a levitation spell in public—and sure enough I spotted Nixie at a desk. Her head lay on its surface while one hand hovered in the air, her fingers dancing as though playing the keys of an invisible piano.

I spied a clump of tiny pebbles resting by the curb. Those should work nicely. I bent to brush the small rocks into my hand. I stood back up, then brought the heel of my palm to my lips. I took a glance side to side to make sure no one was watching, then blew air out in a gentle stream.

The pebbles floated up in the sky, twirling gently in the lamplight, headed toward the house. Up and up the little cloud went until it splattered against Nixie's window.

I hopped a few times again to see if she had heard it.

She was sitting bolt upright in her chair, so I was willing to guess she had.

I waited for her to come to the window, but after a minute or two, I realized that was not going to happen.

"Oh, come on," I muttered. I then bent down to sweep up another pile of pebbles.

I repeated the entire process. This time after only a few seconds, Nixie came to the window. She pushed it up and leaned outside. I stood directly in the pool of light coming from the streetlamp and waved at her.

"Brynn?" she called out in a tired whisper.

I rolled my hand for her to come down.

She pushed the window shut and disappeared.

I brushed the remaining dust from my hands and stepped up onto the sidewalk.

Seconds later, Nixie came out, in an oversized purple and white tie-dyed crop sweatshirt with matching jogger pants. She dragged herself across the lawn, her pink ponytail swinging limply side to side. "What are you doing here? You scared me half to death."

I frowned. Normally Nixie was thrilled to see me regardless of the context. I studied her carefully. She was exhausted, her eyes bloodshot and watery, her shoulders slumped. "You look like you haven't slept in a week." Or at least since I had given her the spell. "I'm hoping it's because you were out partying with friends?"

Nixie glowered at me. "Said no adult ever."

"Let me guess—you've been practicing the spell non-stop since I gave it to you."

She looked down at the sleeves of her top covering her hands and shrugged.

"Dare I ask how it is going?"

She rolled her eyes up to mine. "Awesomely well."

"Really?" I raised an eyebrow.

She threw her head back and groaned. "No! Of course it's not going awesomely well!"

"Has anything at all happened?"

She spun in a tight, angry circle. "I am so close!" She shook her fists at the sky. "I know I'm close."

I ran my hand over my face, then quickly pulled it away; it still had some rock dust on it. "Maybe it's time you took a break."

She gave me a look that spoke to how ridiculous she thought that suggestion was. "I just need a couple more tries."

"And how many tries have you given it so far?"

"I didn't count."

"Ballpark figure."

"Not that many."

"In the tens?"

She squinted and tilted her head side to side. "Maybe higher."

"Hundreds?"

She grimaced, put a thumb in the air, and jabbed it skyward.

My chin dropped to my chest. "Thousands?"

She shrugged tiredly. "Maybe more. It's hard to say."

"Nixie," I said, drawing out the syllables of her name. "This is exactly what I was afraid of. I knew I never should have given you that spell. I was worried I'd get your hopes up for something that has about a zero percent chance of success. And now look at you. You're exhausted. And sad. And not at all Nixie-like."

"I know. I know," she said with an angry stomp. "But I'm telling you. I'm close. I can feel it. You don't have to worry. I'm going to make you so proud."

Make *me* proud? She didn't need to make me proud. I knew, though, that Nixie had a strained relationship with her family. She had told me that she never felt like she fit in. Not that her family believed anything about witches or witch hunters. Actually, that was the problem. Nixie didn't talk to them about her *beliefs* anymore, but she had in the

past; and it had left them with the impression that there was
something a little off about her. All this to say, I think Nixie
felt more accepted when she was around my family. And
that was far more important than any spell. I didn't want to
press her on any of that right now though. She was already
discouraged. She'd figure out soon enough that the spell
wasn't going to happen, and I needed to make sure I would
be there for her when that time came.

"Well, you are an adult, so only you can decide when
enough is enough. Just don't let it get in the way of your
studies. And promise me you'll get some sleep tonight."

"Okay, witch mom."

The corner of my mouth twitched. "Anyway, that's not
why I'm here. I need to see your tattoo again."

"What?"

"The *N*," I said waving my hand out. "Show me the *N* on
your arm."

Nixie straightened and slid the sweatshirt sleeve up to
her elbow. "It's faded now. Why do you want to see it?"

I grabbed her arm and leaned in to get a better look. I
then took the business card out of my bag and placed it
alongside her arm. They were almost identical. "Where did
you get the inspiration for this tattoo?"

"I copied it from this scrap I found."

"What kind of scrap?"

"A candy wrapper."

Chapter 29

WHERE? HOW? DO you still have it? Did it say Naff?"
I knew I was hurtling questions at Nixie at an alarming rate. I could tell by the way her eyes were widening. But I needed to know how it was she had a wrapper from Mort's box of poisoned chocolates.

Nixie blinked a few times, then said, "Outside. I picked it up. No, I threw it out after I copied it. And yes, it said Naff." She beamed. "And you thought I was tired."

"Where exactly did you find it?"

"It was right outside of the gift shop. There's a crevice by the front door where old leaves gather. It was hidden underneath them."

I frowned at her. "If it was hidden under the leaves, how did you know it was there?"

She frowned back at me. "I don't know. Maybe it wasn't hidden. It was all shiny and gold, so I must have seen it glinting in the sunlight."

Hmm. Charmed Treasures wasn't far from the Sweetes' Shop, but it was a fair distance from the town gazebo, where

Mort had taken his fateful bites. It was unlikely it could have blown there from that distance. But Mort had said the store never used the wrappers with Naff printed on them because of the branding. So where did it come from?

"I can tell you where it came from if that helps?"

I raised an eyebrow. Nixie may not be able to do spells, but she certainly had something going on in that blood of hers.

"Where?"

"Okay, well, I copied the tattoo design from the wrapper I found outside the shop." She stopped her explanation briefly to duck away from a bug that had flown close to her face. "But that was only after I had gotten rid of all of mine."

"All of yours? Why did you have candy wrappers?"

"I got them from the box of chocolates that was delivered to the store. We all got them," she said. "All the shops on the street. At first, I thought it was pretty presumptuous, given that we already have our own town candymakers, but then I realized it was a charm offensive."

I shook my head. "I have no idea what you are talking about. What charm offensive?"

"Fredrick Naff. You know him. I think he's staying at the B&B. He's the awesome guy with the twirly mustache and cane?"

"Yes, I know who he is. My aunt was thinking of setting me up with him."

Nixie made a face. "I don't think you're his type."

"*And* he's not mine."

"Anyway, I heard he wants to buy the Sweetes' Shoppe. I mean, the box came with a note that said something to the effect of hoping to serve you all soon. So, I think he was trying to ingratiate himself to the neighborhood so that Cookie would sell the shop to him first. Which I am all for because my family does not need any more stores in Evenfall."

"Surely your aunt and uncle can't expect you to clerk at them all?"

"No, they'll just bring more of us to town, and do you really think Evenfall needs more witch hunters running around?"

"As a general rule, no. But you are quite lovely."

"Aw, thanks, Brynn."

I frowned.

"I said, *thanks, Brynn.*"

"Sorry, no, I'm just thinking."

"I mean the wrapper I used for the tattoo could have come from anywhere, but Jodi at Furry Tales told me she caught Cookie throwing things out in the street garbage can."

My gaze snapped back to her. "And that's a no-no?"

"That is a *huge* no-no. You're only supposed to use the dumpsters in the alley. We have to keep Main Street looking clean for the tourists. That's why those cans are emptied so regularly."

There was so much to process, and I didn't know what any of it meant. Yet. "When did everyone get these boxes of chocolates?"

"About a month ago. It was funny. I only thought about the tattoo idea after I had thrown all the packaging out. I was so bummed I didn't keep it. But then it just turned up."

That had to be what Fredrick meant when he said *fool me once.* Maybe Cookie had previously led him to believe the shop was for sale? She was the only one that made sense. Mort and Les had both told me they didn't want to sell. Something had obviously changed Mort's mind in the hours before his death, but he seemed certain about wanting to keep the shop before that. There was Angie, of course, and her talk of moving closer to her daughter, but I couldn't see her doing anything as bold as approaching a potential buyer behind Mort's back.

"And when did you find *this* wrapper?"

"The morning Mr. Sweete died. That's kind of a hard thing to forget. I was tracing the tattoo when I heard the news. Wait a minute. Does this have something to do with Mr. Sweete? Is that why you're so freaked out?"

"I'm not freaked out."

"Then why are you chewing your thumbnail?"

I dropped my hand from my mouth. I hadn't realized it had gotten up there. "Truthfully, I don't know what I'm thinking."

"That's a lie."

I swatted her arm. "Would you stop doing that? Sometimes, there are things I'm not ready to share. It would be irresponsible. Kind of like giving a spell to a witch hunter."

"That is some non sequitur-type argument you're making there. I'm sorry I didn't keep the wrapper though. If I had known it was important, I would have hung on to it."

"It's okay. It's probably not. I have to go, but thank you." I walked a few steps toward my bike, then whirled back around. I knew this was probably a bad idea, but I had to ask. "Nixie, would you say you thought *a lot* about the wrapper after you had thrown it out?"

"Only like all the time. I was so mad at myself. It was the perfect *N*. I wished over and over that I still had it."

I tried to keep my face still, but I think my eyebrow twitched. That was all it took.

Nixie's eyes widened to a degree I didn't think was possible. Her mouth dropped open too. She then raised a hand in the air and pointed at me. Repeatedly. "You think I called it back to me!"

I shook my head.

"You're lying!"

"Would you please stop doing that! I am not lying! At least not really. I mean, it's just that it's quite the coincidence." And there seemed to be a lot of that going around.

"I've got to go!" Nixie shouted, spinning on her heel.

"Where do you have to go?"

"To practice the spell!"

"Would you keep your voice down?"

She spun back around. "I told you I had magic in me."

"Nixie, this doesn't mean anything. It was probably just one of those fluke things."

"Or it could mean my magic is so strong, it's just erupting from me." She mimed miniature explosions with her hands.

I sighed. "You're not going to get any sleep tonight, are you?"

"Probably not a wink."

Chapter 30

WHEN I GOT back to the B&B, instead of going up to my loft, I went to the screened pergola in the back corner of the garden. I didn't much use it even though it was tucked away in the property's fragrant lilac bushes. We left it mainly for the guests. Given how late it was, I didn't think I would run into anyone, though, and it was a beautiful space to enjoy the garden. There was also an added benefit. The wooden chairs underneath it, while cushioned, probably would stop me from falling asleep. Not that I was tired or wanting to sit.

I wanted to pace. I had a lot to puzzle out.

As much as I liked Fredrick Naff, I couldn't deny that he had designs on the shop. He had told me as much. But if Mort had emailed him, he wouldn't have had a motive to get him out of the way. *If* he was telling me the truth.

And then there was the outstanding issue of the love letters. I was no closer to finding out who had written them, but the sender had to be someone clueless or extremely coldhearted. As coldhearted as a murderer?

Related to that subject was Elias Blumenthal and his poison garden. Now, I liked Elias, too, but I couldn't help being suspicious of him. Maybe it was all the stories about his deceased wife floating around.

Last but not least, there was Cookie. Nobody had much good to say about her; and it seemed she, Les, and Mort had a lot of history behind them. It was clear she resented the shop, too, and it was Mort who was responsible for keeping it going as long as they had. Maybe she had had enough of it all?

Suddenly a strange picking noise found its way into my consciousness. I looked over to find Faustus plucking the screen door like a banjo.

"Looking for company?"

The cat picked the screen again.

"Okay, okay," I said, walking over. "You don't need to tear a hole in it." I held the spring door open for him to step inside. "Let's be quick about it. You're going to let all the bugs in."

Of course, he wasn't quick at all. He strolled in leisurely with his fluffy tail straight up in the air. He moved to the center of the space and sat himself down.

"I guess I'll just pace around you."

I set to doing just that. I needed more evidence. I did already have a number of clues, but I couldn't seem to get them to point in a conclusive direction. And I was running out of time. Mort's days to walk this plane unaffected were few. I needed to do something drastic. Force the killer's hand. I pressed the spot between my eyebrows. I couldn't help but think the gardening society meeting might just be my best—

Tap! Tap! Tap!

I looked under my hand, following the noise, to see the tip of Dog's head peeking over the lower part of the door-frame.

"You want to come in too?"

Tap! Tap! Tap!

I sighed and walked over. I then looked back and forth between the crow and the cat. "Are you two going to play nice? This is a small space. I don't want any fights breaking out."

Faustus, who had been licking his paw, gave me a look. Dog didn't say anything, just hopped in when I opened the door.

I resumed my pacing, winding an awkward path between the two creatures. Now, where was I? Right! The meeting. There was a good chance Fredrick, Elias, and Cookie would all be there, but how could I use that to my advantage?

Faustus chittered.

"Could you keep it down? I'm trying to concentrate here."

I closed my eyes and took a breath to clear my mind.

Now, the meeting. There had to be a way to get the killer to reveal something. But how? I needed—

Dog squawked.

"Really?" I peeked an eye open. "I don't have any peanuts if that's what you are looking for."

I took another turn around the pergola. As I began my second pass, I noticed both Dog and Faustus were following me. I looked over my shoulder and said, "I'm not sure the conga line is helping, but thanks for the support."

Okay, focus, Brynn.

I needed a plan. And maybe some information that only the killer knew. Then I could use that information to—

Dog and Faustus cried out at the same time.

I spun on my heel. "What is it you two want?" But before I had finished the question, I knew.

"You have got to be kidding me," I whispered.

The two were perched on the armrests of a chair, looking a bit like gargoyles, but on the seat between them lay a book.

The History of Dressage.

How on earth did that get out here?

I was certain I had left it up in the loft. Of course, I did leave the loft unlocked most days. Izzy often brought over leftovers and sometimes sleepwear, and Nora, well, Nora on occasion needed to come by and beat my electronics to death; but why would either one of them take the book? Had Gideon tipped them off to something?

Maybe it was a sign.

Once again, for whatever reason, I wasn't particularly comfortable with that idea.

I carefully picked the book up. It felt prickly to the touch, like it had its own current of electricity.

I frowned at it. "Why are you tingling?"

The book didn't answer. Not that I had really expected it to.

"You are a funny little thing, aren't you?"

Despite having learned nothing of use so far from the text, I couldn't ignore the fact that I did feel drawn to it. Like I knew it wanted to tell me something.

My frown deepened. Aside from reading it cover to cover—a thought which did not excite me—there was only one other way I could think of to test the theory.

"If I am completely off base, I am very sorry for what it is I'm about to do."

I lifted the book to shoulder height, shut my eyes tight, and dropped it.

Smack!

Faustus and Dog jumped from their posts to get a better glance at the pages the drop had revealed. I lowered down to my knees and took my place between them.

Huh.

This particular chapter was all about the importance of a rider's posture during training exercises.

Couldn't really see how that helped.

I read the entire two pages just to be sure I wasn't missing something, but aside from making me think I really needed to work on keeping my shoulders rolled back and down, I didn't find them all that helpful.

"I knew it," I muttered to my companions. "There are no signs." I made a grab for the book to lift it off the ground, but it slipped from my fingers, turning a single page.

Dog and Faustus leaned in once again. Faustus went so far as to plant a fluffy paw on the top corner of the open text.

"What?" I asked, looking back down. The right page was filled with type, but the left had a large photograph of a horse standing in front of a flowering bush.

Stars above.

"That's it," I whispered as chills raced up and down my arms. "That's the bush I saw in Elias's garden." The one that had its branches hacked.

My eyes darted over to the type. The title at the top of the page read, *Plant Toxicoses in Horses*.

My gaze flew down to the caption under the photograph.

Oleander.

Chapter 31

"BRYNN, AM I hearing you correctly? Are you telling me you could not identify an oleander bush on sight?"

I closed my eyes and inhaled deeply. I had not called this meeting to discuss my failings as a botanist.

My aunts and I were seated around the circular table in the library, a number of grimoires scattered about between us. A low fire burned in the hearth.

The real reason I had gathered us here was to brainstorm ideas for the gardening society dinner—despite the fact that things were still awkward between Izzy and me. I wasn't mad about the brunch anymore, and I didn't get the sense she was mad about my missing dinner, but we still had a lot to work out. I was dealing with the tension by pretending everything was fine. Izzy, on the other hand, was handling things by heaping sunshine on me.

"I think it's marvelous Brynn has discovered yet another talent. A book whisperer, who would have thought it?" Izzy remarked, eyes twinkling with excitement.

Apparently, book whispering was a thing.

"You know, with the number of talents you keep uncovering, I think you could be a master witch someday."

I gave her a wan smile. She was laying it on pretty thick.

Being a master witch wasn't exactly a goal of mine. All it meant was you were a witch with multiple talents. Regardless, I wasn't convinced that what had happened in the pergola was a new gift revealing itself. "Why don't we work on solving Mort's murder first and see where things go from there?"

"Quite right," Nora said. "Let's get back to the topic at hand. Oleander. It is a rather basic but potentially effective choice under the right circumstances."

"So, it could be used to poison someone in chocolate?"

"It's hard to say. Unless the murderer was able to find a recipe, it would be difficult to ensure its effects," Nora mused. "It would be quite easy to kill say a child though."

"Evanora," Izzy said, grimacing.

"I'm not saying *I'm* thinking of killing a child," Nora said, shooting her sister an indignant look. "Shame on you if you were."

Izzy's eyes widened with horror.

"My point is there are a lot of factors at play. Like how much of it was consumed? A few leaves could kill a small"—Nora paused, briefly meeting her sister's eye—"*human*, but an adult might be able to survive the same amount. Usually, though, the death is prolonged by several hours at least. But I've heard of at least one or two instances where that wasn't the case. Mort's health issues must have played a role. His arrhythmia in particular."

Izzy sighed. "While this is all very good to know, it doesn't really help us, does it?"

"I beg your pardon," Nora snapped.

"No," Izzy began, "I mean, it is important to have the details, but it doesn't bring us any closer to uncovering the identity of the killer. Even if Elias Blumenthal was the only person in town to grow oleander, which is a big if, I assume his garden isn't locked down?"

I shook my head. "Even locked, an adult could get over the fence. So yes, we still need something to help us narrow in on our suspect."

"I have an idea." A sly, somewhat scary, smile slid across Nora's face.

"I don't like the sound of that," Izzy said.

Nora laid out for us her plan in great detail. Once she was through, an uncomfortable silence fell over the library, like a cold, heavy sea fog.

Izzy and I were both stunned, but she was the one to recover first.

"Are you mad? Absolutely not." She scissored her hands over the table. "We are not even contemplating doing that."

"Whyever not?" Nora asked with a scowl. "Given the history, I think turnabout is fair play."

"I don't think I should have to explain to you *why not*."

"Brynn," Nora said, turning to me. "What do you think?"

I studied my aunt's face, trying to gauge her seriousness. The conclusion I came to was not reassuring. "You know how badly I want to find answers for Mort, but no. Of course not! We are not doing that."

"I agree!" a tinny voice sounded from the iron register near the ceiling.

"Thank you, Gideon," Izzy said.

Nora groaned. "I truly do not see the issue. There would be a *little* discomfort at most for those we target. Nothing too painful. In fact, they might even find the experience *tasty* depending on which option we chose to go with." For a moment Nora looked like she might lick her lips. "I would make sure the guilty party did not die."

"And if you made a mistake?" Izzy asked.

"Well then, yes, I suppose much like a lightning strike,

or winning the lottery, someone could theoretically die, but—"

"No!" Izzy and I both shouted at the same time.

Nora leaned back against her chair, rolling her eyes to the ceiling. "It would have been perfect, given the theme we're working with."

"We are trying to uncover a murderer," I said. "Not plan a party."

Nora rolled her eyes back down. "I was under the impression we were doing both."

That was technically true. "You know what I mean."

"I don't see why it is that Izzy here gets to spell people with food in order to lower their inhibitions," she said, waving a hand in her sister's direction, "but I can't use my magic to help."

Izzy scoffed. "I am merely making people comfortable and—"

"Don't you mean vulnerable?" Nora asked, raising an eyebrow.

"You make it sound so ugly." Izzy twisted her hands together. "I create my food with love."

As my aunts continued bickering, a fledgling idea swirled in the back of my mind. It had started the moment my aunt had used the word *vulnerable*.

"Besides, that was just one suggestion. I was, what do they call it?" Nora waved her crimson fingernails in the air. "Spitballing ideas. I have many others. I could, for example, alter the atmosphere of the greenhouse to literally scare a confession out of the guests."

"Evanora, please," Izzy said, pressing her fingertips to her forehead. "There are innocent people to consider. Besides, our spells always have a funny way of going rogue when performed in public settings. We have to be careful."

Nora groaned. "I am one hundred percent certain I could come up with a spell that would ferret out our guilty party without anyone being the wiser."

"And I am one hundred percent certain that that is not something you could be one hundred percent certain about," Izzy snapped.

"You always underestimate my abilities."

"Your abilities aren't the problem. It's your ego."

Nora straightened in her chair and folded her arms over her chest. This was not good. I needed her at her best if my plan was to work.

"I think I may have an idea. One that won't involve using magic on any large, flashy scale but will require both of you to use your talents."

Nora slid her gaze over to me.

"What is it, Brynn?" Izzy asked. "What are you thinking?"

I smiled. I was thinking knowing the killer's choice of poison might not be so useless after all.

AFTER NAILING DOWN the details of our plan, I went out searching for Mort. I was excited about what we had come up with. It was by no means foolproof, but it was something. And if anyone could use a little hope right now, I suspected it was him.

I rode around town, trying to make myself available. I didn't know if Mort could sense whether I wanted to speak to him or not, but I hoped all my pains in searching for him wouldn't go unnoticed.

I lingered for a while in the town gazebo. No Mort.

I sat on the bench outside the Sweetes' Shoppe. No Mort.

I even went by his house a few times, but given that Angie's car wasn't in the driveway, I doubted Mort was there.

By the time the sun was getting low in sky, an awful thought occurred to me. What if he had decided to go into the light? Maybe he had gone without telling me. It was his choice, of course. He didn't owe me anything. But the thought hurt far deeper than I would have expected it to.

I decided to ride by Mort's house one last time before calling it a night.

Golden sunlight filtered through the tall trees lining his street, and the birds were in the midst of their nightly orchestra. I slowed to a stop once I reached the small cottage with the climbing pink rosebush. The car was back in the drive.

The gauze curtains were drawn across the front window, but I could make out Angie's silhouette on the other side. She was seated in an armchair, hunched over, her elbows resting on her knees. Her hands were clasped together and pointing out. There was a fainter silhouette kneeling in front of her. One that only I could see. Mort had his hands over his wife's, and his head was bent close to hers so that their foreheads touched.

My chest tightened with familiar pain. I turned to leave, but as I did, Angie got to her feet, and Mort vanished, only to reappear a second later by my side. "Ghostie?"

"I'm sorry," I stammered. "I didn't mean to interrupt."

"What's happened? You look upset."

I lowered my bike to the ground and sat on the curb. "I've been looking for you all day. I thought maybe you went into the light without saying anything."

He sat down beside me. "You sure do have a thing about goodbyes, don't you?"

I peeked over at him. "I could say the same about you."

"That's true. I've never liked them."

I wanted to press the point. We were running out of time. But I didn't have it in me to fight.

"Truth is, I am getting ready to go though. Can't see much reason to stick around."

"That's not true. We still need to find out what happened to you."

He gave me a weak smile. "I know it's what I said I wanted, but the thing is, staying, well, it's starting to hurt more than it helps." He glanced across the street. "That's not my house anymore. It was the house Angie and I shared. But now it's hers. Hers to do with as she pleases. I hope she sells it. Moves down to Florida to be closer to Amanda. Our baby girl could sure use the help."

"Did you go see her? Amanda?"

He nodded. "She's by her husband's side as she should be. The doctors think he's going to pull through, so that's something. You know," he said, turning back to look at me, "I think she might have felt me there. I put my hand on her shoulder, and she placed hers on top of it. Or maybe *through*." He shrugged, bewildered.

"I'm sure she felt you there."

"I went to check in on the grandkids after that. They were at school having a blast." His face brightened by about a hundred times. "Seeing them happy did my heart good."

I smiled. "That's wonderful."

He looked back again at the house. "Letting go of Angie is all that's left."

"I don't think you ever really let go. In fact, I know you don't."

He looked at me with so much empathy, it nearly broke my heart. "You've been through a lot, haven't you?"

We both fell silent as a group of kids raced by on their bikes.

"Mort," I said suddenly, "do you believe in signs?"

"What do you mean?"

"My uncle asked me not too long if I thought there might be a reason for our paths crossing." I waved my hand back and forth between the two of us. "I told him it was coincidence, but, I don't know. I've been having some weird experiences lately." I told him all about the book and Nixie's tattoo. When I was through, I said, "I guess it sounds pretty funny that a witch is having all this trouble believing in signs."

"No, Ghostie, it doesn't. Given the way you lost your husband, I think it makes perfect sense."

Mort's words hit with unexpected force. He was right. That was it. I hadn't been able to pinpoint it before, but he was right. I hated all this talk of signs and serendipity because if such things existed, why hadn't *the powers that be* given me a sign that Adam had a heart defect? Why was Gideon given the vision of my parents' death too late? Why was Mort murdered? Why hadn't he been given warning?

"I don't know much about signs," Mort said, "but there is another theory that I've always been partial to."

I raised an eyebrow. "What's that?"

"Guardian angels. I think maybe there's some things that can't be changed—whether it's because of some plan or just bad luck—but I like to think that every once in a while those who have passed can give us a helping hand or a blessing when we need it most."

"That's a nice thought."

"I guess the trick is knowing when one of those angels is pointing you in a good direction." Mort gave me a phantom bump with his elbow. Of course, it went right through. "You're a good egg, you know that? I'm glad I got to know you before I—" He jabbed a thumb up at the sky, then grimaced. "At least I hope that's where I'm going."

I knew he was trying to lift the mood, but I was filled with a strange sinking feeling. "For a man who doesn't like goodbyes, that's starting to sound an awful lot like one. And I'm telling you, right here and right now, I'm not having it."

The ghost frowned. "You were just upset when you thought I'd left without saying goodbye."

"Yes, I want you to say goodbye, but not until I've helped you."

Mort chuckled under his breath. "You already have helped me. So much. I'm not sure what these past few days would have been like if I didn't have you to talk you. And maybe drive a little crazy." He winked. "I don't want you worrying about me anymore. You've done your job."

"No, I haven't. And I swear by every star in the sky I am going to find out who did this to you." I knew that was a promise I shouldn't make, but I meant it just the same. "I've got a plan."

Mort blinked. "That sounds scary."

Not really. Nora's plan had been scary. Mine was much more cautious but, hopefully, still effective. "You should be there to see it." I gave him the details for the meeting being held at the B&B.

"Well, I appreciate you trying. I really do, but—"

"No buts. I'll see you there." I jumped to my feet, pulled up my bike, and threw my leg over the seat. I pressed down hard on the pedal, not waiting for Mort to object. When I was a good distance away, I shouted, "And, remember, no leaving without saying goodbye!"

Mort wasn't the only one who could make an exit.

Chapter 32

IZZY TRULY OUTDID herself.

Dinner was a smashing success. And for a small-town gardening society meeting, it turned out to be quite the elegant affair. Not that anyone was dressed up exactly. It wasn't a black-tie type of event, but the evening held a certain sophistication. We ate outside at two long tables nestled between the gardens. All the trees were glowing with lanterns, and the air was fragrant with the rich heady scent of lilacs.

It was, dare I say, magical?

In fact, the night had such an enchanted feel to it, I asked Nora if she had used her powers to boost the bewitched atmosphere. But, of course, as soon as I asked her, I wished I hadn't.

Me? Use my powers in public? What a terrifying suggestion.

It left me to wonder if somehow the property itself had risen to the occasion. The Warrens had, after all, been living on the plot for nearly four hundred years. It seemed entirely possible that some of that generational magic had found its way into the earth. Either way, it was wonderful.

And the food itself was marvelous. Not that I ever had any doubt. There were so many dishes to choose from that when the guests first sat down, many were overwhelmed. From what I could tell, though, the wild-caught scallops pan-seared with brown butter lemon sauce was probably the favorite. Although the apple bourbon roast chicken was a close second. My stomach growled. I would have liked to pick my own favorite. I really wanted to try the triple-threat onion galette. It looked quite flaky. But the food wasn't for us.

My nerves started to build the moment the servers came to clear the tables. Izzy had hired a handful of local university students to help out. She often did that when we hosted larger events. The servers cleaning up meant the second part of the evening was about to begin, and that was the part on which all my hopes rested.

I twisted my hands together as the society members got to their feet and drifted off among the many gardens. Everyone who I had hoped would come tonight—Elias, Cookie, and Fredrick—had in fact shown up along with a few people I hadn't expected. Angie was first on the unexpected list. Elias had asked her to come under the pretense that it wasn't good for her to be alone. I could only hope that if Mort did decide to come, he wouldn't be too upset. Theo had also shown up. I had waved at her when she had first come in; and it looked like she wanted to have a word with me, but I hadn't had the chance to speak with her yet. In truth I wanted to keep my attention focused on my suspects.

Nora mingled throughout the group. She was quite the marvel tonight. The epitome of an excellent hostess. Charming. Charismatic. Engaging. Maybe even warm?

I smiled. I couldn't help but think her performance was at least in part inspired by the fact that she had been purposely overlooked in the first place. She would show those society members. She would show them all!

Just then my aunt looked over.

The smile dropped from my face.

Nora had long denied that mind reading was one of her talents, but sometimes I wondered. It would be just like her to have the ability and not tell us.

She sashayed over to me. What was particularly remarkable about her ability to charm the crowd was the fact that she was able to do it in what she was wearing. No, this was not a black-tie affair. It really wasn't. For everyone but Nora. You could say she had gone a little over-the-top. Her long red curly hair was piled up on her head with a few tendrils elegantly falling to her shoulders along with her gold pendant earrings. Moving down from there, she wore an emerald green kaftan—the shade picking up on the color of her eyes—with a gold embroidered collar that ran all the way down to its hem. Every time she reached out an arm, the fabric draped with an elegance that was just a bit stunning. A fact she was clearly aware of because she was pointing at a lot of things. Far more than she normally would. Finally, on her feet she wore gold thong sandals, her toenails painted her signature crimson.

I brightened my smile as my aunt floated up to me. "Have I mentioned you look spectacular tonight?"

"Really?" She placed a gold-ringed hand on her chest. "I forgot I had this old thing in my closet."

Uh-huh. If I had to guess, she had begun working on it the day we met Elias. Sewing was another one of Nora's many talents.

"And I must say, Brynn, you look, adorable."

I had pulled my hair up into an Audrey Hepburn–style bun and thrown on a simple but cute cream-colored sleeveless dress with tea-length skirt. I did look adorable. I almost said thank you, but Nora cut me off by adding, "For once."

I glowered at her.

"Kidding! I'm kidding." She hugged me. Once again showing off the folds of her kaftan to great effect. "I know fashion's not your thing."

I pulled away.

"Still kidding," she said with a melodious giggle.

"You're in an awfully good mood, considering the circumstances."

"I am in an awfully good mood *because* of the circumstances," Nora said, her eyes flashing in the light of the lanterns. "I feel quite alive."

I was tempted to probe that further, but she went on with, "Listen, I wanted to have a quick word with you about two topics before we all head into the greenhouse."

"Okay," I said carefully.

"First, have you noticed the battered leather portfolio Elias Blumenthal is carrying around?"

I had not.

"Well, never fear, my darling niece, your aunt Nora is on the case. Would you like to hazard a guess as to what is inside?"

"Gardening notes?"

"Gardening notes, indeed. *Typed* gardening notes."

I studied my aunt's face just to be sure she wasn't still toying with me.

"I think we should make an effort to get our hands on at least one page of those notes so that you can compare it to the widow's anonymous letters, don't you?"

I nodded eagerly.

"Well, I have an idea, but I may need help. You'll know what to do when the time comes."

"I, uh, okay." Nora was really coming through tonight. I hadn't even noticed Elias's notes, and to think Izzy and I had been nervous about all of her *plans*. "What's the other thing you wanted to discuss?"

"Oh, that." She leaned in and lowered her voice, "So, while I do think this plan of yours has merit, I wanted you to know I've come up with a backup should it fail." She leaned away, offering me a satisfied smile.

Oh dear.

"I realize both you and Izzy pooh-poohed my initial suggestions, but I assure you what I've come up with is quite safe and yet still manages to stay true to the initial theme. I have it all ready to go. We just need a signal should you wish me to use it."

"No, no," I stammered, trying to hide the terror in my voice. "I don't think any signals or backup plans will be necessary. I'm fairly certain my idea will work."

"But if it doesn't," Nora persisted, "I don't want you to worry because my plan is, again, all ready to go."

I grabbed my aunt by the elbow lightly—I didn't want her to hurt me—and walked her a few more steps away from the crowd. "Nora, I am worried. Very worried. I take it Izzy doesn't know about your backup plan?"

"Stars, no," Nora scoffed. "What my sister doesn't know won't hurt her."

My eyes widened. "But will it hurt the rest of us? That's what I'm concerned about."

My aunt laughed again. "Don't be silly. After all of your protestations, you'll be pleased to hear I've decided to go in a nonpainful direction."

"Well, that's good, but—"

Suddenly Nora's eyes flashed neon green. "At most, some of our guests might feel a small *squeeze*."

"What does that mean?! Nora, what did you do?" I forced a smile as one of our guests walked by.

"I hardly think now is the time to go into details," my aunt said. "But I suppose I could give you another hint."

I stared at the familiar catlike expression on her face, feeling like I, along with everyone else in attendance, was a mouse.

My aunt straightened to her full height and waved out her hands. "I call it *in vinea veritas*."

"In *vinea*—what? What does that mean?"

"You will have to give me the sign in order to find out," she trilled, swirling away. She then clapped her hands in the air. "Everyone! Everyone! Let's retire to the greenhouse, shall we? I have many wonderful things to share with you. Come!"

The crowd coalesced and followed Nora toward the doors of the conservatory as I watched on helplessly. A moment later Izzy came to my side in her black chef's coat.

"Are you okay, darling? Are you nervous about what we have planned?"

I put a hand to my head. "I sure am, but I'm even more nervous about what Nora has planned."

"Nora has something planned?" Izzy's eyes darted over my face. "Oh, I'd better get in there." She hurried away as quickly as she had come over.

I took a deep breath to steady myself, then headed after the group.

My step faltered when I noticed Dog perched on top of greenhouse like a weather vane. "I'm not sure if your being here is a good sign or a bad sign."

Dog flapped his wings and soared away.

Chapter 33

NORA'S GREENHOUSE WAS always beautiful, but tonight it was enchanting. The structure itself was quite large, running nearly the entire length of the property. The rectangular framework was all cast iron, and the roof had a bulbous curve that tapered up to a long running peak, ornamented with filigreed cresting. Normally, inside, there were three long tables, one at each side, overloaded with plants, and one running down the middle that served as a work space. For this evening, though, the one that ran down the center had been removed and replaced with rows of cushioned folding chairs. At the back wall, some of the cabinets had been moved around to make room for a podium. We had also opened a few windows to lessen the humidity and hung lanterns from the ceiling to give off a warm glow against the darkness pressing in from the outside.

Even though all the guests had gathered inside, it was very quiet. Nobody, it seemed, wanted to break the enchanted atmosphere. Many looks of wonder, though, did come over the gardeners' faces as they moved from plant to plant. Nora had removed the more *unusual* ones from her collection to safer locations, but I knew there had to be a few left behind that would amaze.

I squeezed my fingers into tight fists, then shook them free as my gaze ran over the crowd, eventually settling on Mort's wife. I hoped she would be okay, given the topic of Nora's lecture.

Just then a prickle ran up the back of my neck, and a voice whispered, "Angie?"

The sparkling specter manifested at my side, adding an unearthly glow to the already mesmerizing surroundings.

"Mort, I'm so glad you came."

"Didn't seem like something I should miss, but what's Angie doing here?"

"I don't know," I murmured. "I haven't had the chance to talk to her." I didn't want to mention Elias, but unfortunately Mort had already spotted him, touching his wife's arm and gesturing to side-by-side chairs up near the podium.

The spirit's eyes bulged. "That man did not just touch my wife."

"Mort, don't—"

And just like that, he was gone, reappearing by Angie's side. I thought I saw Elias shudder. I did know from experience that Mort could give quite the cold shoulder. I sighed. Well, this was off to a marvelous start. Maybe it was better if Mort was distracted though. Someone would eventually notice me whispering to myself in the background.

And speaking of distracted, I spotted Izzy looking just that. Her crush, our family lawyer, was here. Beatty Barnes. He was a lovely man. Reliable. Courteous. Warmhearted. He and Izzy had one of the slowest-moving relationships in history. They never really got beyond chance encounters. But the look on both their faces when they were together, well, it was downright adorable. I once suggested to Izzy that she invite Beatty out for coffee. The idea had not gone over well. The mere thought of it had sent Izzy into a tizzy. But looking at them now, maybe it was time I suggested it again.

My face twisted up in a grimace. Or not. I couldn't exactly insert myself into her love life when I had explicitly forbidden her from inserting herself into mine. I crossed my arms over my waist. Huh, when the shoe was on the other foot, I had to admit—to myself, not to Izzy—that the situation was annoying. I mean, I wanted her to be happy! Which is, of course, exactly what she had said to me. But the situations were entirely different. She didn't have my history.

I shook the thought away. I couldn't be distracted by any of this right now. We had a plan to see through.

Obviously, Nora had been thinking the same thing because she called out, "Everyone! Please take your seats." She strode through the throngs of people, sending them swirling like whirlpools around and into their chairs. "Let's get started, shall we?"

My pulse quickened.

This was it. The moment of truth.

I would like to say I had come up with a foolproof plan to uncover the identity of Mort's killer, but I hadn't. That being said, what I *had* come up with wasn't terrible, and it did involve the talents of both my aunts. Perhaps, unsurprisingly, the part that involved Izzy had to do with what Nora had said about her food making people vulnerable. Now, I didn't want Izzy to make anything that would leave our guests completely defenseless against our charms. That would be pretty dark magic. After all, I was fairly certain there was only one killer in this room, and everyone had eaten Izzy's meal, so that kind of spell would not be justified. No, what I was looking for from her was much more subtle. I wanted her dinner to leave everyone happy, relaxed, and maybe with *slightly* lowered guards.

It was the perfect setup for Nora's part of the plan.

My aunt had always intended to give the talk tonight. Every meeting had a lecture on one topic or another, and Nora wanted to show off her knowledge. I had simply come up with the idea for the subject matter.

Poisonous plants.

Now the topic was tricky, but maybe not for the most obvious reason. Given that Elias Blumenthal was president of the society and had a poison garden, I was sure the group had had lectures on toxic plants before. Nora assured me it wouldn't be a problem, though, given that they had never heard *her* lecture on toxic plants. And while that was all well and good, the purpose of the talk was not to entertain our guests but rather to make them uncomfortable. One guest in particular. The plan was for Nora to turn up the poisonous pressure, so to speak, until it became almost unbearable—at which point she would introduce the oleander bush. Izzy and I were then supposed to observe our suspects carefully for any sign of distress. And by distress, I mean guilt. If any of our suspects did give up a tell, we would figure out where to go from there.

So again, not a foolproof plan, but one that would hopefully yield results. We all needed to be in top form though. Nora had no doubt that she would be able to perform her role to its fullest, and Izzy—

Izzy was still talking to Beatty even though everyone else had taken their seats. I snapped my fingers. A second later, Izzy jolted like someone had just pinched her on the backside. I don't know how she explained herself to Beatty, but she was able to get him to take his seat. She then hurried over to where I was standing at the back of the room.

"Sorry about that," she whispered, looking flushed.

"Distracted, were you?"

She swatted my arm.

"Welcome, everyone," Nora called out once the crowd had settled. "I can't tell you how honored I am to have

Evenfall's most esteemed gardeners gathered all together in my humble greenhouse."

Izzy and I exchanged glances. Hopefully Nora wasn't planning to lay it on quite this thick through the entire lecture.

"Now I know all of you have probably already heard rumors about the topic for tonight's lecture, and I'm pleased to say if you were thrilled by what you heard, I can promise you won't be disappointed. As a collector of unusual plants, I thought I would show you some of my most prized horticultural specimens."

An excited murmur ran through the crowd.

"But be warned," Nora said sharply, dragging a pointed finger over the many faces. "This particular tossed salad I've thrown together has quite the bite." She gnashed her teeth together, then laughed at her own theatricality.

"I think your aunt missed her calling," Izzy whispered dryly. "All she needs is a top hat and whip, and she could have her own three-ring circus."

I smiled. Izzy wasn't wrong, but so far I liked where this was headed. Nora had the crowd entertained but just a wee bit on edge. I glanced over at Mort. He didn't seem to be taking in much of what was going on. He had moved off to the side so that he was no longer hovering over Angie, but she still had all of his attention.

"Now," Nora called out, "while I have amassed some of the most dangerous florae on the planet for your viewing— not touching—pleasure, I should begin by warning you all to be careful. After all, most plants are at least a little bit wicked. Think of even your most benign vegetable. Eat too much of it, and—" Nora cut herself off by putting a hand on her belly and puffing out her cheeks in a comically nauseated expression.

The crowd laughed.

"But what am I saying?" Nora threw her arms wide.

"You already know this. Your president has one of the most impressive poison gardens I have ever seen."

Elias waved a humble hand in the air. And while he did that, I noticed Nora looking at me. Pointedly.

Okay. Not sure what to make of that.

A second later, she turned her attention back to Elias. "Don't be modest. It is quite spectacular. I'm sure you've all heard the reasoning behind his choice of garden before, but I am new to your society. I've never been invited to attend a single meeting." Her tone had gone icy, revealing the tiniest crack in her otherwise flawless veneer. I cringed. To her credit she recovered quickly. "Why *did* you decide on a poison garden, Elias?"

"That man has a poison garden?" a voice shouted in my ear.

I clutched my chest. "Mort, you have to stop doing that. And you know Elias has a poison garden. Didn't he take you on a tour?"

"I wasn't paying attention!"

Izzy looked at me. Thankfully, I didn't have to explain. She was used to me talking to people she couldn't see.

"Mort," I whispered. "Please. I want to hear what Elias has to say."

"Do you think he murdered me? Because I'd be more than happy to get on that train."

As I waved a hand for him to shush, I caught Nora looking at me again. Once she had my attention, she turned her gaze down to the leather portfolio Elias had on his lap. What was I supposed to do about that now? There was a page sticking out of the top, but that didn't exactly help, given everyone was looking at him.

"In truth"—Elias's voice rang out in his somewhat clipped but elegant tone—"I find the cultivating of poisonous plants to be an almost meditative experience. I can focus on nothing but what it is I'm doing. I must take great care or suffer the consequences. It helps to remind me that life should never be taken for granted."

Izzy sighed dreamily beside me.

"Oh brother," Mort drawled. Thankfully, he decided to pop back over to Angie.

"Thank you, Elias. How lovely," Nora said. "Don't you think that's lovely, Brynn?"

All the members of the gardening society swiveled in their seats to look at me, and, as they did, I saw Nora reach for the sheet of paper sticking out of the top of Elias's folder.

"I . . . yes! Lovely. Just lovely. Meditative."

Nora shot me a dry look as she spun back around, headed for her podium.

That had been easy. Hopefully the rest of the evening would go as smoothly.

I took a breath to settle my nerves. My aunt was about to move to the main event.

"Now," Nora said, tucking the sheet away without anyone being the wiser, "instead of boring you all with some sort of lecture, I thought we all could play a game. Are you up for it?"

The crowd murmured its assent.

"I call it *Who am I? Botanical Edition.*"

Chapter 34

L ET THE GAMES begin.

    Nora shifted from the podium to stand behind the small table she had set up, covered in plants. She rested her hands on the edge, surveying her deadly sampling. "Ready to play? I will provide you all with some clues, then you can guess which plant I'm referring to." She cleared her throat and gestured to one of the potted specimens. "Greek mythology claims I sprung from the saliva of Cerberus, the three-headed hound. Who am I?"

"Oh! Oh!"

I followed the ohs over to the speaker. They came from our neighbor Mr. Henderson. Yet another surprise guest. I hadn't realized he was a member of the gardening society but was glad he was expanding his interests.

"I've been meaning to ask you something," I whispered, leaning toward Izzy. "Have you noticed anything strange about Mr. Henderson lately?"

"Mr. Henderson is always a bit strange," she answered. "Why?"

"He seems to be fortifying his property with pillows and wooden stakes. The spell you cast on him, did it go okay?"

"I think so." Her eyes jumped side to side. "I mean, I was startled. It wasn't my best work. You don't think he's experiencing some sort of side effect?"

I leaned back. "I'm probably just borrowing trouble."

Nora's eyes searched the crowd. "No one else would care to hazard a guess?"

"Monkshood!" Mr. Henderson shouted, not waiting to be called upon. "You're monkshood!"

In fairness, it most likely would have taken Nora a while to select him. She had little patience for our neighbor's foibles.

"Yes, monkshood. Others may know it as wolfsbane or leopard's bane or mouse bane or *woman's* bane." Nora rolled her eyes. "But I think my favorite is devil's bane." She winked. "Of course, the more formal designation is aconite. I'm guessing you've all heard the story of how it came to be called monkshood?"

The room fell silent.

"It all started with a dinner party, not unlike this one," she said, giving the crowd a mischievous look, "in a small Scottish village called Dingwall sometime around 1850. A servant had been sent to the garden to dig up horseradish, but instead he uprooted the deadly aconite." Nora glanced at the potted plant resting nearby. "Not realizing the servant's mistake, the cook used shavings of the plant's root in the sauce for the roast. While a few of the guests did manage to survive, sadly, the two priests in attendance did not fare so well." She shrugged. "*C'est fini* for the poor padres. Hence the name *monkshood*." She gave the crowd an assessing look. "Terrible way to go. *Poisoning*."

The word rippled through the greenhouse. I studied my suspects, but all were expressionless. Actually, not Fredrick. He looked like he was enjoying the show immensely.

"Sounds ghastly," Birdie Cline called out. "Maybe I should have inspected my dinner plate more closely."

The crowd giggled.

"Oh, don't worry, Birdie," Nora said, eyebrow cocked. "I attended to your plate personally."

My eyes widened.

"Don't worry," Izzy whispered. "I didn't let her near that dish."

"Anyway," Nora went on, "aconite can be found in gardens and in the wild throughout North America, so don't be fooled by its innocuous appearance. Even the slightest brush can cause cardiac symptoms."

At the mention of cardiac symptoms, I looked over to Mort but was unable to get a read on how he was coping.

"Now," Nora said, bringing up a dish tucked away among the plants, "let's move on to a species that may be a touch more difficult to identify, given that you will have only its seeds to observe before you make your guess." Nora passed the dish to Cookie and gave her a sharp look. "Do remember to keep your fingers to yourself. Unless, of course, you are experienced in handling poison."

Cookie accepted the dish, but she kept her eyes on Nora as she passed it to the person seated beside her, refusing to look at its contents.

The small bowl traveled through the rows of gardeners. When it hit Fredrick, he mused, "My, they do look rather delicious, don't they?"

The crowd tittered.

"So, are there any guesses?" Nora asked. "Would you like another clue? These seeds are from a fifty-foot tree, and they were used by an infamous serial killer to get rid of not only a troublesome wife but an inconvenient girl-friend he wished to dispose of while attending medical school."

"Strychnine! It's strychnine! Dr. Cream!" Mr. Hender-

son shouted, jumping to his feet. Under the weight of Nora's gaze, he lowered back down.

"You are correct. These deadly seeds from which
strychnine is derived are from the *Strychnos nux-vomica*
tree. And indeed, it was Dr. Cream who opted to take this
poisonous route to commit his dastardly deeds. He was
turned in by the wife of a patient who also happened to die
of strychnine poisoning. When the poor woman realized
she was being fitted up as the prime suspect, she was able
to put the pieces together and identify the real culprit."

"He did it again after serving a decade in prison," Mr.
Henderson called out. "In London after he moved."

"Once again, you are correct. I was just about to add
that." Nora gifted Mr. Henderson with a smile, but it looked
as poisonous as the plants on her table. She didn't like being upstaged. "It boggles the mind, doesn't it? What kind
of *fiend* resorts to poison to dispose of another soul?"

Nora carried on with her lecture, presenting poisonous
plant after poisonous plant, each more unique and deadly.
The energy in the greenhouse, once calm and enchanting,
now had a peculiar edge. As my aunt's horrid tales continued, the once polite smiles elicited from the mild-mannered
gardeners transformed into wicked grins, their laughs into
cackles. If I had to guess, Nora's magic was seeping into
her words, enthralling the crowd. She appeared to be enjoying herself too. And I wasn't the only one who noticed.

"I think we'd better move to the grand finale soon," Izzy
whispered. "I need to get some dessert into these people."

Fortunately, having anticipated the possibility of tonight's festivities going awry, Izzy had prepared a luscious
dessert. A chocolate fondant with caramel center. She made
it with the intention of stirring up feelings of goodwill,
community, and comfort. She was also sending everyone
home with a box of sweet dream sugar cookies. The name
was self-explanatory. They were sugar cookies that gave

sweet dreams. The way these people were coming off, I intended to partake of one myself before heading to bed.

"I'm going to get closer to Nora," Izzy added, "in case things get out of hand."

I nodded, and she moved to stand by one of the walls about halfway up to the podium.

Nora clapped her hands together. "Now, it's time for our star leafy green devil." She disappeared behind a number of tall plants that had been moved to the back of the greenhouse. A moment later, she returned rolling out a large flat dolly with a potted bush on top.

A noisy murmur ran through the crowd.

"What is that?" Mort asked, appearing at my side.

"It's oleander," I whispered. "We think that's what was in the chocolates you ate the night you . . ."

He nodded grimly.

"I can see you all know what this is," Nora said. "In 77 AD, Pliny the Elder documented the oleander bush's poisonous properties. But, in addition to its toxic effects, dear Pliny believed it could also be used an antidote for snake venom. And he was right. Oleander can indeed relieve the suffering caused by a venomous nip." She paused dramatically. "In the form of death."

I wanted to stay focused on my suspects, but Mort had gone uncharacteristically quiet. His expression was stoic, but it reminded me of the face of a child trying to be brave. Maybe inviting him hadn't been the best idea.

"Oleander, if ingested, can kill its sampler relatively quickly. And painfully. Even honey made from the plant's nectar is toxic."

"Mort," I whispered, "if you want to go, I can tell you later what we find out."

Just then Izzy waved a hand at me, jerking my attention away. She mouthed the words, *It's not working.*

My gaze bounced from Elias, to Cookie, to Fredrick.

Fredrick still seemed to be having a wonderful time, Cookie was stone-faced, and Elias only seemed concerned for Mort's wife.

"You need to stop this," the spirit suddenly said. "Angie's upset."

I glanced back over to her. The widow trembled in her seat as she twisted a handkerchief in her hands.

Mort was right. This had gone far enough. Yes, I wanted to get him answers, but if I wanted those answers more than he did, maybe I was going about it in the wrong way.

I raised my hand to get Nora's attention, but she was already staring at me. With her eyebrow arched. In question. Like she was looking for permission to move to plan B.

Yes, it was definitely time to call it a night.

I strode toward the aisle between the rows of chairs just in time to catch Minnie Abernathy whisper, "This is the strangest meeting I've ever been to."

"What did you expect?" Birdie drawled. "It's Nora."

My gaze snapped back up to my aunt.

It's Nora.

Gideon's story flashed to mind as two red circles bloomed on my aunt's cheeks. No. Why? Out of all the careless comments Birdie could have made! And Nora had been having such a wonderful—

"You need to stop this," Mort pleaded, appearing in my path. "Right now!"

"Okay." I nodded. "Okay, yes."

The instant the words left my mouth, he vanished, and I realized my mistake.

Even though I had been looking directly at Mort, to Nora it would have appeared as though I was speaking to her. Giving her the signal to move to plan B.

A slow smile spread across my aunt's face.

Oh dear.

Chapter 35

I HAD TO HAND it to her. Nora performed the charm so subtly that no one noticed a thing.

No one but Izzy and me, that is. We both saw the quick dance of my aunt's fingers and her lips mouth the words of a charm. A rush of energy rippled through the greenhouse, raising the hairs on my arms. A second later, Nora snapped her fingers and the lights went dim. The crowd oohed and aahed. "I think we have time for one last topic. A surprise grand finale."

Izzy hurried to my side and hissed, "What just happened?"

I cleared my throat. Suddenly it felt quite tight. "I may have inadvertently given Nora permission to move to plan B."

"Plan B?" Izzy replied, struggling to keep her voice down. "Plan B! Please tell me plan B isn't what I think it is?"

I grimaced.

"But we all expressly forbade her from using—"

"Ordeal poisons!" Nora announced to the crowd.

Izzy swayed on the spot. "I feel faint." She reached her hands out, searching for something to grab on to.

I clutched her elbow and pulled her in to my side. "Don't worry. I talked to her before we came in, and whatever she has planned, she doesn't intend to actually poison anyone." Saying the words out loud really brought into focus just how wrong they were.

"We can't take any chances." Izzy took a sharp breath and gathered herself up. She then marched toward the aisle between the rows of chairs. "Everyone? Everyone! Who's ready for dessert?"

The entire society turned as one to face her. They were a little frightening.

Izzy dropped her hands.

Nora frowned sympathetically. "I think they'd like to hear the rest of the lecture before we head out."

Izzy backed away under the glare of the gardeners and didn't stop until she had returned to my side. "Our coven needs to adopt a new rule," she murmured. "No more plans that involve your aunt public speaking."

"Now, where was I?" Nora's voice rang out. "Oh yes, ordeal poisons. Is everyone here familiar with the concept? No? Well, allow me to educate you on the beastly practice." She took a full, deep breath as she pyramided her scarlet fingernails beneath her chin. "Since time immemorial humans have been faced with a problem. When a crime has been committed, how do you determine the innocent bystander from the guilty felon?" She flipped her hands out to either side. "It's certainly not something you want to get wrong. You could condemn an innocent person to prison. Or worse yet, death." She clapped her hands together. "If only there was a way to know for sure." She dragged her gaze over the crowd. "What if there was a plant that could prove a person's innocence simply by having them ingest it? Everyone would want to use it, wouldn't they?"

Sinister-sounding chuckles rippled through the gardeners as Mort shot me a desperate look from where he stood by Angie's side.

"Ah! I see a few of you have already guessed the catch. The herbal ingested, of course, is poisonous. During the ordeal, the person in question consumes the plant, and if said person is innocent, they simply vomit it up. If not, well, we all know how that story ends."

"It's just like what they used to do with witches," Mr. Henderson blurted out, once again up on his feet. "By dunking them in water."

A chill filled the air as Nora's gaze landed on him.

Mr. Henderson slowly dropped back once again into his seat.

"Yes," she hissed, "just like that."

Back in the library, when she had originally tried to sell us on this plan, Nora was tickled by the thought of witches putting humans through an ordeal. But, just as Izzy and I suspected, while theoretically enjoyable, the reality of it was a bit less *ticklish*.

"Throughout history many plants have been used in the pursuit of justice," Nora continued. "The Calabar bean. The tanghin nut. Sassy bark. Strychnine, which we've already discussed. The sap from the upas tree. All were options with varying levels of toxicity. But, regardless of the chosen botanical, the concept was, of course, ludicrous. As vast as creation is, even I am not in possession of a plant that could show me your deepest, darkest secrets." I swear she made eye contact with every single person in the room. When she was through, she laughed merrily. "The idea is preposterous."

Another chuckle ran over the crowd.

"Or is it?"

The laughter quickly died away.

Nora paced back and forth in front of the podium. "I've always been one to believe that plants are far more attuned to the animal world than any of us *animals* would care to believe." She flashed her teeth in a big smile. "I mean, everyone's heard that plants grow better when talked to or when surrounded by music. But I think they can pick up on—and perhaps *act on*—much more. Obviously, there are botanical species that are predators in their own right. Venus flytraps for example. They love to consume mortal flesh. It makes one wonder what else plants might be capable of."

I didn't want to wonder about that at all.

"Are we sure we don't want to move on to dessert?" Izzy called out weakly.

Nobody answered.

"What if plants could react not just to our voices but to our very thoughts?" Nora posited, strolling back over to stand behind the podium. "Let's try an experiment, shall we?"

A handful of people nodded, but the energy of the crowd was shifting. Angie still looked miserable, almost ill, and she had all of Elias's and Mort's attention. Cookie also looked, if not miserable, certainly uncomfortable.

"Okay, let's all imagine that each of us has committed a terrible crime. The worst crime possible." Nora slapped the podium with her palms. "Murder."

There was no more nervous laughter, but I thought I heard a few gulps. Minnie Abernathy may have even cried out a little. The slightly maniacal energy I had felt coming from the crowd earlier was transforming to something more frightful.

"Now I know none of you sweet souls could be capable of committing such an act, but let's pretend." The lights dimmed further.

Izzy tried to work a finger charm to undo her sister's spell and get the lanterns back up glowing at full strength, but she was having no luck.

"Imagine there's a plant in this very room that could ferret out guilt."

"There's no such plant," Mr. Henderson said, folding his arms over his chest.

Nora batted her eyelashes. For a second I was terrified her irises would flash fluorescent green, but she restrained herself.

"My dear man, have some self-preservation," Fredrick Naff quipped, "before *you* become fertilizer."

"Thank you," Nora said, giving Fredrick a nod. "Now, let's all be quiet, stir up our most guilty thoughts, and see if any of my plants react."

"Look!" Mort gasped, reappearing at my side. He tried to swat me on the arm, but his hand went right through, sending shivers up from my elbow to my shoulder. I looked to where he was focused. A small vine tendril had uncurled and dropped down from between a cluster of plants on one of the side tables to creep across the floor.

In vinea veritas!

I should have known.

It was the spell Nora had used on me as a child when I was sneaking a taste of the icing from her birthday cake. Except this time instead of using her spell on a mischievous witchling, she was using it on a room full of people!

"What?" Izzy whispered. "What is it?"

"Quiet in the back," Nora called out.

I pointed at the vine. "I could be wrong, but I think *that* is headed straight for our guilty party."

"It's going for Elias," Mort shouted. "Straight for Elias!"

It *was* headed for Elias. Had Nora really done it? Was Elias Mort's killer?

I was so focused on the vine that I didn't see Izzy sneak behind me and pick up a spade. She walked over to the vine and dropped the blade directly on its corded body, severing it like a guillotine. The sound of the metal clanging against the tiled floor caused several people to jump. Minnie Abernathy screamed.

"Sorry!" Izzy said with a laugh. She then gave Nora a deadpan look. "It slipped."

"Does that mean Elias did it?!" Mort asked me. He sounded so relieved. So happy.

"I don't know. I think it maybe—" I cut myself off at the sight of another vine slithering across the floor. *Oh no.* This one was headed for Fredrick Naff.

I shuffled as discreetly as I could over to the back wall and grabbed a set of shears off a hook. I then scurried over to the vine to cut it in half.

Mort appeared again at my side and pointed. I followed his gesture to yet another vine. One that was headed for Cookie. "Please stop this," he begged. "Whatever this is, it isn't working. And you're going to scare the pants off everyone here!" He met my gaze, a sick look in his eyes. "I don't want this. I know you want to help, Ghostie, but I never should have started any of this. Coming to you the way I did, it was . . ." He let the thought go. But I knew what he was going to say.

Coming to me was a mistake.

Vine tendrils were now slithering out from every corner of the room, traveling across the floor like thin snakes. They were all headed in three main directions though. Elias. Cookie. And Naff. Nora's spell was a bust. Maybe somehow the vines had picked up on our ideas about who the guilty party might be? Why couldn't Nora have listened? Our spells never worked in public!

Suddenly a rumble of thunder sounded in the distance.

"Is that a storm?" Minnie asked. "The forecast didn't call for rain."

"Yes," Izzy announced. "That most definitely was thunder. Time to take this party indoors."

I knew that tone. It took a lot for Izzy to get mad, but

when she did, it was frightening. I also knew the incoming storm was not the result of shifting weather patterns.

"So soon? Are you sure?" Nora asked. "We haven't quite accomplished everything we set out to."

"Oh, I'm sure," Izzy said. "If we're not careful, some-one's life could be at risk." By the look on her face, the life in question was most definitely her sister's. "Besides," she went on, "it really is time for dessert. Isn't it, *Evanora*?"

"I guess so," she replied sulkily. She knew Izzy meant business when she used her full name.

"I promise what I've whipped up for you all is even better than dinner."

"Better than dinner?" Minnie Abernathy jumped to her feet. "How is that even possible?"

Izzy sighed. "I don't know how I do it, but I do. And it is." She rolled her hand like a big wheel. "On your feet. Out the door. Let's get inside before the rain starts."

As the crowd stumbled toward the door in the low light-ing, miraculously only one person tripped over the vines. I watched helplessly as Birdie Cline lost her footing and stumbled toward one of the tables. She did manage to catch herself by slapping both hands down on its surface, but, unfortunately, that spot just happened to be covered in loose compost. A cloud of dirt shot into the air, coating her in a thin layer of grime.

"Do watch your step," Nora called out sweetly.

Birdie huffed, smacking the dirt from her front, then headed for the door.

I searched the crowd for my suspects. Cookie strode out first, her expression wooden. Next came Elias holding An-gie's arm as he escorted her to the door. I heard him ask her if she would like to head home and she nodded, dabbing a tissue to her eye. Fredrick strolled by after that, tapping his cane and sporting an amused smile.

Once the last person had made it through the threshold

and back over to the B&B, Izzy's eyes flashed bright green and an enormous crack sounded above our heads. Well, maybe not *our* heads, more Nora's, who flinched ever so slightly.

Having made her point, Izzy left.

Nora strode after her muttering, "It was worth it."

I watched them leave, then turned to face Mort, but he was gone.

I wasn't the least bit surprised this time.

I closed my eyes and ran my hands over my face as a vine curled around my ankle. I kicked my foot free as a voice said, "Well, that sure was something, wasn't it?"

My eyes searched the room for the speaker and landed on the rounded lens of my former boss's glasses flashing in the low light. She had been tucked away in the shadows at the back corner of the conservatory.

"Theo, I . . ." I had no idea what to say. Other than, hopefully, she hadn't seen Izzy's eyes. And I couldn't say that. "We should get going," I said, moving for the door. "We don't want to miss dessert."

"In a moment. I need to tell you something." Theo looked around the greenhouse as though searching for something, a strange look on her face. "It could be important."

"What is it?"

"Mort's near-death experience," she said, eyes settling back on me. "I remember what it was."

Chapter 36

"THERE WAS A fire."

I brought over two chairs so that Theo and I could sit. I was incredibly anxious to hear what she had to say, but I didn't want to rush her and have any details slip through the cracks.

Rain streamed down the glass walls of the conservatory as we settled ourselves, but at least the thunder had ceased. That was the problem with calling up a storm: you couldn't just put it back in the box after you were through with it.

"I remembered last night as I was falling asleep," Theo said. "I was toasty underneath my quilt when it came to me. Of course! The fire at the Sweetes' Shoppe!"

"I don't remember ever hearing about a fire." Given Evenfall's close-knit nature, an event like that would have had everyone talking.

"It must have been at least thirty years ago," she explained.

"What happened? How did it start?"

Theo frowned. "It was a kitchen fire. I know that much.

The back of the shop was a write-off, but the main structure stayed intact."

"What about Mort? Did he try to put it out? Is that how
he got hurt?"

"I don't know those details, but, as I said back at the
bookstore, I do remember him ending up in the hospital."

I stared into the darkness beyond the glass panes sparkling with rain, trying to process what this meant. There
was so much to unpack, but one uncomfortable realization
stood out.

Mort had lied to me.

I had asked him if he had ever had a near-death experience, and he had said no. A fire? Spending time in the hospital? Those were not things a person easily forgot. Granted,
I had asked him about it at the memorial, and he had been
upset. But still.

"There's something else," Theo said. "Now, I'm not one
to spread rumors or half-truths, but I have pieced together
a little of what you do, Brynn, and I remembered something
else that could be important."

It was hard to say exactly how much Theo had pieced
together, but once again I was grateful that she was willing
to let sleeping witches lie, so to speak.

"I don't remember what drove me to think this, but I do
recall a distinct chill forming between Cookie and Mort
around that time. They had never been bosom buddies; but
I believe it was after the fire that Mort's disposition toward
her changed. It went from friendly disinterest to something
more hostile." Her eyes were downcast and tracking side to
side as though searching through her many years' worth of
memories. "I think Mort blamed Cookie for the fire."

I did my best to contain my shock, but I couldn't stop my
hand from covering my mouth.

Why? Why had Mort kept this from me?

So not only was there a fire that put him in the hospital,
but if Theo's memory was to be trusted—and I had known

her long enough to put a great deal of faith in her faculties when it came to these types of matters—Mort blamed Cookie for it. Maybe that was why he had been so quick to accuse her of his murder in the beginning? Had she tried to kill him once before?

It made no sense. Mort had never tried to hide his feelings when it came to Cookie, so why keep this story secret?

"Well," Theo said, slapping her thighs, "I wanted to tell you what I remembered, and now I have. It probably would be best for you to confirm these details with another source though." She tapped her temple. "This old brain ain't what it used to be."

"I'd say it's still sharper than most by half. But I will check it out. Thank you."

She pushed herself to her feet. "You're very welcome." Once standing, she gave the conservatory another look over. "I hope it helps you."

I nodded, but I didn't think her words were meant for me.

A FTER TALKING TO Theo, I decided to skip dessert. I needed answers, and I knew where to find them.

I hurried around the side of the B&B, sticking close to the shadows. Moonlight peeked through clouds Izzy had gathered as I guided my bike out from the garage.

I rode over the wet streets, barely registering the early bats flapping overhead. Within minutes, I was at Mort and Angie's house. Their little cottage with its black shutters, nestled in the low-lying mist, looked so peaceful tucked back from the glow of the streetlamps. I leaned my bike against the picket fence, clicked the gate open, and walked the path up to the front door.

I raised my fist to knock, then hesitated. Suddenly I could hear Mort saying, *I thought I could trust you.*

Well, trust went both ways.

This wasn't just about him. Or Angie. The crime that had been committed was bigger than all of us.

I rapped my knuckles against the door.

Before long, Angie peeked through the window beside the door. A second later the lock turned.

"Brynn, this is a surprise. I just got home. What are you doing here?"

I twisted my hands together. "I apologize for calling on you so late."

"It's fine. I probably won't get much sleep," she said, tightening the tie of her bathrobe. "All that talk of poison and murder? It was a bit much for me." New light flashed in her eyes. "Is it Mort? Is that why you're here? Have you heard from him?"

The desperation in her voice resonated deep within me. "No. I'm sorry. That's not it. At least not in the way you think."

As the hope drained from the widow's face, a strange new intensity took its place. "He doesn't want to talk to me. That's it, isn't it?" Her face twitched with emotion as she locked me in her gaze. "I saw you at the memorial. You were talking to someone. And again, tonight, in the greenhouse."

I thought I had been careful but clearly not careful enough.

I couldn't deny it. I couldn't lie to her outright. Not again. But I couldn't admit it either.

"When did you first hear from him? Was it before you came to see me?"

"Angie, I want to tell you everything. I really do."

"Then do it," she said, her words shaking with emotion. "Just tell me the truth. Whatever it is, I can take it."

I struggled to find an explanation that would make things better. One that wouldn't have me betraying any more of the promises I had made to Mort, even if those promises were unfair, especially given all that he had kept from me.

"I came here to ask you something. It could really help pull things together. And then maybe—"

"No. No. I'm so confused by all of this. Why would Mort not want to talk to me?"

"I wish I could explain, and I know you have no reason to trust me, but, Angie, I need to know about the fire at the Sweetes' Shoppe."

"The fire?" She gripped the doorframe for support. "Why? It was years and years ago."

"I know. I'm sorry. I . . ." I clenched my jaw. "I just think it could be important."

"It's not something any of us likes to talk about."

I couldn't help but think by *any of us*, she meant herself, Mort, Les, and Cookie. So, it was a secret the four of them were keeping together. And I already knew Mort didn't like to talk about it. He had lied to me so that he didn't have to.

"If I tell you what happened . . ." She shook her head. I was worried she was about to ask me to promise to tell her about my communications with her husband as a quid pro quo, but instead she said, "Just know Mort was not supposed to be there."

"You don't mean"—I paused, unsure if I wanted to hear the answer to the question I was about to ask—"someone intentionally set the fire?"

"It's not how it sounds," Angie pleaded. "Cookie, she was going through a terrible time."

Based on what Theo had told me, hearing Angie say Cookie was responsible for the fire shouldn't have been a shock, but it was. It wasn't a mistake. Or an accident. She had done it deliberately.

"She wasn't in her right mind. And Les spent so much time away from home." Angie glanced over her shoulder back into her house. I knew she was debating shutting the door on me and this whole mess, but then she sighed and dragged her tired eyes back up to mine. "She put a pan of oil on the stove and turned the burner to high. She didn't know Mort was in the other room doing taxes. He had fallen asleep. The firefighters found him. They pulled him out in time. He had to go to the hospital, but he was fine."

"But the police," I said, "wasn't there an investigation?"

"Mort told the authorities he had done it. That he started cooking something, then fell asleep."

"But why? Why would he protect her like that?"

Angie closed her eyes. "Cookie had lost a baby. She had miscarried before, but she was late in her pregnancy this time. She was out of her mind with grief. Les convinced Mort not to tell anyone what really happened. Swore us both to secrecy. He felt so guilty. We all did. Cookie wasn't always the easiest person to love, but we knew she was struggling, and we didn't intervene. The truth was, Les never felt for Cookie the way a husband should for a wife. But in that moment, when he realized just how desperate she had become, he resolved to do better. And we all made a pact to say it was an accident."

I struggled to piece together what Angie was telling me with what I already knew. What did it all mean? It was a terribly sad story, but I didn't see what bearing it could possibly have on Mort's death thirty years later.

"I'll admit," Angie said, "I was so mad at first, I didn't want to sweep it under the rug. Mort could have died. But if you had seen Cookie then—" She cut herself off with a shuddering breath. "Say what you want about her, but losing that baby, it nearly killed her."

I blinked, speechless.

"Now, you tell me what is going on. Why doesn't Mort want to talk to me?"

I was about to answer—to say that I didn't know—but before I could speak, Mort appeared.

"Not one more word."

Chapter 37

"WHAT ARE YOU looking at?" Angie asked sharply. "Is he here? Is my husband here?"

I backed away, shaking my head.

"Mort?" Angie called out into the dark. "Talk to me, sweetheart. *Please*. I don't understand."

I looked to the spirit and Angie followed my gaze. She rushed out of the house then stopped abruptly, standing inches away from her husband. "Please, Morty. I just want to know you're okay." She looked back at me, eyes flashing with tears. "Tell me what he's saying!"

I stared at Mort, begging for the permission to finally give Angie the comfort she had been seeking, but the only response I received in return was a furious glare. "I can't," I mumbled. "I'm so sorry."

"Stop apologizing!" She swatted a tear away. "I don't understand what's happening, but . . . I can't do this anymore. I don't want to see you again. Not unless you're willing to tell me everything." Angie ran back inside, slamming the door behind her.

Mort whirled around to face me. "I told you she wasn't ready for this. Does she seem like a woman ready to hear her husband was murdered?"

I don't know if it was witnessing all of Angie's pain or once again bearing the weight of all the forced promises I had made, but a scalding wave of emotion crashed over me. One I wasn't prepared to handle. "No, to me she looks like a woman desperate to hear anything—*anything at all*—from the love of her life."

The ghost I had come to think of as a friend recoiled from me.

I knew I had crossed a line, but I couldn't stop myself from going on. This fight between us had been building for some time. "It's not fair what you're doing to her."

"I'm doing this *for* her."

"No, you're not," I said, shaking my head in a quick, tight motion. "You're afraid. Too afraid to let her say good-bye to you. Tell me, Mort. You're always saying you want to make things easier for Angie. But who are you really making things easier for?" I didn't give him time to answer. "You told me you don't like goodbyes, but you are doing just that every time you see her. That's why you're still here. That's why you haven't gone into the light. You're saying goodbye to your wife. But she doesn't get that. It's not fair."

Mort stood motionless, sparkles floating around him as I waited for his response. I wanted his answer, his explanation for all of this. I wanted him to try to refute my claims. I was so sure I was right. Which left me completely unprepared for what he then said.

"You talking about me and Angie, Ghostie? Or you and your husband?"

The ground tilted beneath my feet.

"I am so sorry," he said, floating back toward me. "I know how much you want to help, but I also know what it's costing you. It's time to let it go. It's done. I'm dead. And finding out what happened, it won't bring me back. You're right. I should have gone into the light already. I'm just making people upset hanging around here. I never should have dragged you into any of this."

I knew what he was about to do, but I didn't know how to stop it.

"Please," I said, reaching toward him. "Don't go. Not like this."

"It was nice getting to know you, Brynn. You're a good kid."

"Mort, wait!"

He was gone before the words had left my mouth.

NONE OF THE sleepless nights I had experienced in the last week or so compared to what I suffered through that night. I lay in my bed without moving, second after endless second ticking by on the clock. I couldn't even say I was thinking about anything. It was all too much. I was numb.

It seemed like years had passed since that sunset on the back porch with my aunts. I had wanted so badly to help spirits again. I thought it would be easy to jump back in. I had truly believed that I was whole again after losing my husband. That I had resolved all of my own issues. But Mort had shown me the truth.

In the early morning hours, I must have drifted off to sleep because when a soft knock sounded at my door and I blinked my eyes open, the loft was filled with sunlight.

I rubbed my hands roughly over my face before padding my way over to the door and pulling it open.

"Izzy," I said, unable to keep the surprise from my voice.

She lifted a coffee decanter. "You got in so late last night. I thought maybe you could use this."

My eyes welled with tears.

"Oh, darling," my aunt said, rushing in. "What's happened?" She put the decanter down on the kitchen table and buried me in a hug. "It can't be that bad."

"It's pretty bad," I said, pressing my forehead into her shoulder. "I've messed everything up."

My aunt ushered me over to the table and poured me a cup of coffee before sitting down across from me. "Tell me."

I told her everything that happened after the lecture. I didn't want to. I was so ashamed of my behavior, but somehow I couldn't not tell her either. I finished with, "So now I'm not any closer to finding Mort's killer; Angie's devastated, worse than before, because she doesn't know why her husband won't want to talk to her; and Mort's gone." I planted my elbows on the table and dug the heels of my palms into my forehead.

"Brynn," my aunt said, rubbing one of my arms, "you can't take on all the responsibility for this. You had the best intentions."

I peeked up at her. "Isn't there a saying about that?"

She smiled.

"The worst part is Mort was right. I pushed so hard, went against all his wishes, because it was what *I* wanted." I placed a hand on my chest. "I never got the opportunity to talk to Adam after he passed, and I couldn't understand why Mort wouldn't jump at the chance. I was supposed to help him, but I made everything about me."

"Sweetheart, if it makes you feel any better, I probably would have done the same thing. Mort should have taken the gift you were offering him, but . . ."

"But?"

She inhaled deeply. "I think it's time I told you a story from my past. It involves something you don't know about me."

I studied my aunt's face, trying to guess what it was she could possibly have to say. I could tell by her tone it was serious, but it was hard to imagine what it might be. I certainly didn't know everything about my aunt—Nora and Gideon had insinuated as much—but I thought I knew everything important.

"Brynn, once, a very long time ago, I was engaged."

Chapter 38

"ENGAGED?"

A gentle breeze floated in from the window above my kitchen sink, ruffling my aunt's hair. "Yes, I was supposed to be married, and it wasn't some flighty promise made after a whirlwind romance. We were deeply in love and committed to spending our lives together."

"How did I not know this?"

The corners of my aunt's eyes creased with guilt. "Because I purposely kept it from you." She looked away, scratching the back of her neck. "With your parents and Lydia, I didn't want to give you any more reason to believe in the family curse."

"Izzy, please tell me this fiancé of yours didn't die."

She laughed. "Oh darling, no. Thank the stars. Harry did not die. He's alive and well."

"Harry?"

A heartbreakingly beautiful smile came to my aunt's face. "Harry."

"He sounds sweet."

She closed her eyes. "He was. So sweet. And kind. And a little bit quiet. Nora would tease him about that. But he had a steady strength to him. An unshakable understanding of the world and his place in it. He was a farm boy from Oregon of all places."

I cupped my coffee mug to my chest and leaned back in my chair. "How did the two of you meet?"

"At a mutual friend's wedding. He was going to college nearby. He always planned on running his family's farm, but his parents insisted he go to school first. They wanted him to experience the world before he took on the responsibility of that life. But he never wavered. That farm was in his blood. We planned to get married as soon as he was done with his degree."

My chin dropped to my chest. "You were going to move to Oregon?"

"I had my bags all packed."

"But what about Ivywood Hollow?"

She shook her head. "I knew my siblings were more than capable of taking care of the house, and I planned to visit often. Harry had taken me to visit the farm. I could really see myself there." She met my eye to show me the depth of her sincerity. "It had this wonderful large sunny kitchen with a tin ceiling. Oh, and the garden. I could grow any vegetable I desired. There were fruit trees and berry bushes too. And I could cook with fresh eggs every day if I wanted. I was in heaven."

"Sounds like it."

"In my heart, I already lived there. Harry always wanted four kids, and I could see us in that old house, surrounded by fields and mountains, raising our children with love and laughter." She sighed. "There was just one problem."

My breath caught as I waited for her to finish.

"I never told him I was a witch."

A powerful sadness settled over us the both of us. I felt like I had heard this story a thousand times before, and it never ended happily.

"Your mother tried to warn me. She was the only one I told. My, she was relentless, going on and on about what a mistake it was not to tell him. She said that it wasn't fair. That Harry deserved to know who he was marrying. That I deserved a husband who loved all of me." Izzy inhaled sharply, reliving the memory. "But I told her right back that it was my choice, and that I knew what I was doing."

"So, what happened?" I was afraid to ask, but I had to know.

"Well, she kept my secret for a while, but eventually she told the rest of the family, and you can imagine the uproar that caused. But I had it all worked out, you see." Izzy tapped the table with her fingertip. "I've never been one for the big flashy spells. I thought I could stick to using my magic through food. I pictured myself in that kitchen, cooking up my enchantments and helping my neighbors much like we do now." She smiled as she described the life that she had imagined for herself. "I wasn't exactly sure how I would handle things once we had children, but witching genes don't always come through when mixed with human blood, so I didn't even know if it would be an issue. It's amazing how such things seem so manageable when you're in love. I felt invincible." Her smile dropped away. "Then it all went wrong.

"The morning we were supposed to get married. Harry snuck into the house. Everyone knows the groom isn't supposed to see the bride before the wedding. I never dreamed he would do such a thing. He was always so traditional." She frowned at the puzzle she still hadn't been able to sort out after all these years. "But he did, and he snuck up to my room. He wanted to give me a wedding day gift. A necklace. A white opal pendant."

"I've seen it," I whispered. She had it tucked away in her jewelry box. I never understood why she didn't wear it.

"I was so stupid that morning. So careless. I was giddy with excitement, and I let it all out through magic. I filled my room with flowers, and rainbows, and bluebirds." She put her hands over her face. "I stopped short at the dancing mice."

"Oh, Izzy," I said, touching her elbow. "You wanted your Cinderella moment."

She nodded miserably. "I wanted my Cinderella moment." She dropped her hands. "The look on his face when he saw me, really saw me." She blinked and rolled her eyes to the ceiling, steadying herself. "He dropped the necklace and ran. He was terrified." She shook her head. "But even so, I thought we could still make it work. Obviously, we couldn't have the wedding that day. Harry was in shock, and your grandmother wanted to spell him, wipe away all his memories of me, but I wouldn't let her. I couldn't stand the thought of our love story being erased. So, I made her promise not to, then I found Harry. I told him everything. And do you know what he said when I was through?" My aunt's face contracted in pain as she tried to smile again. "He held me in his arms and said everything would be okay. He said it didn't change anything. That he would always love me."

"We talked about having another wedding, eloping maybe. But, as much as we both wanted to be together, seeing me that morning changed everything. Harry loved me as much as he ever did, but he was afraid. He had constant nightmares. He lost weight. He saw the world as this new, frightening place, and he no longer understood his role in it. I told him, when I first explained who I was, that I could take away all his memories of us, but he was so against it. Like me, he couldn't stand the thought of obliterating our love. But after one particularly bad night, I asked him again, and he said yes."

I grabbed my aunt's hand. I couldn't imagine how terrible that must have been for her. Erasing herself from the heart of the man she loved.

"After that, Harry went on with his life. He took over the farm, married a girl from his town, and had four beautiful children." She looked down at our hands and nodded. "So, it was for the best in the end."

Maybe she was right, but it didn't feel like it.

"Now," my aunt said, gathering herself up with a shudder. "I didn't tell you all this to make you sad. I guess part of me felt like I needed to explain why I've been behaving so badly. I gave up on love after I lost Harry, and I don't want you doing the same thing."

"Izzy, I—"

She held up a hand. "I've also come to realize something else. Just like my siblings couldn't make me tell Harry the truth before it all went wrong, I can't make you do what *I* think is best. There are some things we need to figure out on our own. Or in my case, learn the hard way. Maybe that applies to ghosts too."

I knew she was right. I hated it. But she was right.

"The point's moot, anyway," I said. "Mort's gone."

"If that's the case, all you can do is learn from this."

I nodded. Maybe Mort had been brought into my life to teach me this lesson. It certainly wasn't one I enjoyed, but maybe it would help me do better in the future. And, hopefully, Mort, too, had taken something away from our paths crossing. "Thank you, Izzy," I said softly. "For everything, but especially for sharing Harry with me."

"I should have done it sooner." She got to her feet, and once again opened her arms to me. I stepped right in.

"So, do you forgive me for brunch?"

"I don't know. It was pretty awkward."

"So awkward."

I laughed. "Of course I forgive you. You're done setting me up, though, right?"

"So done."

My aunt leaned back and smoothed a lock of hair away from my face, tucking it behind my ear. "Promise me something?"

I raised an eyebrow.

"Don't be too hard on yourself. The road to hell may well be paved with good intentions, but without them, there would be no way into heaven at all."

I TRIED TO TAKE Izzy's advice to not beat myself up, but that was easier said than done. I had handled everything so badly, and I couldn't think of a way to fix it anymore. With Mort gone, it was too late.

Despite the coffee my aunt had brought me, after she left, I went straight back to bed.

This time around, I fell into a deep dreamless sleep. It was one of those sleeps where the world falls away, and you lose all sense of time. I was in such a deep sleep, in fact, that when some part of my consciousness registered a pressure on my chest, I had to fight just to open my eyes. When I finally did manage to blink them open, I was so stunned by what I saw, I thought I was still dreaming.

It didn't help matters that the room was pitch-dark.

I carefully reached to my side table to click on the lamp. Once the soft light illuminated the room, I realized I *was* actually seeing what I had thought I had been seeing.

"Dog?"

Chapter 39

WAKING UP TO find a cat on my chest was one thing. I had experienced that many times before. When Faustus was hungry, there wasn't much that could stop him from getting *someone's* attention, but I could honestly say I had never awoken to the sight of a large crow staring down at me. His beak looked super sharp from this angle.

I blinked a few times, then moaned, "Go away." I didn't even bother to ask him how he got in this time.

The crow didn't move.

"Can't you see I'm busy feeling sorry for myself?"

Dog cawed, which might not seem too bad, but I don't think the average person can truly appreciate just how loud a crow's caw can be unless they've had one do it while standing on their chest.

I wiggled my index fingers in my ears. "Thanks for that."

He said nothing, just regarded me carefully.

"Seriously," I said, matching the crow's deadpan look,

"what do you want? You have any more ribbons tucked away underneath your wings?"

Dog hopped in the air, dropping back down on the soft part of my belly.

I grunted. "What is your problem?"

His wings twitched like he might do it again, so I stammered, "Wait. Wait. I get it. You think I should be up doing something, not lying around in bed having a pity party, am I right?"

Dog chittered and adjusted his footing.

"I get it," I said with a small shrug. My motions were quite limited. "I don't disagree. But, Dog, there's nothing more for me to do right n—"

And we were back to the earsplitting caws.

I closed my eyes. "That felt uncalled—or perhaps *uncawed*—for." I peeked one eye open. "Get it? Uncawed for?" I was still very tired.

The bird glowered at me, looking mightily unimpressed.

I let my hands flop to my sides. "I don't know what you want from me. I get that you have a special relationship with the dead. And I can appreciate that you are disappointed with the way things have turned out. I am too! But I tried to help, and I failed. Mort's gone."

Dog cawed again, but it sounded different this time.

Wait a minute.

I gave the bird a sideways look. "Are you trying to tell me Mort isn't gone?"

The crow bobbed up and down in what looked like a full body nod. My eyes widened. That was new. And totally amazing. "Dog, did you just nod at me?"

He did it again.

This was a huge turning point in our relationship, and one that might very well save my hearing. "Okay, okay, let's try this out. Did you see Mort somewhere? Does he need me?"

The crow didn't move.

"So, you're not trying to get me to go anywhere?"

He stayed frozen.

"But Mort *is* still here?"

He nodded again.

A smile spread across my face. *Mort wasn't gone!* What did that mean? Maybe he was still saying goodbye to Angie? Or maybe some small part of him was holding out hope for answers.

"Dog, did you come here just to tell me Mort was still around?"

The crow didn't answer.

"I'm missing something, aren't I?"

Dog squawked lowly, but I already knew it was the truth.

I brought my hand up to my mouth to chew on my thumbnail. It was not a habit I wanted to encourage, but apparently, it helped me think.

I *was* missing something. Some detail. Some clue.

I searched my memories, going over everything I had learned so far. All that I had been told. All the people involved. All their motives. The problem was I could make a case for everyone, and I couldn't count on anything I had been told. No, personal accounts were never reliable. I needed to go back further. To something I *could* count on.

As my thoughts raced, my eyes searched the loft. I wasn't thinking I would find anything that would help in the outside world. I wasn't even conscious I was doing it until my gaze landed on my grandmother's cauldron.

That was it! The reenactment spell.

What exactly had I seen in the cauldron? I needed to go over it again. Slowly. Step by step.

I took a breath and closed my eyes, trying to once again re-create Mort's death, this time from my own memory.

What *had* I seen?

The first thing I remembered was Mort hopping up the steps to the gazebo and then sitting down. His movements sure and vital. After that, he had placed the box on his lap and lifted the lid. I saw him in my mind's eye, selecting one of the chocolates and unwrapping the gold foil. That's when he had looked at it and said, *X, O.*

I grunted in frustration. What did those letters mean? The obvious answer was hugs and kisses, but I had a feeling there was more to it.

What happened next?

I recalled Mort saying, *Well, that's unexpected*, but—

Wait. That wasn't right. He had done something before all that. I remembered the funny look that had come over his face. He had been confused. I remembered because ghost Mort had made the exact same expression when I turned from the cauldron to look at him. What prompted that confusion?

I needed to go over it again.

Mort sat down. He lifted the lid from the box. He picked up a chocolate, unwrapped it, and . . .

No. I had forgotten. It hadn't seemed important, and I had been so focused on the letters, but . . .

Mort had smelled the chocolate before taking a bite. That's what had caused that look. Mort had smelled the chocolate, but I never smelled the wrapper! I had put it directly into the plastic baggie, wanting to preserve it in case the police needed it for evidence.

"Dog! Get off!"

The bird shifted side to side, dancing on my abdomen.

"Get off! Get off! Get off!"

And I was cawing like a crow again. But it worked. Dog flapped his wings and jumped down off me to the other side of the bed. I whipped my covers back and lunged for my messenger bag on the floor. I flipped it open with one hand, the other diving inside, searching for the baggie.

In seconds I felt the slippery plastic against my fingertips. I pulled it out and pushed myself back up to sit on the bed. Dog waddled up close to my elbow.

The gold foil protected by plastic glinted in the lamp-light.

It was a long shot, but . . .

I pulled open the seal of the bag, brought it up to my nose, and inhaled sharply.

My body knew what was wrong before my thoughts could catch up.

The scent was unmistakable. Alcohol.

This wrapper had held a chocolate made with liquor. That's why it had been wrapped in foil.

But that wasn't right.

Naff told me Mort wasn't a fan of liquor in his chocolates. He could have been lying about that, but I didn't think so. Fredrick had been the one to bring the topic up. If he was Mort's killer, why bring up a clue only to have to lie about it? It could have been a mistake, but I didn't think so.

So, maybe the killer didn't know Mort's preferences? Elias might not have known. But that didn't seem to fit either. Something about Elias being the killer had felt wrong since the beginning. Unless he was an expert chocolatier on top of being a master gardener, I didn't think he would have been able to make the chocolates. Not with the hand stringing.

I thought back to the conversation I'd had with Fredrick. There was something else there. Again, he had said Mort didn't like liquor in his chocolates, but . . .

Les brought all of his creations home.

Sickening dread raced through my veins.

Oh no. What if . . .

What if the chocolates were never meant for Mort? What if they were meant for Les?

Someone did have a motive to kill Les. A motive with a time limit. Fredrick said his offer to buy the shop would only last until midnight tonight! Les could still be in danger!

I glanced at my watch. Eleven thirty-five.

I jumped to my feet, sending the wrapper spinning to the floor. I bent to pick it up, but yanked my hand back before I reached it.

The chocolate markings didn't look like *X*, *O* anymore.

No, the wrapper had landed, turned by one quarter, and now instead of looking like letters, the chocolate markings came together in a symbol.

A skull and crossbones.

Poison.

Chapter 40

I TORE THROUGH THE streets on my bike, my magic fueling my ride. I was being reckless, my airborne wheels gliding above the pavement, traveling at a speed no human could hope to achieve, and I wasn't making any effort to conceal myself, but I couldn't worry about any of that now.

I had to get to Les and Cookie's house.

I whipped around a corner onto a dirt path, a shortcut that Adam and I used to take to get to his old house. Cookie had told me they lived directly across from it. Towering hedges on either side closed in around me.

Please. Please don't let me be too late. As I had the thought, a cloud of sparkles formed twenty, maybe thirty feet ahead of me.

"Ghostie," a disembodied voice called out, "where you going in such a hurry?"

Mort materialized just as my bike sped through him,

sending sparkles flying. A deep cold washed over me, but I couldn't stop.

"Wait!"

I didn't answer. There was no time to explain.

I took a wide turn onto Adam's old street. Thankfully there were no cars.

"Stop! Tell me what's happening?"

I heard Mort's ghost, but I could tell he was having trouble materializing with the speed I was going.

Adam's old house sat in the distance, so I headed for the opposite side of the street. When I made it to the house across from his, I dropped my bike to the ground and sprinted up the lawn.

I stopped when I reached the steps leading up to the door. A movement in a window had caught my eye. I could see through to the kitchen. Cookie and Les were arguing. Cookie was at the island, banging her fist on a stack of papers on the counter, long knife clutched in her hand.

I ran up the steps and twisted the doorknob. Locked.

There was no time for this. I closed my eyes, reaching for the power swirling in my belly, calling on it to grow. If I had to, I would blast through the door.

Just before I released the spell, I felt a familiar tingle travel up the back of my neck. I opened my eyes—knowing my irises were glowing bright green—to meet Mort's spectral gaze.

"I can't let you go in there," he said, cringing back from my flashing glare.

"You don't understand." My voice sounded different, thick with the power running through me. "Those chocolates weren't for you. They were never meant for you."

I raised my hands to blast through the door, waiting to see if my words registered, but Mort's expression remained unmoved. He still looked uncertain at the change that had come over me, but he didn't look surprised by what I had told him.

No, he didn't look surprised at all.

The power roiling through me drained away in a sudden rush.

"But you already knew that."

Chapter 41

TOADS CHIRPED AND croaked from the lawn as a tiny moth fluttered around the light beside Les and Cookie's door. I struggled to understand what was happening, but I couldn't make any sense of it.

"I wanted to tell you, Ghostie," Mort said, looking as miserable as I had ever seen him. "I knew how hard you were trying to help me."

My head shook side to side slowly of its own accord. "Why? Why would you want to protect Cookie?"

Mort turned his gaze completely away.

"Oh no." I brought my hand to my mouth. "No, it can't be."

All the pieces fell into place—the despondency on Mort's face bringing them together—but I didn't want to accept it.

"You don't have to do anything," he pleaded. "Just walk away. Pretend I never involved you in any of this mess."

I glanced over to my bike but didn't move.

"I don't know all the details," he went on, his tone desperate, "but I know it was a terrible accident. Nothing more. Les never would have tried to kill me."

And there it was. Les had made the chocolates. He just hadn't made them for Mort.

"They were meant for Cookie, weren't they?" I asked, my voice barely above a whisper.

Mort and I stared at each other. Every part of his being radiated sadness.

Finally, he shrugged, defeated. "He never would have gone through with it."

I clutched the sides of my head. This couldn't be happening. Out of all the possibilities this had to be the most tragic. I didn't want to believe it. But it all made so much sense now. The way Mort kept disappearing when we found out something new. The way he didn't want me talking to Angie or asking questions in the candy shop. He never wanted me to find out the truth. "You've known this entire time."

"I didn't know," he said, shaking his head. "Not for sure. I suspected when you guys did that spell. I wouldn't just eat chocolates unless I assumed that they were samples Les left for me to try. Then when you went to Elias's, I remembered that tour of his garden. Les had joked at the time about making Cookie a poison batch. But it was a joke! Then in the gazebo, when you found that foil, that made me wonder too. It's normally used for liquor fillings. I've never liked them. But Cookie . . ." Mort gave me a bleak smile. "But all of those things, they weren't proof. Only suspicions. It wasn't until I got a good look at the inside of the wrapper. The *X, O left behind by the chocolate*? It looked a little funny, but I'd recognize Les's hand stringing anywhere."

"It wasn't *X, O* at all, was it? It was a poison symbol."

"Les has always struggled with depression. He and Cookie were never happy. I think it might have been a grim joke, but it also proves he never intended for Cookie to actually eat them. He put a warning right on the top!"

"Except you ate them."

He gaze dropped away.

"You've been eavesdropping, too, haven't you?"

"I had to know what you were up to. You're smart, Ghostie. And determined. I tried my best to keep you off the trail." He looked at Les and Cookie's door. "But here we are."

I closed my eyes.

"You can just walk away. I'm the victim. I should decide what happens. Just walk away."

"You're not the only victim, Mort."

"But—"

Just then the door opened.

"Brynn Warren," Les said with a tired smile. "I'm glad you're here. Please. Come in."

Chapter 42

I HAD ONLY CROSSED the threshold when a panic-stricken Cookie rushed toward us. "Oh, Brynn, hello." She tried to make the words sound light, natural, but she failed miserably. "Les, can I talk to you a moment?"

"No, I've made up my mind."

"You don't have to do this," she said, moving closer to her husband.

"Is he here?" Les asked me.

Before I could answer, Cookie jumped in. "Is who here? Les, you're tired, dear." She reached for his arm. "Why don't you go on to bed?"

Les flinched at his wife's touch. "I am not tired," he snapped. "We both know she's some sort of medium. You're the one who told me how she helped your uncle. And we both know why she's here."

Cookie backed away, her palm pressing against the wall for support.

"Don't you see?" he pleaded. "All this lying. Me always

doing whatever you say with a *Yes, dear.* That's what got us to this point." He turned back to me. "Is he here?"

Judging by the look on Mort's face, I don't think he had ever seen this side of his cousin. I nodded.

"Good," Les said. "I want him to hear this. I want him to know what happened. I can't live with the guilt anymore."

"But it was an accident," Cookie whispered.

Les looked back at his wife, all trace of anger and frustration gone. "I'm not innocent, Cookie. Not in my heart. We both know that. It's time you faced it."

MINUTES LATER, WE were seated in the married couple's living room. The atmosphere had an almost bizarre quality to it. Like at any moment, either one of them might offer me tea or suggest we pull out a board game. I don't think any of us expected to find ourselves here. Not like this.

I was seated on a floral print sofa in front of a coffee table. Cookie and Les took the armchairs at either end so that they faced each other. Mort stood alone by the window. I knew he didn't want to be here. He didn't want to hear Les say the words, but his cousin and best friend needed him to hear his confession.

"I want you all to know. This wasn't something that I planned. Cookie and I had our troubles, but it wasn't as though I had been harboring some plot to kill her all these years."

Cookie flinched, but it didn't stop Les from continuing. "We were never a good fit. You know that. But I didn't want bad things for you. I just . . ." It seemed like Les would let the thought trail away, but then he said, "I just wanted you to leave me alone."

It took everything in me to look back at Les's wife. I didn't want to see the pain on her face. "What happened?"

Les looked down at his hands. "Cookie's been after me for years to sell the shop. From the beginning, really. She hated it. It was the one part of my life she couldn't control. But I couldn't give it up. The shop was the one place I could be myself. No one was trying to change me there."

I didn't look at Cookie this time. Imagining what it must be like for her hearing all of this was enough.

"Why did you two get married?" Out of all the questions I needed to ask, that one wasn't the most important, but I couldn't help myself.

"Yes, why did you marry me?" Cookie asked bitterly.

"Truth?" Les threw his hands up and then let them drop down between his knees. "Mort found Angie, and I knew I would be alone. It's not like I proposed. One day Cookie just told me, *We're getting married in the spring, Les.* At least she gave me a couple of months to get used to the idea."

Mort grunted, but when I looked over, he had his face still turned away.

"I thought it would be fine," Les went on. "It's what people do. They get married. They start families. But I knew it was a mistake. Right away. As soon as we moved in together, I knew we weren't suited. Everything I did annoyed her."

"Poor Les," Cookie said with a sniff. "Such a bully for a wife."

"I tried to do things the right way. Her way. But it was never good enough. I spent more and more time at the shop. That's how we were able to work. I could get through the time I spent at home because I knew I could go to the shop. I thought things would get better when we had kids."

At the mention of children, Cookie brought her fist to her mouth, choking back a sob.

Les looked at his wife. "I did feel for you then. I know how badly you wanted a family for us. When you lost that—" He closed his eyes. "When *we* lost *our* baby, I knew how much it hurt you." He turned back to me. "It was like she had been turned inside out and all the world was just there to cause her pain. I promised myself then that I'd do better. I'd be a better husband. But the years went by, and"—his voice cracked—"it all faded away. And she just kept on talking about selling the shop. She blamed all of our problems on Mort."

The spirit looked over at his cousin, arms folded across his chest.

"She thought if I retired, and we moved away, everything would be fine between us. But the thought of it. All my time with Cookie. I couldn't do it." Les's features went slack, sickened by the thought. "I wasn't worried though. Not at first. Mort wasn't going to sell. He wouldn't do that to me. He knew the shop was my only escape."

"It wasn't though," I said, unable to hide my frustration. "You could have left."

Les dropped his gaze, shamefaced. "I've never been that strong. I'm a coward at heart. Cookie knew that. And she knew Mort wouldn't abandon me either. So, she came up with a new plan. She went to Angie. That was her ace in the hole." Les locked glares with his wife. "Mort could never deny Angie anything. He told me not to worry, but . . ."

"You didn't have to worry," Mort snapped. "We would have figured it out!"

"Mort told me Angie was thinking about downsizing," Les continued, unable to hear the ghost's words. "I knew what downsizing meant. They were moving. To be closer to their daughter in Florida. Their son-in-law was sick. They wanted to help. Then everyone on the street got those chocolates from Freddie. I knew instantly Cookie had gone to him behind my back. He always wanted to be part of the shop." Les smiled, but it didn't reach his eyes. "I didn't blame him for jumping at the chance."

"That deal fell through!" Cookie said, pounding her knee. "You told me no, and I told Fred the deal was off."

"You hadn't given up though. Not by a long shot," Les bit back. "You kept working on Angie. I saw their furniture in the antique shop. That rolltop desk of Mort's in the front window? That's when I knew it was over. I had lost. Mort just hadn't had the heart to tell me yet."

"I wouldn't have done that!" Mort roared. "I would have found a way." Suddenly the emotion dropped from his face. If I had to guess, he was remembering something. I wanted to ask him, but I didn't want to take the chance that it would derail Les.

"I went walking. Thinking about how I could end it. End *me*. Then I walked by Elias's, and before I knew it, I was in his yard. I don't even remember going in. He'd given us a tour of his poison garden. I couldn't remember what was what, except for the oleander bush. I took a branch. I wasn't thinking straight. I was going to use it on myself, but when I got back to the shop, I was overcome with how much I loved the place. All my best memories were there." A light sparked in his eyes, but died away quickly. "I was so angry. Angry in a way I had never been before. I would never confront Cookie. I'd never been able to do that, so I made the chocolates. Did it on a whim. The entire time I was working I was arguing with myself. Were they for me? Or were they for her?"

"The wrappers though. They said *Naff*," I interjected. "You don't use those in the shop."

Les gave me a funny look. He knew I must have gotten that from Mort. But even when people say they believe in what I do, it's still hard for them to really accept it. "I got them as samples. It was petty. I thought she'd notice the label before she bit in. Then she'd know why I had done it."

"But you're saying you never intended to go through with it." I was skeptical. He had obviously put a lot of thought into this fantasy of his.

"No, don't you see? I didn't know what I was thinking. I didn't know what I would do. Part of me was so angry. But the other part just wanted out. I was confused. And upset. But no. No, I never really intended to give them to her."

"I believe that," Cookie said quietly. "I know that may be hard for you to believe. How could you possibly understand? You seemed so happy with Adam. You wouldn't know how strange and complicated a marriage can be."

I didn't understand. At least not yet.

"I made them early evening," Les went on. "Then I just stared at them for a good long time, wondering how I let my life get so bad. As the hours passed, so did the anger. And the despair. Coming that close to the edge? It was a wake-up call for me. I did start to think there might be another way. I could talk to Cookie. People divorce all the time. Maybe I could follow Mort to Florida."

Cookie flinched. "You never told me that. You had a whole life planned without me?"

"I don't like hurting people. Your pain does not bring me joy. But you need to know the truth." He turned back to me. "She came to the shop late that night to find me. I didn't have a chance to get rid of them, but I knew I could do it in the morning. I was always the first one in. Always."

"I remember," Mort said. "I remember why I was there."

Les tracked my gaze to the window. "What is he saying?"

I held up a hand for him to wait.

"I had a late-night brainstorm. Angie wanted to sell the shop. We both knew we had to help our baby girl. It was the right thing to do. But I also knew what that meant for Les. I tossed and turned in bed that night, going over and over it in my mind. Then it hit me like a thunderbolt. I could sell my stake to Fred. I never liked the guy, but Les and him got on like a house on fire. Fred would give Les the strength to keep going. To not give into Cookie's wishes. They would make the perfect team. I couldn't sleep after that, so I went to the shop. I had Fred's contact information there and all the business papers. I wanted to come up with a proposal. I

must have spotted the chocolates and thought Les left them
for me to try."

I repeated what Mort had said.

Les buried his face in his hands.

"When did Cookie get involved?" I knew Les had been
careful not to implicate his wife in any of this, but, as difficult as it was for me to understand, I knew she had a
played a role.

Cookie looked at her husband. "Go ahead, tell her the
rest. Don't act like you care about protecting me now. You
want to clear your conscience? You can't have it both ways."

Les took some time to gather himself. "When we got
home, I told her I wanted out. She said it was all nonsense.
We were never going to get a divorce. She wouldn't let me.
So, I told her what I had done. I told her about the chocolates. She didn't believe it. Didn't think I had it in me. I told
her to go see for herself. I didn't care anymore."

"So, I went," Cookie interrupted before he could finish.
"I got there just in time to see Mort leave the shop. Candy
box in his hand."

Chapter 43

I DIDN'T BELIEVE FOR a second Les had actually done it," Cookie said, picking up the story. "It's *Les*. He's not a violent man. The thought was laughable." She chuckled unpleasantly. "So, I decided to watch. I was going to tell Les I saw Mort eat his so-called poison chocolates. Oh, how I planned to gloat. The thought actually made me happy. But then Mort did eat a chocolate." She plucked at the armrest of her chair. "Even when it was happening, I didn't believe it. I actually thought they were playing some sort of prank on me. That Les had called Mort after I left the house, told him to rush over to the shop, make it look like he was dying, just so they could laugh at me. I thought it was all some big performance. But I'd get the last laugh. I believed that until . . ." Her face twisted at the horror of what came next.

"Until you realized it wasn't an act."

"I checked his pulse," she said. "That's when I knew."

"Why didn't you call someone? Why didn't you go to straight to the police? Why did you clean up the evidence?"

"It seems so simple, doesn't it? That's what you do." She held up her hands. "But I was in shock. It was ludicrous! My husband had made chocolates to poison me? That knocks a girl back a few steps. And Les is not a killer. He had confessed to me what he had done. It was an accident," Cookie went on desperately. "And you heard your aunt. Oleander poisoning usually takes time. For all we know, Mort died of a heart attack. A natural one."

Mort scoffed from his post by the window.

I rubbed a hand over my eyes. We all knew she was reaching. It didn't change the fact that Les had made those chocolates.

"I know you don't understand," Cookie said, frustrated tears spilling down her cheeks. "But I've been in that place where it feels like all hope is gone, and Les was the one who got me out of it. That one thought broke through it all. He covered for me when I needed him to, and I was going to cover for him. So that's what I did."

"I'm sorry. It still doesn't make sense to me."

"Then maybe I can put it another way. As terrible and toxic as our marriage is, I don't know who I am without it." Her voice dropped to a murmur. "And it was an accident."

"I don't want you covering for me," Les said. "Not anymore. I'm going to tell the police everything. I hate living like this. Mort was the person I loved most in the world. I don't know if you can really talk to ghosts or not, Ms. Warren, but if you can, you tell Mort I'm sorry. He'll never know how sorry. I don't expect him to forgive me though. It's unforgivable what I've done."

I didn't have to look over to Mort this time. I already knew he was gone.

Chapter 44

LES WENT TO the police station. I followed to be sure, but I already knew he couldn't live with his guilt a second longer. Cookie went with him. They didn't speak much on the way over.

I spent the rest of that night and the following day in the loft by myself. My aunts checked in on me, of course, but I was fine. I just needed time to process everything. I was also hoping Mort might visit, but that didn't happen. He had been through so much, and I think hearing Les's confession—even though he already knew for the most part what happened—was more than he could handle.

And then there was the fact that Mort didn't like goodbyes.

By the second morning I resolved to get on with things, so I got myself up and headed over to the B&B. I wasn't surprised to find Izzy in the dining room, clearing up breakfast, but I was a little taken aback to see Nora there too. She was more of a night owl.

"Darling," Izzy called out in greeting, "I was wondering

if you'd join us. There's plenty of food left." She rushed over to the side table to make me up a plate. I knew she was worried, given all that had transpired, and feeding me was always a go-to coping mechanism of hers to show care. Given the amount of bacon she was putting on the plate, she cared *a lot*.

"Have all the guests gone?"

"Fredrick has headed into town, and the lovebirds left first thing this morning. They were anxious to get on to the next stop of their honeymoon tour."

"That's too bad," I said, lowering myself into the free chair across from Nora. "I would have liked to say goodbye."

"Don't worry. We'll see them again. They've already made a reservation for next year," Izzy replied, stacking the plate with miniature pancakes.

Nora regarded me over her coffee mug. "How are you doing?"

"I'm fine. All things considered."

Izzy set the enormous plate of food down in front of me. I clutched my silverware almost in self-defense.

"Have you seen any sign of Mort?"

I shook my head.

Izzy pulled another chair up to the table. "It's all so incredibly sad."

"For everyone," Nora mused. "But you did the right thing. It may very well have been an accident, but Les needs to be held accountable for his actions."

We fell into silence.

Not too long after, Nora said, "I almost forgot. I found something in the greenhouse when I was tidying up from the other night." Izzy made a noise low in her throat. It almost sounded like a growl. I guess she still wasn't over plan B. Nora eyed her cautiously, then carried on. "I thought you might want to take a look." She swept up from her chair, holding out a finger for me to wait, then walked over to the buffet, retrieving a sheet of paper. "It's the page I stole from Elias."

Izzy sighed dreamily. "I'm so glad he didn't turn out to be the killer."

Nora scoffed. "I don't know what it is you all find so attractive about the man. The only thing remotely interesting about him is his garden." She handed me the typewritten page. "Well, his garden and his wife's many deaths."

With everything that had happened, I had almost forgotten about the love letters.

The notes were in German, but I didn't need to understand the language in order to analyze the type. I scanned the page until I found what I was looking for. "It wasn't him." I tossed the sheet onto the table. "He didn't write the letters."

"Are you sure?"

"Of course not," I said with a dry laugh. "It's hard to be sure of anything these days, but the letter *d* lines up on this page. It was off in the love letter Angie gave me." It was too bad that I couldn't have solved that mystery for her. "Thank you for bringing it to me though."

"My, it has been a strange week or so," Izzy said. "I'm actually kind of glad the B&B will be quiet for a day or two."

"So, Fredrick is checking out?"

"I think so," Izzy said, sipping her tea. "He had some business to attend to this morning. I think it depends on that. Not that he's any bother."

I couldn't help but wonder if he still intended to buy the shop. All the news of what happened would have had to have reached him by now. "You know," I said, looking at my aunt, "I had breakfast with Fredrick the other morning. He is pretty charming, but I was surprised to hear you wanted to set me up with him."

Izzy nearly spit out her tea. "What? Set you up with Fredrick Naff? What are you talking about?"

"Gideon said that you were going to set me up with our guest."

"Not Fredrick," Izzy spluttered. "Our other guest."

I cocked my head. "What other guest?"

"You know who I'm talking about. The handsome one. With the Jeep."

"Not this again," Nora said, reaching for her coffee mug. "I already told you that would never work."

"What other guest?" I repeated with more gusto.

"Why wouldn't it work?" Izzy asked, shooting her sister a questioning look. "What's wrong with him?"

"There's nothing wrong with him per se," Nora said, mug hovering under her lips. "It's just an unsuitable match."

"Why?" Izzy and I both asked. We exchanged looks.

I wasn't saying I wanted to be set up with anyone. Again, I had made it quite clear that I wanted just the opposite. But even so, I was interested to find out what kind of man Nora deemed unsuitable for me.

She squinted against the sunshine coming in through the window. "It's hard to explain exactly. There are some things you just know. Or rather *I* know."

"Oh nonsense," Izzy said. "You know no such thing. He was quite the catch. What was his name again?"

Nora's mouth opened briefly, then snapped shut. She frowned. "That's odd. I'm sure I know it."

"Well, whoever he is, he didn't sign the ledger," I said, remembering how I had checked it.

"Now, that's nonsense," Nora replied. "I watched him sign his name right under Naff's."

"I'll show you." I went to retrieve the book, then hurried back. I placed the heavy ledger down on the table in front of my aunt.

Nora stared at the empty line underneath Fredrick Naff's elegant signature. "That's impossible."

I shrugged. "Maybe you misremembered."

Nora gave me an indignant look, then squinted back at the page. She ran her finger over the spot where she thought the name should have been. "You did this," she said, turning on her sister.

Izzy placed a hand on her chest. "I did no such thing. Why would I erase the name of a guest?"

Nora straightened. "Obviously to make me go to see the eye doctor. Or to trick me into believing I am afflicted with spring fever!"

"Here we go," Izzy drawled.

"Spring fever aside," I said, holding my hands out in what I hoped was a placating gesture, "did this mystery man ever tell either of you what he was doing in town?"

"Visiting family."

"Business."

My aunts frowned at each other.

"Well, that clears it up."

"This is all very peculiar," Nora said, looking again to her sister.

Izzy matched her serious expression. "I think there is something more going on here. Brynn, are you still having that funny feeling of yours?"

"Not in the last few days."

Nora shot to her feet. "I don't like this. Someone or *something* is fooling with our magic. We Warrens don't just have funny feelings."

Izzy joined her sister in standing. "I remember reading about something similar. The book is in the library. We need to do some research."

"I agree," I said, also rising to my feet. "But you guys are going to have to get started without me."

"What? Why?" Izzy asked. "Where are you going?"

"I have something I need to do."

Nora blinked. "Now? What could possibly be more important than this?"

Chapter 45

SURPRISINGLY, I DID have something more important to do. Something that I could no longer put off.

I had to try to speak to Angie.

Given the way we'd left things, I didn't know if she would listen to anything I had to say, but I owed it to both her and Mort to try. She was due an explanation. I was also hoping that maybe—despite everything—I could bring her some measure of comfort.

It took a while to explain all this to my aunts—they were understandably focused on our other issue—but once I had, I headed out. Again, I didn't want to put this off any longer.

Given that was the case, it might have seemed strange that as soon as I turned onto the sidewalk from the B&B, I stopped dead in my tracks.

Oh dear.

Mr. Henderson was standing in the middle of his lawn surrounded by a smattering of pillows and a circle of stakes.

Yet another problem I had forgotten about.

After Izzy told me the story of her failed engagement, her actions regarding Mr. Henderson suddenly made a lot more sense. I could see how his initial fear and horror at discovering our true nature may have triggered her to spell him without giving it proper thought and consideration. I just hoped whatever was going on with our neighbor wasn't a result of bad magic. Either way, it was time to get to the bottom of this.

"Good morning, Mr. Henderson!" I called out brightly. "How are you today?"

"Fine. Fine."

I had been hoping he would simply offer an explanation for his behavior, but clearly we were going to have to do this the hard way. I walked up his lawn, picking my way around the pillows and stakes, to join him. "Everything okay here?"

He straightened his glasses. "Sorry?"

I pointed half-heartedly at the pillows scattered across the lawn.

"Oh, those," he said, glancing at his handiwork. "Don't worry. They're all going back inside. I need to do it before Birdie Cline rings my neck."

"Can I ask why they were out here in the first place?"

My neighbor blushed, then pointed to the top of the tree.

I rolled my eyes up, nervous about what I might find there. I didn't see anything at first, but then I caught sight of a flapping set of wings. A robin. I followed the bird as it ducked into a crevice between the branches. A second later a nest erupted in chirping.

"Oh, baby robins! How wonderful!" I looked back at my neighbor. "But why would you need pillows and—" I gasped. "You were hoping to break their fall." A smile spread across my face. "Mr. Henderson."

He waved a hand out. "I know. I know. It's ridiculous. Birdie set me straight. Told me in no uncertain terms that I was going to do them more harm than good."

"But it was a very sweet idea."

He shrugged and shuffled his feet.

"But why the stakes?"

"I was going to wrap chicken wire around them."

I raised an eyebrow.

He sighed noisily. "There's potential threats all over this neighborhood. You've got that beast of a cat, and Minnie is always walking that rottweiler of hers."

"Honey," I said, nodding.

Mr. Henderson suddenly looked uncomfortable. I think he thought I was flirting with him.

"Minnie's dog. Her name is Honey."

His eyes lit with understanding. "Right. Well, I wanted to give these baby birds a chance before they became somebody's lunch."

I pinched my lips together. "That is adorable."

"Anyone would do it."

I didn't think that was true. For a number of reasons. But I didn't want to embarrass him any further. "I should be on my way. And don't worry. I'll make sure our beast of a cat doesn't get anywhere near your baby birds."

"It's appreciated. Oh! And, Brynn, could you return this to your aunt?" He moved to pick up a mallet off the grass.

"Of course. Just leave it there," I said, headed for the sidewalk. "I'll grab it on my way back."

"Don't forget. I wouldn't want to make Nora angry. I know what can happen when you Warren women get angry."

I froze.

His voice dropped to a mutter, "I could go a lifetime without seeing those glowing eyes again."

I turned, slowly. "What did you say?"

Mr. Henderson's eyes widened. "Did I say something?"

I gave him a sideways look.

"Nope, I'm pretty sure I said nothing at all. Not a word." He leaned toward me and put the side of his hand to his mouth to block the view from absolutely no one at all. "And I can promise you I never will. We neighbors need to keep each other safe."

My jaw dropped.

"I should get these inside." He pressed his pillow close to his chest then scampered away.

I WALKED TO TOWN in a daze. Izzy's memory spell had not worked. It had not worked at all. Mr. Henderson knew the truth. He had known for at least six months or so. And he hadn't told anyone. Or lost his mind. Maybe Gideon was right about spring being the time for new possibilities. I certainly hadn't seen this one coming. I still needed to tell my aunts. I wasn't sure how they would react, but—

That was a problem for another time.

I had enough on my plate today.

As I reached Main Street, my shock subsided against the cheerfulness of the day. Children were laughing and chasing one another, and the tourists were already out in full force, window-shopping. There was a general feeling of excitement and anticipation in the air.

I let the surrounding happiness fill me up. Today would be difficult. I needed all the reinforcement I could get.

Just as I had the thought, I reached As Time Goes By. The rolltop desk still stood displayed in the window. Les had said it was Mort's. My heart ached, remembering all of his and Angie's plans to move to Florida. It was such a tragedy the way their future had been stolen from them.

My eyes trailed over the elegant old desk. I smiled, conjuring up in my mind's eye a vision of a young Mort sitting before it back in the days when he and Angie first met. Hmm, back in the days when they first met. I wonder . . .

I reached for the antique shop's door when a voice called my name from across the street. It seemed all of my ongoing issues were demanding attention today. Gideon would probably read something into that too.

Nixie stood outside Charmed Treasures, her neon pink ponytail shining brightly in the sun. I couldn't read her expression. And it wasn't because she was standing on the other side of the street either. No, I could see her just fine. But she looked *funny*.

I moved to join her, but she held a hand up for me to stop. She then looked up and down the street, making me do the same. There were a few people in the distance on both sides but no one particularly close.

My pulse quickened as she held out her other hand, palm turned to the sky. There was something resting on top of it. A feather?

Chills raced down my spine.

No.

Nixie dropped her other hand, hovering it above the first, palm down this time.

No way!

Her lips began to move.

This was not happening. I suddenly really, really wanted it to happen. But it was not happening. It was impossible!

Agonizing seconds passed, as my young friend worked the charm. I was surprised by how badly I wanted this for her. But as I much as I wanted it, my hopes were nothing compared to how much I knew Nixie wanted this for herself. I reached out to the powers, pleading for their support on her behalf; but somehow, with a sense I couldn't explain, I already knew they were here, watching.

Come on, Nixie. Come on.

Suddenly the feather leapt up into the air.

The fluffy plume hovered in the space between her hands, then turned slowly, revolving in a tight circle.

"Nixie!" I shouted. "You're doing it!"

"I know!" She nodded in a big motion like she couldn't believe it either.

I was so happy! Yes, I was going to be in so much trouble with my aunts. Nora might find the energy to turn me into a toad after all. But I was so happy!

I jumped as the door behind me opened. Nixie clapped her hands together, pinning the feather between them. She then rushed back into Charmed Treasures.

I wheeled around to meet a concerned-looking Marjorie, standing at the threshold of her shop. "Is everything okay out here? I thought I heard a shout."

"Yes. Yes, I'm fine." I couldn't stop myself from beaming. "I'm wonderful actually."

The antique dealer's concern deepened.

"It's just that my friend"—I glanced back at Charmed Treasures. "She accomplished something today I never thought she could."

"Oh my, that is wonderful. Good for her."

I nodded, my smile growing bigger still. Then I remembered something. "Now that I have you, though, is Simon around?"

"He certainly is."

"How fortunate," I observed. "I'd love to have a word with him. It's about the desk in the window."

NOT LONG AFTER, I stood at the picketed gate of Angela Sweete's house, warm sunshine at my back. Deep pink tulips, petals sparkling with late morning dew, had sprung up along the fence, encouraging me on with their cheerful beauty.

It had been a remarkable day so far, miraculous even, but I still feared what was to come next.

I clenched my hands together. I knew there was a chance Angie wouldn't open the door when she saw who was on the other side, but, again, I had to try.

I had spent countless hours over the past day or so, turning words over in my mind, struggling to string together the perfect ones that would convey everything in my heart, but in the end, I knew it was of no use. It wasn't my heart Angie wanted to connect with. No matter what I said, hearing only from me would be a disappointment.

Despite Izzy's reassurances, I couldn't help but think I had failed. My gift was to connect the departed with their loved ones. I had no right to be here alone.

My steps, slow and measured, carried me up the path to the door. When I reached the halfway point, an unexpected tingle ran up the back of my neck. I faltered, then whirled around, searching the quiet street for any sign of life—or *death*—but was unable to spot a soul.

Wishful thinking.

I resumed my walk, only to be stopped again a half second later by another prickle, but this time it came accompanied by a cool breeze rustling through the bushes and over the grass. I spun around again, looking in all directions.

My heart soared when I spotted the sparkling current of wind, dipping and swirling in the sky. After a few somersaults, the glittering wind gust dropped down to the ground, and a man materialized in front of me.

"Mort, you're here."

The spirit held his hands open. "In the . . . I was about to say in the flesh, but that isn't right."

My eyes stung as I smiled.

"Now, don't you start," he grumbled. "It's far too early in the game to be getting all emotional. You've still got a job to do."

I threw my shoulders back and straightened to a posture that would make even Nora proud. "And what job is that exactly?"

He led my gaze over to the door.

"Are you sure you're ready?" I certainly didn't want to discourage him now, but I had pushed him pretty hard on this topic. I wanted it to be his choice.

"Ghostie, everything you said was true. I've done a lot to try to stop you from finding out what happened to me. I did all that to protect him. But that wasn't why I tried to keep you away from Angie. I *was* afraid." He heaved a phantom sigh. "The pull of the light, though, it's gotten so much stronger. I think it's my last call, and I don't want to miss the chance to say a few words to my wife."

I studied him a moment, then moved to knock on the door. A minute later, it opened.

Angie stood before me, her eyes carrying a mixture of exhaustion and mistrust. "Brynn . . ."

"I know I'm the last person you want to see. But I've brought someone with me this time. Someone who would like to talk to you."

O NCE WE WERE seated in the living room with me on one end of the couch, Angie on the other, the spirit resting on the coffee table in front of her, I relayed the story of everything that had happened since Mort's passing. When I was through, all Angie could muster was, "I don't know what to say. The police told me Les had come to them, but . . ." She pressed her fingers to her lips and shook her head.

"Tell her she doesn't have to say anything if she doesn't want to." Mort tore his gaze from his wife to meet my eye. "But there are a few things I'd like to say if she's up to hearing them."

I relayed the message to Angie, then turned back to her husband. "You say whatever it is you need to. I'll repeat it exactly."

He nodded grimly, then took some time to gather his thoughts. "Angie," he said, laying his hands on hers. "I'm sorry for what I've put you through by not talking to you sooner. I needed some time to get my head right." He dropped his chin to his chest and stared at their hands.

"Truth is, I don't want to mess this up. Brynn here knows I've been too afraid to talk to you. Not because it hurts. Although it does. More than I ever thought it could," he said, peeking up at her. "But because I've been afraid of what I might say."

The confusion on Angie's face mirrored my own. I thought I had imagined all the things Mort might want to say, but apparently my ghost friend still had a few tricks up his sleeve.

"I am far from a perfect man. Everyone in this room knows that." Mort shot me a wink. "But there's one thing I know for certain. The best part of me is the part that loves you. And more than anything, I don't want to say something now that will make things harder for you going forward. Especially when it comes . . ." He clenched his jaw, gathering himself. "Especially when it comes to things like you moving on."

"Mort," I said, filling my tone with question. I hadn't yet told Angie what he had said. "I'm not sure now is the time to—"

"There is no other time. She already knows I love her. I don't want anything else left unsaid." He caught me in his gaze. "I know this is hard on you, given everything you've been through, but can you do this for me? I've asked too much already, but you're all I've got. And, while I could be wrong, I have this feeling like maybe you're supposed to hear this. Our paths crossed for a reason, Ghostie. You said so yourself."

I frowned at the spirit. "I don't understand."

"Well, we both know all that you've done for me. Maybe hearing this part is my gift to you."

I shook my head then looked out the window, swallowing hard against the tension building in my throat. I had to make sure I had control of myself before repeating Mort's words to his wife.

She reacted much as I expected her to.

"Mort," she said, straining to see the man hidden from her, "you have to know I'm not thinking of that. I can't even begin to think about moving on. You've given me enough love for an eternity of lifetimes."

He nodded. "That's all well and good, and it fills my heart to hear you say it, but loneliness is a terrible thing. And life is meant for the living. If the time ever comes, if you ever meet someone who makes you happy, I don't want you to let that opportunity pass by. Not on my account. And not even if it's with someone like Elias Blumenthal."

I raised an eyebrow.

"I've been following him," Mort said sheepishly. "He's not a bad guy. I heard him on the phone, speaking German." His eyes widened. "Turns out I can understand German now. Don't know how that works. Anyway, he was giving money to the hospital that cared for his wife when she had cancer. He donates every year. I caught a bit of the conversation on the other end. You'd think the man was some sort of saint."

I relayed Mort's words to Angie, leaving out the last bit about Elias.

When I was through, all she could do was shake her head.

"Let me say this, and then I'll leave it be. Nothing could ever change the love between us. Not one bit of it. What we've shared, it's forever." Mort rubbed the top of her hand with his thumb. She looked down at it. "But one day life may surprise you, and if it does, just know I'm in your corner. Always. Until the edge of doom."

As the final word left Mort's mouth, I gasped, startling them both. I knew I needed to relay what he had said, but I couldn't stop myself from reacting. "I forgot to tell you something. It's really important." I grabbed my messenger bag off the floor. "Angie, it's about the letters."

"Oh, Mort," she said, her gaze searching the air in front of her. "There's something I need to tell you."

"He knows all about it," I said quickly. "Your husband is a bit of an eavesdropper."

Angie smiled. "Thank goodness. I don't know who sent them, but—"

"Mort did!" I shouted. I was too excited to stop myself.

They both looked at me, gobsmacked.

"Well, at least I think he did. Simon at the antique shop said he found them in the old desk you sold him. The thought struck me when I saw it in the shop window. I thought it was a long shot, but it turns out Simon found the first letter, slipped behind a drawer, when he was repairing the desk. Being the introvert he is, he put it into your mailbox without ever telling you who it was from. He figured you'd know. He found the second letter a few days later."

Mort frowned. "Let me see these letters."

I held out the one I had while Angie rushed out of the room to get the other.

"I don't believe this," Mort whispered. "I remember these. I wrote them back in high school. I was too shy to ever send them."

"Mortimer Sweete, you did not write these letters," Angie said. "They sound nothing like you."

"I did. I did. I was just so in love with you, Sweetness. I was beside myself. I must have written a hundred of them. I thought I got rid of them all. I was so embarrassed. But I guess these two . . ."

Angie clutched the letters to her chest as I relayed his words. "These two were meant for me."

Chapter 46

I CAN'T SAY THAT the goodbyes between Angie and Mort weren't hard. They were. Terribly hard. But I felt honored to be able to help them.

Before I left, Mort pulled me aside. He wanted to ask me for one more favor. He didn't want to take any anger or bitterness with him to the other side, so he asked me to tell Les that he forgave him, that he still loved him, and that he hoped he could find peace. We then thanked each other and said goodbye.

Well, kind of.

I said goodbye. Mort said, *I'll be seeing you, Ghostie.*

And, really, that was all I needed.

I didn't stay for Mort's actual parting. That was something he and Angie needed to do alone even if they couldn't share any words. Being in each other's presence was enough to transcend the distance between them.

After I left, I walked to the gazebo. I needed some time to reflect and watch the people go by. New moms and dads pushing babies in strollers. Children playing. Teenagers tossing footballs and Frisbees. Older couples walking hand in hand. It never ceased to amaze me how the world worked, with its infinite endings and beginnings happening all at the same time. I was overcome with the same sensation I'd had looking at the stars with Gideon. That feeling of awe and wonder. I didn't know if there was some master plan holding it all together, but I no longer hated the thought.

After that I went home.

My aunts tried to drag me into the library to go over everything they had learned about the strange symptoms we had been experiencing, but they quickly realized my heart wasn't up for another investigation just yet.

Fortunately, when I woke up the next morning, I felt much more like myself. Gideon was right. Spring was a special time. A time of possibilities. New hope for things to come. I had so much to be grateful for, and I was excited for my future. It wasn't the future Izzy wanted for me, but it was one I couldn't wait to meet. Despite Mort's beautiful words to his wife, I knew what I wanted for myself, and it didn't involve finding that kind of love again. I was happy and grateful for the life I had, and I was ready to get on with the business of both the living and the dead.

First living soul I needed to check in on?

Nixie.

What she had done was truly incredible. Full-blooded witches would have trouble performing a spell for the first time without guidance. We had to celebrate! And maybe figure out a way to tell my aunts we had a new coven member.

Main Street was packed with tourists by the time I made it into town. I knew there would be a good chance Charmed Treasures would be packed, too, but I could wait.

I had almost made it to the shop when a strange rustling sound caught my attention. And not just my attention. Several people stopped to look in the direction of the noise.

Wind.

A strong breeze rushed down the corridor between the buildings lining either side of the street; and when it hit the large cherry tree, just past full bloom, at the town's four corners, the petals exploded into the air, showering everyone below with a riot of fuchsia blossoms. A number of people gasped in wonder as they raised their hands to catch the falling flowers.

I marveled at the sight, but then something else caught my eye. In among the petals, there was a flash of gold. I watched it fall to the ground, then tumble over the sidewalk. A tiny scrap of paper, shining in the sun.

Chills raced up my arms.

The gleaming wrapper rolled and flipped over the sidewalk and across the street, driven by some force I couldn't see. It tumbled over a few more times before landing at my feet. I bent to pick it up.

A candy wrapper.

But this time it didn't say *Naff.* No, the fine script read *The Sweetes' Shoppe.*

My gaze turned up to the fluffy white clouds rolling over the bright blue sky. It could all be coincidence, of course. There had to be more than a few candy wrappers from the Sweetes' Shoppe rustling around Evenfall, but somehow I doubted it.

Just then a new, much colder, wind gusted up out of nowhere and snatched the wrapper from my hand. I spun to grab it but lost its trail, distracted by the sight of three men standing outside of the candy store, Fredrick Naff, Martin Quigley—a real estate agent—and someone else that I couldn't make out, standing in the shadow of a tree. Martin was switching out the For Sale sign to one that read *Sold.*

I had forgotten to ask Angie about it, but it looked like Fredrick had followed through with his plan to buy the shop after all, but who was that other man? Every time I tried to focus on his face, a flash of sunlight reflecting from a silver sign, with some sort of promotion for Furry Tales Pet Shop, wavered in the wind, blinding me.

Well, I could fix that.

I worked a quick finger charm and murmured the word *still* beneath my breath. My spell traveled across the street, its current distorting the air with a telltale shimmer. Just before it reached the sign, the enchantment splattered like it had hit some sort of invisible wall or shield.

Stars above, what was happening now?

I was about to try again when the proprietor of Furry Tales fixed the problem for me. Jodi came out and tightened the strings holding the sign, securing it in place. I blinked, then turned to get my glimpse of the man with Fredrick Naff, but as I did, a cloud moved over the sun.

The change in light was so abrupt I was blinded once again. Or maybe not blinded. No, the man was now hidden in even deeper shadow, much like the darkness I had experienced in the alleyway not so long ago.

This man . . .

This was the man responsible for interfering with my magic. It had to be.

My eyebrow arched. Right, then, if my spells wouldn't work around him, I would simply go over and introduce myself. I took a step toward the curb and pitched forward, my knees momentarily giving way beneath me. I righted myself quickly, threw my shoulders back, and patted my hair down. I didn't know how the man was doing this, but once I found a way across the street, I was going to . . . well, I wasn't entirely sure what I was going to do, but I was fairly certain it would involve me giving him a piece of my mind.

I stepped forward again, and my ankle gave way. I lunged toward a nearby bench, clutching its back for support.

This was ridiculous! I felt like I was learning to ice-skate for the first time, or . . . or like I was Gideon in that story Nora had told me. Well, I was no lovestruck teenager. No, I was a fully grown Warren w— I yelped as my feet slipped out from under me once again. Thankfully, someone caught me before I hit the pavement.

"Brynn! Are you okay?"

"Nixie." I grasped both her arms to regain my footing. "Thank you. I'm fine. I just can't seem to stay upright."

Nixie looked me over from top to bottom. "Are you dizzy? Feeling faint?" She smiled. "Shocked by my stunningly impressive spellcasting skills?"

I laughed, releasing her arms. "That must be it."

"You're impressed, aren't you?"

"I am."

"Proud even?"

"I . . ." I didn't mean to take away from her moment, but the cloud had moved from the sun. Before I could get a glimpse at the man though, Nixie stepped into my view.

"Brynn?"

"I'm so sorry. It's just . . ." I pointed across the street. "It looks like the Sweetes' Shoppe sold after all."

"Don't remind me," she moaned. "So, what's next? Do I get my own cauldron? Broomstick? Will there be an initiation ceremony into the coven?" She gasped. "Do you think Nora will make me a dress?"

"I don't know. Anything's possible. You proved that. Nixie, do you know who that is?" I pointed over to the man with his back now turned across the street.

She glanced over. "That would be Fredrick Naff's newest business partner, now co-owner of the Sweetes' Shoppe. Although I think they have plans beyond sweets." She sighed. "He also happens to be my very annoying big brother."

Brother. Nixie had a brother.

"I guess I should probably introduce him to you now that he's staying," she said dryly. "Or did you meet him when he was staying at the B&B?"

Staying at the B&B? It was all coming together. The funny feeling on the second floor. The signature disappearing from the ledger. My aunts not being able to remember his name. Whether Evenfall's newest proprietor realized it or not, his witch hunter blood seemed to be providing him some sort of natural protection against all the witches in town.

"I told him there was no way he was bunking with me in the attic. He's such a neat freak and he goes running at six. Who does that? Oh, and don't mention anything to him about me being witch. He's pretty conservative."

No, I certainly would not be doing that. This needed to be handled carefully. I had to speak to my aunts. There was no telling what danger this man might present.

"Nick!" she shouted, waving her hand in the air. "I can't believe he's going to be living here now. I mean, I love the guy, but it's bad enough having my aunt and uncle watch my every move. You know, it's funny. One minute I'm on top of the world, and I still am, but then, in almost the same breath, this happens."

I tried to focus on what Nixie was saying, but at his sister's call, the man finally turned and stepped into the light.

Suddenly I felt both heavy and weightless, outside of time and traveling at the speed of the light. It was like I didn't exist, and yet I had never felt more alive. The only thing I knew for certain was that I was *falling*.

"Brynn!"

It was hard to say how much time passed before I heard the faraway voices reaching through the darkness.

"I don't know what happened! She said she was having trouble staying on her feet, but she seemed fine."

"The ambulance is on its way."

"I called her aunts. They'll be here any second."

I blinked against the blinding sun before a shadow moved over me. I squinted, making out the silhouette of a man, his features coming into focus one by one. His brow. His lips. His cheekbones. The thin scar running over his jaw. But I couldn't see his eyes. They were on his sister. "Did she say anything before she fell?"

"I was talking about how quickly life can change, and then just before she dropped, she said—"

"Life may surprise you." The man turned, his eyes the color of spring leaves, locking on mine.

"Um, that's exactly what she said," Nixie whispered, leaning in close to her brother. "How did you know that?"

The man blinked. "I'm not sure."

A thousand half-formed thoughts swirled through my mind, but only one stood out in the chaos. It was the only one that made any sense.

One tiny little thought that could be summed up in a single word.

Uh-oh.

ACKNOWLEDGMENTS

Many thanks to my editor, Jenn Snyder, whose invaluable insights are always welcome. Thank you also to Mary Ann Lasher and Vikki Chu for yet another beautiful book cover, and to all the amazing people at Berkley Prime Crime and Penguin Random House for bringing this book to life.

As always, many thanks to my agent, Natalie Lakosil, for continuing to believe in me and my work, and to the readers, librarians, and bloggers who make up the cozy community for all their support.

Finally, forever love to my husband and children. I couldn't do it without you guys.

Ready to find
your next great read?

Let us help.

Visit prh.com/nextread

Penguin
Random
House